Readers Love *Those Who Lie*

'Deliciously dark and twisty'

'Very well written, keeps you guessing!'

'Great book, couldn't put it down'

'Fantastic plot! Terrifying and romantic!'

'Highly recommended'

DIANE JEFFREY grew up in North Devon. She lives and teaches English in Lyon, France. She is the mother of three children, and the mistress of one disobedient Labrador and one crazy kitten.

Those Who Lie is her debut psychological thriller.

Diane has a BA Joint Honours degree in French and German from the University of Nottingham and an MA in English Literature and Linguistics from the Université Jean Moulin Lyon III.

In her free time, she devours novels and chocolate. She also swims a lot and runs a little. Above all, she enjoys spending time with her family and friends.

Diane's imagination often runs amok and gets her up in the night to scribble down ideas for her writing. Incredibly, her supportive long-suffering husband puts up with this.

Readers can follow Diane on Twitter or on Facebook
@dianefjeffrey
facebook.com/dianejeffreyauthor

Also by Diane Jeffrey

He Will Find You
The Guilty Mother

Those Who Lie

Diane Jeffrey

ONE PLACE. MANY STORIES

HQ
An imprint of HarperCollins*Publishers* Ltd
1 London Bridge Street
London SE1 9GF

This paperback edition 2020

1

First published in Great Britain by
HQ, an imprint of HarperCollins*Publishers* Ltd 2020

MIX
Paper from
responsible sources
FSC
www.fsc.org FSC™ C007454

ISBN: 9780008389116

Printed and bound in Great Britain by
CPI Group (UK) Ltd, Croydon CR0 4YY

For my grandmother, Carrie. We still miss you.

~ Part One ~

Chapter One

~

Oxford, August 2014

Emily Klein doesn't know she has killed him until the day of his funeral. Her loved ones, including, of course, her husband, are all at the church rather than at her bedside. That explains why there are no familiar faces around her this time when she regains consciousness.

The room swims in and out of focus, and, at first, she has no idea where she is. But then it comes back to her. She's trying to remember why she's here when a cough to her right startles her. She isn't alone. Her neck hurts as she turns her head, expecting to see Greg, or her sister, or at the very least her mother. Instead, her eyes rest on the broad chest of one of the two strangers sitting beside her bed.

'Good afternoon, Mrs Klein,' the stranger says in a deep voice.

Emily looks up into the kind face of a burly man. He appears to be around the same age as her. He has a bushy moustache containing far more hair than he has on his balding head. He's smiling at her a little lopsidedly. Emily attempts to smile back, but her lips feel as if they're glued to her teeth.

Next to him sits a thin woman who also seems to be in her mid-thirties. She has a dour expression on her pretty face, and her hair is cropped very short and dyed a copper-red. She inches her chair forwards, closer to Emily's bed. The legs of the chair make a scraping sound on the floor. Emily feels intimidated.

'I'm Sergeant Campbell,' the woman says, fixing her piercing, green eyes on Emily, 'and this is my colleague.' She waves her hand towards the robust man as she introduces him by name, but Emily only catches the word 'Constable'.

Emily must look bemused because the constable smiles at her again from beneath his impressive moustache. He means this reassuringly, she supposes, but the right side of his face appears more animated than the left, and Emily finds his crooked grin rather unsettling.

What's going on? What do the police want? Emily can't shake off the unnerving impression that something is very wrong.

'What can you tell us about your movements on Friday the first of August?' asks the redhead officiously, whipping out a notebook and a pen from a pocket in her uniform. She has a lilting Scottish accent that mitigates the hard edge to her voice.

Emily tries to speak, but she's very thirsty and no sound comes out. She clears her throat.

'May I have a drink of water, please?' she asks.

Her head is pounding.

The constable pours some water from the transparent, plastic jug on the cupboard and presses a button on the remote control to raise Emily's bed. Then he gives her the glass. He watches her, a concerned look on his face, as she takes a few tentative sips before handing back the glass.

'The first of August, Mrs Klein,' the sergeant repeats, 'what happened on that day?'

'Well, that's my mother's birthday,' Emily begins. Her throat is still dry and her voice sounds strange. 'Oh, that's right; I'd sent her some flowers and bought her a necklace. I rang to wish her a happy birthday. She turned sixty-five.' Emily plucks at the stiff, white sheets before she adds, 'She is... um, she has been ill recently, for a long time really, and... well, she's doing a lot better at the moment. We're so proud of her.'

'We?' the sergeant echoes.

'My sister and I,' Emily says, and then the thought strikes her. 'Where is she? Where's my sister?' she asks. Amanda was there last time Emily opened her eyes, she's sure of it.

The sergeant ignores Emily's outburst. 'What happened after that?'

Emily shifts her gaze to the friendlier face of the constable. *Are these two police officers real?* They seem like caricatures, characters from a bad television series.

'I met my husband for lunch,' she answers, wondering where Greg is.

The constable doesn't give her a chance to voice her concern. 'Where?' he asks, sounding genuinely interested.

'At Gee's. It's not far from my husband's shop.'

'Oh, I know that restaurant,' the constable says. 'The one on Banbury Road? I've only eaten there once, though. It's a bit pricey, isn't it?'

Emily isn't sure if she's meant to reply, so she remains silent, trying hard to think. She's in hospital. She's groggy. She's in pain. She knows all that. But she can't get beyond that. She's having difficulty associating her two new acquaintances with her surroundings. Shouldn't there be doctors and nurses or family and friends by her bed rather than police officers? *What on earth am I doing here?*

Emily's gaze flits from the constable to the sergeant. She scans as much of her room as her neck will allow. Hers is the only bed, so she's in a private room rather than a hospital ward. There are flowers and fruit next to the water jug, so she's had visitors. Greg and Amanda, probably. But for some reason, they're not here now.

'Can we get back to the interrogation?' Sergeant Campbell reprimands her colleague, clicking her pen off and back on.

'Is this an interrogation?' Emily asks, bewildered. She almost asks what she has done wrong, but stops herself just in time. She wonders if she's dreaming. She certainly feels sleepy.

The sergeant looks vaguely uncomfortable and squirms in her seat. 'No, not really,' she says, her voice softening a little. 'That wasn't the right word.'

'Not at all,' the constable says. 'It's a routine investigation after—'

'Mrs Klein… Emily, we just want to know what happened that day,' Campbell interrupts. 'For our report. Did you drink anything with your meal?'

Something doesn't feel right. Emily's mind is even foggier, and she's struggling to organise her thoughts. What had the constable been about to say? A routine investigation after what? Into what? It must be serious if these police officers have been waiting for her to wake up. Or are they here for her protection?

Campbell repeats her question.

'Yes. A Perrier water, with a twist of lemon,' Emily replies. 'That's what I always have.'

'I meant, did you have any alcohol? A glass of wine, for example?'

'Oh, no. I don't drink. And anyway, I was driving.'

'Yes, you were,' the sergeant says. 'Why was Mr Gregory Klein, your husband, in the car with you?' Her voice is silky now, but Emily gets the feeling she's hiding something.

'Well, he wanted to have a look at an Edwardian inlaid satin-wood wardrobe.'

Now it's the sergeant's turn to look perplexed.

'An antique wardrobe,' Emily explains, seeing Campbell's expression. 'The owner lived in Staunton Road, in Headington. I didn't have any urgent work that day, so I drove Greg there.'

The policewoman seems temporarily at a loss for words and

purses her lips as she digests this piece of information. Her pale pink lipstick has been applied rather haphazardly, which makes Emily wonder if she had difficulty colouring inside the lines as a young child.

'Did you need new bedroom furniture?' the sergeant asks after a few seconds.

'Oh, no.' Under different circumstances, Emily might have found the question funny. 'My husband's an antique dealer. The wardrobe was for his shop. It's odd, but I'm not sure whether he bought it or not.'

Before Emily can reflect any more on that, the sergeant resumes. 'What did you and Mr Klein talk about in the car?'

'I think we had an argument.' A vague memory stirs and Emily tries to grasp it, but it fades away. Talking is making Emily's head thump even more, and so is trying to call to mind the conversation they had in the car. 'Greg told me something. I've forgotten exactly what it was he said. But I do know I was very angry about it.'

Emily pauses. Sergeant Campbell waits for her to continue. The constable gives her what is no doubt intended to be an encouraging look. 'I just remember Greg asking me over and over: "Who was it, Emily? Who was it?" He was shouting.'

Emily has a sudden image of her husband's furious face.

'Who was what?' asks the sergeant, somewhat impatiently.

'I don't know.' Emily frowns.

'Do you recall your answer to your husband's question?'

'Yes,' Emily replies, surprised, 'I do. The answer was: "My father." I told him that it was my father.' The mere thought of him makes her shudder.

'So, you remember you were arguing,' the sergeant recaps, looking down and pointing her index finger at the notebook on her knee, 'but not what it was about.'

Emily glances at the sergeant's pad. Although for her the notebook is upside down, Emily can clearly see that the police officer has taken no notes whatsoever. She has merely doodled a series of dots in a circular pattern, which reminds Emily of the recurrent spiral motif she uses in her own artwork.

'That's right.' Emily nods, and then scowls as the pain in her head intensifies.

'If it comes back to you, will you contact us?'

'How do I get in touch with you?'

The policewoman produces a card from a pocket in her uniform and hands it to her. Emily looks at it and sees a series of addresses, telephone numbers and a shoulder number under the heading Sergeant Campbell, Roads Policing Unit, Thames Valley Police.

'What's your name again?' Emily addresses Campbell's colleague, thinking it would be infinitely preferable to deal with him than the scary sergeant.

'PC Constable,' he replies.

'Police Constable Constable?'

'Yes, I'm afraid so,' he says wryly. 'I desperately need a promotion.'

Emily tries again to smile at him, but yet another bolt of pain shoots through her head and she suddenly finds him far less amusing. She still can't work out why she's here. She seems to recollect being told last time she woke up that she'd been involved in an accident. A growing sense of alarm overcomes her initial disorientation.

Sergeant Campbell's next question does nothing to reassure her. 'Mrs Klein, do you know what caused you to crash the car?' The police officer clicks her pen again.

Emily has a vision of her car hurtling off the road towards a tree. She feels a wave of panic break over her. Is this what really happened? Or is her imagination running wild? She takes a deep breath. So, she crashed the car. That makes sense. It would explain why she's in hospital and why her head, neck and side hurt so much. But she can't think straight. And she's far too tired to answer any more questions.

At that moment, the door to her hospital room opens and in strides a tall, plump woman wearing a badge that identifies her as Staff Nurse Peterson. She reminds Emily a little of Chummy in *Call the Midwife*. Emily is now almost convinced she's trapped on a TV studio set in a bad dream.

But then the nurse says, 'Oh, Mrs Klein, you're awake again.' She puts her hand on Emily's arm. 'How are you feeling?'

'Very confused,' Emily replies, 'and in pain.'

Staff Nurse Peterson checks the drip, and tells Emily that she'll administer some more painkillers. As the nurse completes her clinical checks and records the data on Emily's chart, Sergeant Campbell drops her bombshell.

'I must say, Mrs Klein,' she says, 'you're taking the news of your husband's death incredibly well.'

Emily senses Staff Nurse Peterson freeze at Campbell's remark. Words swirl round in Emily's head. *Argument… my father… car crash… husband's death.* She tries to suppress the scream rising inside her, and it erupts as a strangled whimper. That's the only sound audible in the room. It seems to resonate in Emily's ears. She cradles her sore head in her hands.

'Mrs Klein hadn't been told yet that Mr Klein was killed in the accident,' the nurse hisses at Sergeant Campbell, who looks unperturbed.

Campbell's mobile phone rings out and shatters the silence that ensues. The police officer takes the call.

Staff Nurse Peterson glares at the redhead while talking soothingly to Emily whose eyes dart from one woman to the other. The sergeant, impervious to the nurse's disapproval, continues to mumble into her phone. When she has ended the call, Campbell taps her colleague on the shoulder.

'Let's go,' she says to Constable. 'I am sorry,' she mutters to Emily who isn't sure if Campbell is apologising or expressing her condolences. Then she turns and heads for the door without so much as a cursory glance in Staff Nurse Peterson's direction.

PC Constable gets up from his seat, and tells Emily how sorry he is for her loss. Then he leaves the hospital room before his superior, who is holding the door open for him.

Emily clearly hears Campbell's words as she follows Constable out: 'The witness has finally turned up at the station to give his statement.'

Just as Emily is wondering if Campbell's phone call and witness have anything to do with her, Staff Nurse Peterson hangs the chart up on the end of her bed and says, 'Don't worry. You concentrate on getting better. You'll be home in no time.'

But Emily barely registers what the nurse says. *Greg is dead*, Emily thinks. *I was driving the car. I didn't kill him. I can't have killed him*. The thought of going home without Greg fills her with despair and dread.

Chapter Two

~

Devon, Christmas Eve, 1995

At half past nine, Josephine Cavendish was already snoring on the sofa in front of the television. Emily decided to go to bed although she knew there was no way she'd be able to sleep. Not tonight.

As she cleaned her teeth, she could hear Michael Stipe's voice coming from the end of the corridor. *Half a World Away*. Amanda stayed up here a lot listening to REM. She also liked Pearl Jam and Nirvana. Even when she wasn't listening to music, she seemed to spend as much time as possible in her bedroom. *Perhaps she feels safe in hers*, Emily thought.

Emily opened the door to her own room, which was larger than her sister's. Through the window she could see it was pitch-black and wet outside. She switched on the lamp by her bed and drew the curtains to shut out the night. She smiled wistfully at the Sarah Kay design. Here the girl was cradling a puppy; there she was holding a basket of flowers. Everywhere she was carefree. The curtains had never been replaced even though they were faded from the sunlight and Emily had outgrown them long ago.

She thought about reading, and walked over to her bookcase. It was crammed with books, from the classics – Dickens, Austen, the Brontës – to modern bestsellers of different genres such as *Jurassic Park, Diana: Her True Story, Captain Corelli's Mandolin* and *The Silence of the Lambs.* Her novels allowed her to escape. And she desperately needed to escape. But she couldn't choose one. She wouldn't be able to concentrate, anyway.

From the top row of her bookcase, at least a dozen teddy bears observed her bedroom through kind, beady eyes. She hadn't played with her teddies for years, and they looked tatty, but she didn't have the heart to get rid of them. Throwing them away would somehow have felt like giving up her childhood. Or giving up on it.

She turned around, imagining what the teddies could see from up there. They seemed to be looking at her double bed. Her parents had given it to her the previous year for her fourteenth birthday, although her mother hadn't really been happy about it. Emily liked the colourful spiral patterns on the duvet cover, but the bed was too big for her.

She pulled on her nightie and climbed into bed. She could still hear the music faintly, although she couldn't make out the song. Another one from the same album, no doubt. *Out of Time.* It occurred to her that her heart was beating too fast; it was out of time with the song. Lying on her side, she brought her knees up and hugged them to her chest. She felt cold in spite of the bedcover. She was wide awake. She looked at her watch on the bedside table. Ten o'clock. She felt sick with nerves.

She'd always been afraid at night-time, although when she was younger, her fears were unfounded. It was just that she was terrified of the dark. Amanda would make fun of her for that, but she'd often sung to her or stroked her head until she fell asleep. Sometimes they would even drag Amanda's mattress along the corridor so she could sleep on Emily's floor. In the end, their father said it was time Emily grew up and he forbade the girls to sleep in the same room.

The music stopped suddenly and a door banged. Emily's throat felt tight and she couldn't breathe. *It's too early. I'm not ready yet*, she thought, alarmed.

Then she heard a floorboard creak on the landing, followed a few seconds later by the rattle of water pipes. She heaved a sigh of relief. It was only Amanda. There was the noise of the toilet flushing, then a gentle knock at her bedroom door.

'I'm awake,' she called out to her sister. She sat up in bed.

The door opened and Amanda came in and walked towards her. She was wearing tartan pyjamas. Her long, mousy hair was loose and wavy from the plaits she always let out at bedtime. 'Night, Em,' she said.

'Goodnight.'

Amanda sat on the edge of the bed and Emily looked into her eyes. They were a murky brown, the same colour as their father's. Emily had inherited their mother's pale blue eyes. Amanda gave her a hug. Emily could feel herself trembling.

'You're cold,' Amanda said, sounding concerned.

That wasn't the only reason Emily was shaking, and she thought her sister probably knew that. But she didn't contradict her. What could Amanda do anyway? She rubbed Emily's arms as if to warm them. Neither of them spoke for a few seconds.

Canned laughter suddenly erupted from the sitting room below, breaking the silence.

'Mum still in front of the TV?'

'Yeah.' Emily didn't need to add that she was dead to the world.

After a while, Amanda pecked Emily's cheek and got up.

'Don't go,' Emily pleaded, but her elder sister had already left the room.

The door to Amanda's bedroom along the hallway closed with a thud, and Emily glanced at her watch again. Half past ten. She became aware of the sound of her own breathing over the indistinct din of the sitcom. She could also hear the wind howling outside and the rain beating against the windowpane. She was alone and helpless. A sob welled up inside her but she fought to contain it. *I have to stay strong*, she thought. She needed to calm her nerves. She decided to read after all.

On her bedside table was a huge stack of books that looked like it would topple over at any minute. At the top of the pile was *Alice's Adventures in Wonderland*. Emily's middle name was Alice. Her father's mother, whose memory was getting bad due to Alzheimer's, bought her a copy of Lewis Carroll's novel every year for Christmas and she dutifully reread the book each time. It had always been her favourite story, and she never grew tired of it. Her grandmother had given her this edition – her sixth copy – just two days ago. When she was younger, Emily had traced and copied the illustrations, and after that she'd created her own sketches for each chapter.

She flicked through the blue leather-bound volume to the part she liked best in the whole book: the Hatter's Tea-Party. She read the bit where Alice was told that they took tea all day long since Time had stood still at six o'clock, in other words, at teatime. *If only time could stand still for me tonight*, she wished silently. But it was nearly eleven now. Her stomach was heavy with dread. She was terrified she wouldn't be able to go through with it.

It was hopeless. She couldn't keep her mind on the book. She still felt cold even though the radiators hadn't cooled yet. Shivering, she pulled the duvet up around her shoulders and contemplated getting out of bed to fetch some thick, woollen socks. Perhaps she should get up and hide. Somewhere he couldn't find her this time.

It was too late. She could hear him swearing loudly from outside. The front door was directly beneath her bedroom window, and she imagined him fumbling with his key and then stumbling into the hall. There was a loud bang as the door was flung open against the wall.

Quickly, she replaced the book on her bedside table, switched off the lamp and lay down. She rolled over onto her side towards the wall, wrapping the quilt tightly around her. She pushed her hand under the pillow and groped around, holding her breath. *Where is it? I know I put it here*, she thought, panicking. Lifting her head slightly and sliding her hand further under the pillow, she found what she was looking for. Clutching it as if her life depended on it, she breathed out.

He'd turned off the television in the sitting room and for a moment there was an eerie silence in the house. She imagined him looking down at her mother disdainfully. He might even take a swig from her bottle of Jameson if there was any whiskey left.

But the silence was short-lived. She could hear his heavy footsteps making their unwieldy way up the stairs. *Oh no*, she thought. *Please, no.*

She sensed her bedroom door open. She heard him lurch into the room and flick the switch. The room was instantly flooded with light. Her heart began to hammer harder and faster. She huddled further into her covers, trying to gain a little more respite. Closing her eyes tight, she pretended to be fast asleep, although she'd tried that before and knew it wouldn't work. She could visualise him looking at her from across the room. It made her skin crawl.

He weaved his way over to her bed, and practically collapsed on top of her. She lay still and tried to swallow down the lump in her throat even as the tears squeezed out from behind her firmly shut eyelids.

'I love you so much, Emily.' Her father's voice was slurred and his smell – a mixture of sweat, alcohol and tobacco – invaded her nostrils and made her feel nauseous. 'You make me love you so much.'

One evening, he'd passed out before he could begin. Perhaps that would happen tonight. But she realised this was just wishful thinking as he pulled back the covers, unwrapping the cocoon she'd enveloped herself in.

She didn't move a muscle as he pulled up her nightie and opened the belt of his trousers. She remained immobile – there was no point in fighting. Instead, she concentrated on the place in her mind she always retreated to when this happened: the beach at Woolacombe.

In one of her happiest memories, she was at the beach with her sister, her parents and her mother's parents. She was little then and this was long before she'd made her father love her too much. They must have gone to the beach often during the summer months and she was never sure if this was just one memory or a mixture of many trips to the seaside.

They were all eating Mr Whippy 99 ice creams with chocolate Flakes. Granny and Granddad said they didn't like the Flakes so Amanda and Emily could have two each. Afterwards, the girls swam in the sea with Mum and Granddad. They stayed in until their lips turned blue and their arms and legs had goose pimples all over them. As the tide was so low, it was a long walk back to the place where their father and Granny were dozing on deck-chairs. Their mum made them run to warm up. Panting with his tongue out like a dog, Granddad pretended to be too old to jog.

It was hard to find the right parasol at the top of the beach because they'd drifted along in the current while jumping over and ducking under the waves, and so they were several metres too far along the beach. Emily was the one who finally spotted the blue and yellow parasol. Granny wrapped a beach towel around her, and then another one around Amanda. Someone had taken a photo – it must have been their father because he was the only one not in the picture, and Emily had kept it. It was in a frame on her bedside table.

She turned her head and focused on this photo now as the familiar pain seared through her. She could almost feel the teddies' cold, glassy eyes on her, and from the open pages of *Alice's Adventures in Wonderland*, both the March Hare and the Hatter stared at her. It was as if they were all watching her, daring her to find the courage to put an end to this. Only the sleepy Dormouse had his eyes closed, as though averting his gaze out of consideration or turning a blind eye to what she was going to do.

As her father's shudder and moan signalled that this was nearly the end for tonight, she reminded herself that there was only one way this would ever stop. She freed her hand from where it was pinned under her father. *I have to do this*, she thought. *I have to do it now, or it will be too late.*

Before she had time to think through what she'd really intended to do, the gun went off.

Long after her father's lifeless body had collapsed onto her for the last time, soaking her in blood and almost crushing her beneath its dead weight, the shot continued to ring in her ears.

Chapter Three

~

Oxford, August 2014

As Josephine Cavendish swings the car into the driveway of Emily's Victorian home in leafy Summertown, narrowly avoiding the gatepost, Emily thinks that it's a miracle she hasn't been involved in another car crash on the way home. She realises she has been pressing her right foot down hard on the floor as though she has an emergency brake on the passenger's side. The five-mile journey from the hospital seemed interminable.

Gently levering herself out of the car, she blanches as her broken ribs protest. She'll take some more of her prescribed painkillers as soon as she's inside the house, she decides. She tries to lift a bag from the boot of the car.

'Go on inside,' her mother says firmly. Peering at Emily over the top of her glasses, which have slipped down her nose, Josephine shoos her daughter away. Emily knows better than to argue with her mother. 'I'll carry these,' Josephine says, hoisting the holdall onto her shoulder. Then she grabs the plastic bags containing clothes, which Amanda brought to the hospital for Emily, as well as the bunch of flowers and another one of grapes.

As Emily walks slowly up the drive, out of the corner of her eye she catches sight of her next-door neighbour. Mrs Wickens seems to be engrossed in her geraniums, but Emily suspects she's burning with curiosity and ready to pounce on them. Anxious to avoid the elderly woman's questions, Emily keeps her head down and escapes, but Josephine isn't so lucky. Snippets of their conversation reach Emily's ears as she takes her house keys from her handbag.

'... a car accident... Mr Klein?... so sad... your elder daughter... she fed the cat...'

Entering the hallway, Emily lets the front door swing closed behind her, shutting out their voices. Mr Mistoffelees pads towards her, mewing. She tries to bend down to stroke the cat, but it's too painful, so she stands still while he weaves himself in a figure of eight around her legs.

Looking around her, she spots several pairs of Greg's shoes and his umbrella. A thought hits her like a punch in the stomach and hurts far more than her injuries: this is no longer their home, but only *her* home. Everything around her looks the same: the light grey walls, the mirror, the rug, Greg's antique furniture incongruously juxtaposed with her own modern paintings. *Something old, something new*, Greg would often joke. And yet, despite the familiarity of her surroundings, Emily doesn't feel at home. *Everything looks the same, but everything has changed*, she realises with a jolt. She has the strange impression that she has just stepped into someone else's life.

She remembers Greg carrying her over the threshold when they came home after their honeymoon in Venice ten years ago. It had been so romantic, they were happy, and the unfortunate incident at their wedding had practically been forgotten. Emily hadn't wanted to think about that, anyway. She'd needed to forgive Greg and build up trust in him again.

Greg spun her around in his arms – both of them giggling – and then set her down in the same spot she is standing in at this very moment. She imagines now that she can hear his laughter echoing in the hall. He'd always laughed louder and longer than everyone else; she'd found his enthusiasm contagious on many occasions. He'd been so full of life. It just doesn't seem possible that he's dead.

Oh, Greg. You can't die. You can't leave me. I didn't mean to—

Emily's thoughts are interrupted when Josephine opens the front door and hauls in the carrier bags, roses and fruit, not without some difficulty. The strap of the holdall has slid down from her shoulder to her elbow. She dumps everything on the rug.

'Come into the kitchen, Emily. I'll make some tea,' her mother says, leading the way.

Emily kicks off her shoes and heads for the kitchen. 'No, I'll do it, Mum,' she argues. 'I need something to do.'

'You'll do no such thing. I've come to stay for a while, and I intend to take care of you until you're feeling a bit stronger. Now sit down.'

Once again, Emily does as she is told. She notices the fridge is full when Josephine opens it to take out a carton of milk. She makes a mental note to thank her sister for her thoughtfulness. She studies her mother who is click-clacking her way clumsily around the kitchen in her high heels.

Having lost a lot of weight when she gave up drinking, Josephine is more discreet physically, but Emily finds her more sociable now, and less withdrawn. Her mother has always been slightly sharp-tongued, though, and this doesn't appear to have changed. She keeps up an endless stream of chatter as she opens and closes the cupboard doors. Emily fixes her gaze on the kitchen table and tries to respond when it seems appropriate until her mother turns to face her and says something that catches her full attention.

'If you need something to do, we could start clearing out Greg's clothes and things.'

Emily is horrified at the suggestion. 'Oh, no, I couldn't do that, not yet.'

'Well, I could do it for you.'

'No! Don't do that, Mum. I'm not ready. He…'

Emily had been about to say that Greg might still come back, but she closes her mouth as Josephine places a mug of tea in front of her. The tea looks as if it has been made without a single teabag. Emily blows gently across the steaming cup and sips at the hot drink. Her hands are unsteady, so she puts the mug down, making a face as she does so. The tea tastes as disgusting as it looks. She is staggered by her mind's ability to think like this when she has just lost her husband. *I'm a widow*, she reminds herself, but it hasn't sunk in yet.

'That's all right,' Josephine says. 'All in good time.'

Emily smiles weakly and asks her mother for some water to take her tablets. She holds the cool glass to her head for a while and closes her eyes. In her mind, she sees an image of herself as a patient, not in the John Radcliffe Hospital in Headington from which she has just been discharged, but in the hospital of her nightmares. The one she stayed in for just one week as a child. It was a long time ago, but the memory still haunts her. She opens her eyes again to make the image disappear.

Just then the phone rings, making Emily jump. Her mother rushes out to the hall, unsteady in her high heels. Then she teeters back into the kitchen with the handset pressed against her ear.

'Well, I don't know if she's well enough to talk…' Josephine's voice trails off as Emily nods, holding out her hand for the telephone.

'Hello? Emily Klein speaking.'

'Sergeant Campbell, here.' Emily immediately regrets taking the call. She has had a strong mistrust of the police ever since she was a teenager. And she has already taken a strong disliking to Campbell. 'PC Constable and I would like to ask you a few more questions, if we may, about the crash,' the sergeant continues, sounding almost friendly, much to Emily's surprise.

'Yes?' she says expectantly. She starts to chew one of her nails.

'Not now. Tomorrow. If you're not feeling up to coming in to the station, we could come to your house. At three p.m.-ish?'

'Fine,' Emily hears herself agreeing while a knot of anxiety twists in her stomach. 'What sort of questions?'

'Just corroborating the statement of an eyewitness to the incident. It would be easier to do it in person. Tomorrow at three.'

'OK. I'll see you then.' Emily tries to keep her voice even, but she can hear it quaver. Hopefully, Campbell can't. 'Do you need the address?'

But the sergeant, true to her original form, has already hung up. Emily becomes aware of the metallic taste of blood in her mouth and realises she has bitten her nail to the quick.

Why did Campbell say 'incident'? Emily wonders disconcertedly. *Surely she'd meant 'accident'?*

'Was that the nasty ginger policewoman you told me about?' Her mother doesn't wait for an answer. 'What did she want?'

Emily is still asking herself the same thing. 'She and her colleague want to ask me some more questions,' she says. 'They're coming round tomorrow afternoon.' She picks up her mug and holds it to her lips, but she can't bring herself to drink any more of it.

Emily wants her mother to reassure her; she wants her to say that this is normal police procedure after a traffic accident. After all, Greg died in this crash. And Emily was driving. She has been trying to shut that thought out, but she knows the grief and guilt will catch up with her.

Instead Josephine says, 'I thought you couldn't remember what happened. What's the point in bothering you about it?'

'Sergeant Campbell said she wanted to follow up a report by a witness.'

'I still don't see how you can help with your amnesia.'

Josephine pulls out a chair and sits down opposite her daughter at the kitchen table.

'I'm not really suffering from amnesia, Mum,' Emily says, avoiding her mother's eyes and staring instead at the mark left by her mug on the table. She puts her mug down, placing it exactly inside the wet circle. 'I've just blanked out the accident itself and what Greg and I were argu… um… talking about. That's all.'

'What did they say about that at the hospital? Will you get your memory back?'

'I haven't lost my…' Emily begins, but gives up mid-sentence. Unbidden, the image of her car about to crash into a tree replays in Emily's mind. She blinks and focuses on her hands gripping the mug. 'They said it might be due to the concussion, or, more likely, the emotional trauma of the accident. I may never remember exactly what happened in the car. According to the doctors, that may be just as well.'

'Well, I suppose it's not the first time you've forgotten something important.'

Emily snaps her head up and looks into her mother's cold, blue eyes. They appear magnified behind her glasses, but Josephine's expression is inscrutable. Emily thinks she knows what her mother was referring to with that barb, but she doesn't know what reaction she was hoping to provoke, so she ignores it.

'And it's not the first time the police have questioned you about a suspicious death.' Emily is still holding her mother's gaze and it takes her a split second to realise Josephine hasn't spoken. This remark has come from a voice in her own head. Deep down, this is what she's afraid of. What if Campbell and Constable don't think it was an accident? *If they find out anything about my past, anything at all, they won't believe me, no matter what I tell them,* she thinks.

Emily sighs. She feels irritable and overwhelmed. Her mother opens her mouth to say something, but Emily doesn't want to hear it. She doesn't want to talk any more.

'Mum, I think I'll go and take a shower and then sleep for a while,' she says, adding, 'if that's all right with you.'

'Yes, that's fine, Emily. I'll potter around down here and make something for dinner later.' Josephine slurps her tea loudly. Then she gets up to busy herself in the kitchen as Emily leaves the room.

Minutes later, as Emily lathers her body with soap under the scalding jet of the shower, she wonders how long her mother plans

23

to stay. She immediately berates herself. Her mother is trying to be helpful. And, anyway, does she really want to be alone right now? As she rinses the shampoo from her hair, a line from the end of *Perfect Blue Buildings*, one of her favourite songs by The Counting Crows, comes into her head. But she can't think of the tune.

Stepping into the master bedroom from the en suite bathroom, she notices Greg's red jumper. It's slung over the back of the antique chair next to his side of the bed. He wore it recently when they went out as it was rather chilly for a summer's evening. They ate at a nice restaurant, then went to a concert at the Sheldonian Theatre. A few bars from the Schubert Sonata that the pianist performed begin to play in Emily's head. She and Greg both thoroughly enjoyed themselves. When they arrived home, Emily recalls, Greg wanted to make love, but Emily pretended to be too tired. She regrets that now.

She wraps the towel around her head, pinning up her shoulder-length hair, and walks over to the wooden armchair to pick up his jumper. She buries her face in it and inhales deeply. She feels weak as she breathes in Greg's cologne mixed with the faint scent of the laundry detergent that he liked her to use to wash his woollen jumpers. There's also the odour of beeswax and polish that permeated all of Greg's clothing. It's a smell Emily would usually find comforting, but in this instant it symbolises every-thing she has just lost. Her legs give way beneath her and she sinks onto the worn, unwelcoming cushion of the chair.

In spite of herself, Emily presses the jumper harder against her face and breathes in again. This time she can detect the hint of a more floral fragrance. She stiffens as a memory hovers at the back of her mind, but it stays stubbornly out of reach. The smell is vaguely familiar, but disturbing at the same time. As the towel slips from her hair, releasing her chestnut curls, she tells herself it's just her conditioner, her own smell mixing with that of her husband. Her *late* husband. Tears start to stream down her cheeks as she clings to the jumper, rocking her body backwards and forwards.

Emily doesn't remember getting up from the chair, but when she wakes up an hour or so later, she finds she's lying in her dressing gown on Greg's side of the bed, still clutching his sweater. She gingerly raises herself to a sitting position, grimacing. She stays on the bed, in a daze, gently rubbing the faded scars on her right forearm with the fingertips of her left hand. It's an unconscious gesture and as soon as she realises she's doing it, she stops and tugs her sleeve down. She can hear the muffled noises her mother is making in the kitchen downstairs, but she doesn't want to join her just yet.

Scanning her bedroom, she notices that most of the things in it are hers. Her paintings are displayed on the walls; her perfume bottles, hairbrushes and make-up are on the dressing table; her ornaments are lined up neatly on the shelves. The antique armchair, on which Greg's clothes were always strewn, was his. She has always found it ugly and uncomfortable, but suddenly she feels fond of it.

Her eyes fall on her MacBook Pro on top of the chest of drawers. Greg bought it for her because she wasn't very computer-literate and he said it was user-friendly. But really Josh, the computer whizz she's employing to set up a website for her artwork, uses her laptop more than she does.

Emily remembers how much Greg had loved new technology. He and his friend Charles would sometimes talk about computers for hours on end, which she found intensely annoying. Thinking how much she would love to listen in on one of those conversations now, a lump comes to her throat. She remembers spending evenings sitting next to her husband, losing herself in the novels on her Kindle while Greg, who had never been much of a reader, was on his laptop or smartphone replying to emails or searching for antiques on the Internet or catching up with friends on Facebook. She makes an effort not to start crying again.

It dawns on her that although all of Greg's close friends and family know he has lost his life in a car crash, several of his old classmates from school won't have heard about it. Now she comes to think of it, many of his work contacts won't know either. She decides to type a short message on Facebook to tell them. She brings her laptop over to the bed, props up the pillows behind her and, sitting with her legs out straight and the computer on her thighs, she boots it up. She knows Greg's password, so she brings up his account. She mulls over each sentence, but in the end she's satisfied with her announcement.

It is with deep sadness that I inform you that my husband Greg passed away on 1st August following a road accident. His funeral was held last week. I'm very grateful for the support I've received at this tragic time. Emily Klein.

Although she doesn't go on Facebook much, Emily does have an account, and she tags herself so that the message will appear on her Timeline, too. Wondering if some people will find an obituary on Facebook distasteful, she hesitates briefly. Then she posts her comment, logs out of Greg's account and connects to her own to check that the message has appeared on her Facebook wall.

Just as she has logged in, she hears the four notes of the message notification sound. She clicks to open the message. The first time, she reads it without fully taking in the meaning, staring uncomprehendingly at the screen. As she rereads the words more carefully, she feels dizzy and struggles to breathe.

Alice, I don't know what's going on. I'll get back to you as soon as I can.

The blue and white bar at the top of the Facebook page seems to flash as if in warning. Then the message becomes an illegible blur. Emily pushes the computer off her lap and jumps up from the bed. The pain in her side is excruciating. The room begins to spin so fast that she feels herself falling. *It can't be. That's impossible.* That's the last thing that goes through her mind before she faints.

Even if the sender's name hadn't appeared in bold at the top of the message, Emily would have known it was from him. Only one person has ever called her by her middle name.

Chapter Four

~

Devon, May 1996

'We've got a lot to get through today,' Lucinda Sharpe began, bursting into the meeting room at the secure accommodation. Emily was being detained in this facility. Then, almost as an afterthought, Lucinda added, 'How are you holding up?' She was out of breath.

'I'm all right,' Emily said. It didn't sound very convincing, even to Emily.

There was a ball of nerves in her stomach that just wouldn't go away. She'd been trying hard not to think about the ordeal she would have to face over the next few days.

'Really?'

Emily looked at her solicitor. Lucinda was blessed with flawless olive skin, beautiful dark eyes and shiny black hair, but cursed with a rather large bottom and a lousy sense of fashion. Emily thought she must be aiming for smart casual, but didn't think she'd succeeded in pulling it off on any of the occasions they'd met so far.

Today, she was dressed more casually and less smartly than

usual, Emily noticed, her buttocks squeezed into unflattering black leggings, and her hair held back with a neon yellow headscarf. She was wearing a denim shirt with too many buttons undone, and, somewhat ironically, court shoes.

Lucinda had often arrived late for appointments and police interviews with Emily, but she was punctual on this particular morning. It was to be their last meeting before Emily's trial began the following day.

Emily was very fond of Lucy, as her lawyer insisted on being called. Lucy talked about her children a lot, and whenever she did, a proud smile lit up her face. She complained that she was always cutting corners, doing her kids' homework for them because explaining would take longer, or heating up frozen pizza when she didn't have time to cook, or putting on a video instead of reading a bedtime story so that they wouldn't squabble while she got some urgent work done.

Listening to Lucy stirred up mixed emotions in Emily. Lucy was a single mother of four, and yet Emily found her accounts of family life attractive simply because they struck her as ordinary. She thought Lucy must be an excellent mum. Emily didn't have any stories to tell Lucy about her family.

What Emily liked best about her solicitor was that she wasn't patronising. She talked in legalese, using complex, complicated sentences, and she explained technical terms only when necessary. During Lucy's visits, Emily didn't feel like a child or an animal, as she sometimes did around the staff and other detainees.

'Tell me the truth. How are you *really* doing?'

'Well, I'm still not sleeping very well,' Emily admitted, 'and when I do manage to fall asleep, I have nightmares.'

Emily's nightmares had got worse and worse since her father's murder. Since then, she'd relived the whole incident several times in her sleep. At the end of the scariest dream she'd had, Graham Cavendish had survived.

'We'll have to see if the doctor can prescribe you some light sedatives.' Lucy kept her caring eyes on Emily as she took some papers out of her bulging briefcase and sat down. 'Are you eating better?'

'Yes.' She told herself it wasn't a complete lie. She was making an effort to finish her meals. She just wasn't keeping them down.

'Uh-huh,' came the response.

Emily realised she wasn't fooling Lucy.

'Are you ready to talk about what's likely to happen to you, Emily?'

'Yes.'

'And I want to go through everything again just to be clear. That will be more for my benefit than yours, though, as you won't have to talk during the trial. The recorded tapes of your interviews will be played in court instead. Firstly there were the interviews with the arresting officers in Barnstaple Police Station on Christmas Day, then those with DC Hazel Moreleigh and DS Michael Tomlinson in the Devon and Cornwall Police Headquarters over the following days.'

Lucy had already told Emily all this, and she felt very relieved that she wouldn't have to take the stand.

'As I've said before, you'll be tried in the Crown Court here in Exeter. Your trial shouldn't last more than a week. My guess is four days. Your sister and your mother will be called as witnesses.'

Here, Lucy paused. Emily realised her lawyer was also dreading the impression Josephine might make. She'd promised Emily she would 'pull herself together'. Emily supposed that meant she would sober up. But although Josephine had attended every one of Emily's interrogations, as the law required, it was impossible to predict how drunk she'd be from one day to the next. Sometimes her presence had been merely a physical one. At best, she smelt slightly of whiskey; at worst, she couldn't walk into the room straight, then tried hard not to doze off during the interviews. Emily could hardly blame her. After all, her daughter had just murdered her husband.

Amanda, on the other hand, had been very supportive. Emily often wondered how she would have coped that night without her sister. When, unbelievably, the gunshot hadn't woken up Josephine, Amanda had decided to wait a while before calling 999. Then she'd gone over the questions the police were likely to ask Emily so she knew what to expect.

The emergency services had arrived two hours later, rather conspicuously in two squad cars and an ambulance with blue lights rotating and sirens blaring. Emily was sitting on the bedroom floor and Amanda was kneeling beside her, gently rocking her and stroking her hair. They were both covered in blood. Emily vaguely remembered her mother, who must have finally woken up when the police arrived, rushing towards them, an anxious look on her face. There were also two police officers. One of them had gone pale at the sight of all the blood while his colleague asked Emily and Amanda where they were hurt.

Amanda had done all the talking. Emily had been very grateful for that. It was Amanda who had used a blanket to cover up their father's body and his gun as they lay side by side on Emily's double bed. Emily had felt proud of her sister for everything she'd done that evening.

Since that night, Emily had often repeated to herself the words Amanda had said over and over to her as they were sitting on the bedroom floor: *It's over now, Emily. He can't hurt you any more.* It had become her mantra. Amanda had been Emily's rock. She felt that she owed her life to her sister.

'I'm sure Amanda's testimony will be very useful,' said Lucy tactfully, bringing Emily out of her reverie and back to the present. 'She was there that night and she speaks very highly of you.'

Lucy leaned forwards and reached across the table to pat Emily's hand. The contact made Emily jump and her knee hit the table quite hard. It didn't budge; the very first time she'd come into this room, Emily had noticed that the furniture was bolted to the floor.

'Now, for the trial itself,' Lucy began, removing her hand from Emily's to adjust her headscarf. 'We couldn't really have raised the issue of fitness to plead. No judge would have found you unfit to plead. It's obvious from your school reports that you're a very bright young lady, so clearly you'll have no trouble understanding the proceedings of your trial. We can't go for self-defence either—'

'Why not?' Emily asked, trying to sound patient, but wishing that Lucy would tell her what arguments she did intend to use rather than what she'd rejected.

'Well, as you know,' Lucy said, 'the police didn't just find the murder weapon; they also found a straight razor with an open steel blade, so it will be hard to rebut either premeditation or intent. And anyway, self-defence doesn't really work like that. No, our best defence is to stress the mitigating factors – the, uh, abuse. Thanks to the examination you had in the North Devon District Hospital just after your arrest, we've got evidence for rape. If we can argue successfully for a special defence of diminished responsibility, you'll only be found guilty of voluntary manslaughter.'

Emily tried to fight against her increasing panic. Lucy had already explained diminished responsibility to her, but this was the first time she'd mentioned voluntary manslaughter. 'What do you mean, *only*?'

Lucy chose not to answer that. 'Furthermore, Dr Irvine's report will help us to exonerate you from the murder charge.' Dr Rosamund Irvine was the psychiatrist who'd been treating and assessing Emily since shortly after her arrest. 'She has said that you're suffering from depression. Your self-harming and suicide attempt support this, according to her.'

Emily had cut into the skin on her forearm with a plastic knife she'd taken from the canteen. She'd also stored up her antidepressants and painkillers for several days and had taken them all together. But the knife had broken easily and she hadn't had nearly enough pills to do herself any real damage. Her psychiatrist had told her it was a cry for help, and that help was here now.

'Dr Irvine has stated that your depression started *before* your father was killed, and that's vital,' Lucy continued. 'This will show that your mental state was too fragile at the time for you to be accountable for, um, your actions. Dr Irvine's conclusions will be backed up by the psychologist you were referred to by your GP last October.'

Emily raised her eyebrows. She'd had just two sessions with this psychologist. He'd seemed completely indifferent to what she'd told him, which wasn't very much.

'Emily,' Lucy's tone was even softer than before. 'I'm very confident that diminished responsibility will be applied. That will allow the judge discretion as to how to pass sentence. It will depend on the judge, of course. But I think we should be optimistic. Given your circumstances and your, um, mental health, you'll be given a hospital order so that you can get the treatment you need rather than a sentence based on punishment.'

'How long?'

'My guess is a maximum stay of three years in a care home. You'll probably be back home in eighteen months.'

Emily flinched.

'Or you can go somewhere else when you're released,' Lucy amended hastily. 'You'll be seventeen after all.'

That was a shorter period than Emily had feared.

'Is there anything that won't work in my favour?'

'Well, in one of your interviews, DS Tomlinson commented on your lack of remorse, but I'm hoping that the judge will be more sympathetic. I can't see how Tomlinson expected you to regret your father's death.'

Emily nodded. Amanda had told her to look contrite in court, but Emily wasn't sure she could manage that. Amanda was a talented actress; she loved participating in school plays. Emily had only ever helped with the artwork for the scenery. Anyway, DS Tomlinson was right. Emily didn't feel at all sorry. Why should she? She was aware that some of her answers in her interviews

32

had sounded unemotional, even cold. She sometimes felt as though all this had happened to someone else.

'The detective sergeant's remark should be countered to a large extent by Dr Irvine's diagnosis,' Lucy said. 'Your psychiatrist will show that you are showing the classic symptoms of a victim of abuse. Depression, and anorexia obviously, and post-traumatic stress disorder. She'll also say that you are showing signs of dissociative identity disorder. Apparently, dissociating can be a coping mechanism after extreme childhood trauma and this explains why you might seem detached at times.'

'What about the evidence?'

'Well, that's nearly all unequivocally against you: your finger-prints were on the weapon – along with your father's since it was his gun, and your sister's since she'd taken it from your hands; the blood on your nightwear matched that of your father…' Lucy counted off each point on her fingers '… the ballistics was incon-sistent with the blood spatter analysis, but there is nothing in either report that will help us, and, finally, you confessed in an interview that was recorded on audio tape.'

Emily tasted the coppery tang of blood and realised she'd been biting her lip. She made a conscious effort to stop. She didn't want to show Lucy just how nervous she was.

'But our defence is not to show you're innocent,' Lucy continued. 'As I said before, it's to highlight the abuse you'd been a victim of for some time. That way, we can have the charge commuted from murder to voluntary manslaughter.'

This time it didn't sound quite so bad, but Emily felt far from reassured despite Lucy's gentle, confident tone of voice. She knew she wouldn't be able to sleep that night.

~

By the time Emily and Lucy had finished talking, night was falling. Emily handed Lucy two pieces of thick sketch paper that she'd kept face down on the table. Emily watched Lucy examine her pictures. One of the drawings was of a tree with different coloured circular swirls on the ends of its long branches. Two girls were sitting under the tree eating ice cream. Emily had tried to use bright colours, but the picture looked a little dark, even to her eyes.

'For your daughters,' she said. 'The other one is for your sons.'

In the other picture, a hammock was suspended from a similar tree. Two black dogs peered from the hammock, their bright red tongues hanging out.

'They're beautiful!' Lucy exclaimed. 'You're really gifted!' Emily forced a smile. 'Don't worry about the trial, Emily. I'm certain it will go well. You're young, and any judge will see you're the real victim.'

Emily was reminded of Amanda's retort that night to one of the arresting officers when he'd realised it was their father's blood on their nightclothes.

'The girls aren't hurt. It's the victim's blood,' he'd said to his colleague.

'Our father is definitely not the victim here,' Amanda had spat at him. Emily had worshipped her sister more than ever for that remark.

'I've got something for you, too,' Lucy said, interrupting Emily's reflection. 'I'll leave it with the director.' She held up a carrier bag. 'For you to wear in court tomorrow.'

Emily was touched by her lawyer's thoughtfulness and generosity, but dreaded what sort of clothes she might have selected. Lucy pulled out a navy knee-length skirt, black shoes, a light blue and white checked blouse and a white woollen cardigan, all from NEXT. Emily was pleasantly surprised.

'Thank you.' Emily managed to lean over the table and kiss Lucy on the cheek before she was scolded by the officer on duty from his position in the corner of the meeting room.

~

That evening after dinner, Emily didn't even need to make herself sick. The following morning after breakfast, she also felt so nauseous that she vomited several times without sticking her fingers down her throat. Emily's hands shook as she tried to do up the button of her new skirt. The waistband was tight around her stomach, which felt bloated even though it was empty.

It was the first day of the court case.

Lucy had informed her that Mrs Justice Taylor QC would be presiding. A female judge. Emily had no idea what effect this would have on the outcome of her trial. When she'd allowed herself to think about the court proceedings, she'd always visualised a male judge. But perhaps a woman would be more sympathetic. Emily hoped so.

Chapter Five

~

Oxford, August 2014

'What the fuck?!'

Philippa Stuart-Barnes has had a fondness for swear words for as long as Emily has known her. Her friend's obscenities always sound at odds with her public school accent, to Emily's ears, anyway.

Josephine sets the tray down on the coffee table a little harder than necessary, making the teaspoons jump as well as Pippa herself. She looks disapprovingly at Pippa over the top of her glasses.

'Whoops. Sorry, Mrs Cavendish,' Pippa says, clapping her hand over her mouth theatrically.

Josephine leaves the living room, her high-heeled shoes tapping on the wooden floor. Emily is suddenly cross that her mother wears shoes in the house. When she and Amanda were little, Josephine had always insisted that they remove theirs as soon as they came through the door.

Pippa takes the hand from her mouth to reveal a cheeky grin and tucks a wayward strand of her straight, dark hair behind her ear. With her other hand, she absent-mindedly rubs her pregnant belly.

Pippa's flippancy annoys Emily, too. This is serious. For Emily, anyway. Then she reasons with herself. Pippa is just trying to provide her with a bit of light relief after the dramatic events of the last few days. But she is irascible today and Pippa will have a hard job lifting her spirits.

'That's like, weird, brah.' This reaction is from Matt, who addresses everyone as 'brah', regardless of gender. He's a handsome seventeen-year-old although his long, unkempt hair tones down his looks. He has striking, green-brown eyes. Emily can see they're slightly bloodshot.

'A message from Greg? That's impossible!' Amanda exclaims. 'What did it say?'

Emily has the impression she's observing this scene, rather than participating in it, and she doesn't realise straight away that her sister is waiting for her to answer. 'He said he didn't know what was going on,' she says. 'He promised to get back to me as soon as possible.'

'Weird,' Matt repeats.

Emily turns towards her half-brother. 'I know,' she agrees.

'What were the exact words? What time was the message sent?' Amanda asks, pouring insipid tea from the pot into each of the four mugs in turn.

Emily notices her sister's hands are unsteady.

'Hang on, I'll fetch my computer and you can see for yourself.' Emily lifts Mr Mistoffelees off her lap and drops him to the floor, then pushes herself out of her armchair. She feels the familiar stabbing pain in her side. She winces.

'I'll go, Em,' Pippa says. 'Tell me where it is.'

'In my bedroom. On the bookcase.' Emily expects Matt or Amanda to offer to go as Pippa's pregnant, but she has already left the room. Emily sits down again. She never knows whether to sit back in her chair or perch on the end of it; either way it's uncomfortable. She opts for somewhere in between, although that's no better.

For a while, no one speaks. The cat jumps straight back up and kneads Emily's thighs with its claws as though punishing her for disturbing him before. Amanda hands out the mugs of tea. Emily catches Matt's gaze sweeping her living room. She looks around the room herself, as if seeing it through his eyes. The flowers she has brought home from the hospital are wilting in a vase on the sideboard. Above it hangs a large painting, *Blue Rotation*, by a Hungarian artist whose work she adores. It provides the only colour in the living room.

Emily realises now with a start that it's the only thing in the whole room she actually likes. It's an inhospitable, minimally furnished room. There's no TV set. There's one in the lounge upstairs, but apart from a few series or dramas, neither she nor Greg ever watched much television. There are no books downstairs either, as Emily tends to read novels on her Kindle.

Amanda puts an end to the silence. 'Mum, can we have some biscuits?' she calls through to Josephine in the kitchen.

'You didn't say please, Mandy.'

Amanda can't stand people using a diminutive of her name, which is, of course, why Matt always does.

'Oh, shut up, Matthew,' she growls, much to Matt's amusement.

Similarly, no one ever calls Matt by his full name except Amanda. Their squabbling has always bewildered Emily. After all, it's not as if they grew up together – Amanda had left home for university by the time Matt was born. Matt claims that it's just good-natured bickering. Right now Emily finds their banter maddening. *I really am in a foul mood. I must snap out of it*, she thinks, reminding herself that they are here to support her.

A moment later, Josephine reappears, carrying a plate of biscuits that she hands to Amanda.

'Thank you,' Amanda says to Josephine as Matt leans over and helps himself to a chocolate Hobnob. Josephine leaves the room again without a word.

'How strange!' Emily says a few minutes later. She has booted up her Mac, which Pippa has brought downstairs for her, and she's sitting with the computer on her lap. She can feel everyone else watching her as she stares in disbelief at the screen. 'It's gone.'

'What's gone?' asks Amanda.

Emily looks up and meets her sister's eyes. 'The message on Facebook. The one Greg sent. It must have been deleted.'

'Maybe you imagined it,' Amanda says. 'They were giving you some pretty strong medicine at the hospital. Perhaps it was hallucinogenic.' She reaches over from where she's sitting on the sofa, and pats Emily's knee.

'I was *not* hallucinating.'

'Well, maybe the drugs were oneirogenic, then. Didn't you say you'd fallen asleep on your bed?'

Emily thinks how much she hates it when her sister uses medical jargon, although she usually gets the gist. It goes with the job, she supposes.

'Onner what?' Clearly Matt hasn't understood, though.

'It's from the Greek word *oneiros* meaning dream,' Pippa explains. Matt looks vacantly at her. 'Amanda means that Emily may have dreamt she received the message,' she adds.

Emily is engulfed by a new surge of infuriation. Apart from Amanda, who seems to think this is all in her head, no one is taking her seriously. Emily looks from Pippa to Amanda to Matt. *I want them to believe me. I need them to believe me.* 'It wasn't a dream,' she says, but she can hear her voice waver. She turns the laptop round towards her sister. 'Look, here's the obituary I posted.'

'Well, the message isn't there now, is it?' Amanda says. 'So you must either have dreamt it or imagined it.' Amanda's tone is soft, but her words seem harsh to Emily. 'Anyway, Greg can't possibly have sent you a message.'

'He might have done,' Matt says, his mouth full of biscuit. 'Weirder things have happened.'

They all look at him. Emily thinks it would be just like Matt to suggest a message from beyond the grave. 'What do you mean?' she asks.

'Well, it could be Greg, couldn't it?' Matt pauses, looking at each of them in turn and stroking his goatee. 'What if he didn't die?'

'What the…?' Pippa refrains from swearing this time.

But Matt has spoken the words Emily really wants to hear. She desperately wants to believe that there's a chance her husband could still be alive. 'Is that possible? I mean, I didn't see his body,' she says. 'I was still in hospital on the day of his funeral.' Thoughts race through her head. *Perhaps Greg has just disappeared? Maybe he's in some sort of trouble and has had to go into hiding?*

'Greg died, Em,' Pippa says gently.

Emily's heart and stomach seem to plummet inside her and it's almost as if she has just found out about the accident all over again. She makes an effort to collect her thoughts. *If Greg really is dead, then there must be a logical explanation for all this*, she thinks to herself. *But surely I didn't imagine the whole thing?*

As if reading Emily's mind, Pippa turns to her. 'Em, I think someone's fucking with you,' she says. 'If that is what's happening here, they'd need Greg's password to access his Facebook account, wouldn't they? How many people know his login?'

'As far as I'm aware, only Greg and I know it.'

That gives Emily an idea and she logs out of her Facebook account and types in the password for Greg's. She no longer has proof she received a message, but she can prove that Greg sent her one.

'So, only one person knows it now,' Amanda remarks humourlessly.

'Wow, Mandy. A mathematician as well as a psychiatrist!' Matt jokes, and takes another biscuit from the plate.

Emily tries to ignore them. She feels crushed as she sees there is no trace of a private message from Greg to her in his Facebook messages, either. She has nothing to show her best friend, her sister and her brother that there ever was a message. Nothing to make them believe her.

'If only you were an information technologist as well, Mandy,' Matt continues as Amanda scowls at him. 'We might be able to solve this, then.'

'Ooh, that's a good idea. Why didn't we think of that before?' Pippa says. 'Emily, why don't you ask Charles? He's good with computers, isn't he? Maybe he can work out—'

'I don't think he knows any more about them than anyone else,' Amanda interrupts. She looks at Emily. 'What time did you say the message was sent, Em?'

'It must have been around 5:15 p.m. It says here I posted my obituary at 5:13. It can only have been a minute or two after that.'

'Maybe you should take a screenshot next time?' Matt suggests.

Emily doesn't want to admit that she has no idea what a screenshot is, let alone how to take one.

'Are you sure it wasn't a message that Greg had sent before his... the accident?' Pippa asks.

'No, I'm not a hundred per cent certain. The message came up when I logged in to Facebook. I thought it had just been sent, but maybe I was wrong. And now I can't check.'

'When was the last time you were on Facebook before then?'

'I don't know.'

'I think Pippa is asking if you'd already been on Facebook since Greg died,' Amanda says.

'*Allegedly* died,' Matt mutters almost inaudibly.

'No, I hadn't.'

'So, the message could have been sent by Greg *before* he died,' Amanda says.

'I suppose so,' Emily concedes. 'But I still don't understand what it could possibly mean.'

'The sender was definitely Greg?'

'Yes, definitely.' But she can hear that she sounds doubtful.

'And anyway, he called me "Alice". No one else has ever called me by my middle name.'

'Yes, but all your friends know he called you "Alice" so that doesn't rule out the possibility that someone is screwing with you,' Pippa says.

'What sort of friend would play mind games like that?' Matt asks. 'That's, like, really sick. Maybe you should call the police.'

'The police are calling on me this afternoon, Matt,' Emily says, feeling nervous at the thought of their visit. She is worried about what they might ask her. 'Maybe I'll talk to them about it.' But even as she says it, she knows that she won't mention the message. They didn't protect her when she needed protection before. They believed her when she lied; they won't believe her now, she reasons, even if she tells them the truth.

'Maybe you shouldn't say anything about it to the police just yet,' Amanda says. She lowers her voice so that only Emily can hear. 'You know, without proof and everything... The last thing you want is for them to make you out to be psychotic.'

'Perhaps you're right.' Emily knows that Amanda understands how reluctant she is to have anything to do with the police.

'Why don't you wait and see if you get another message first?' Amanda suggests.

Emily nods.

Matt takes his mobile out of the back pocket of his jeans and glances at the screen. 'It's a quarter to two,' he says. 'I'd better go. I want to go into town, then I've got to get the train back to Devon this evening.' He puts his mug down on the tray. 'Laters.'

Emily gets up and follows Matt through to the hall. She wants to offer to take him into town, but the thought of being behind the wheel of a car terrifies her. Her handbag is hanging by its strap around the newel cap of the staircase. She takes out her purse.

'Oh, no, Em. I didn't come here to hit you up for money,' he protests half-heartedly. 'I came – we all did – to try and cheer you up a bit. That's all.'

'Take it, Matt. I know you're strapped for cash.'

'Story of my life,' Matt says as Emily thrusts a fifty-pound note into his hand. 'Thanks, sis. When I'm rich and famous, I won't forget you!'

'I know. Don't spend it on dope, Matt, OK?'

'I won't,' Matt promises, giving Emily a peck on the cheek. 'Catch you on the flip side.'

'You shouldn't give him money, Emily,' Amanda says. She has stepped into the hall and is standing behind her sister. Emily whirls round. Although she's older than Emily, Amanda is slightly shorter.

'You scared me!' Emily hadn't known Amanda was there. 'Aw, he needs it, Amanda. I don't.'

'You might do now that Greg has died.'

'I suppose I'll have to look into all that at some point. I'm not up to it yet, though.'

'Just let me know when you are, and I'll help you.' Amanda unties the cardigan from around her waist and puts it on. 'Pippa will give us a hand too, won't you, Pips?'

'Of course I will,' Pippa says. 'Right. We need to get going. Rehearsals. Will you be all right?'

'Of course,' Emily says. 'Mum's here.'

'In that case you'll be fine,' Amanda scoffs. She takes the scrunchie from her wrist and uses it to fasten back her mousy hair into a ponytail. Emily notices that her fringe has been cut. It's a little too short and not quite straight. She wonders if Amanda has cut it herself.

'Don't be unkind,' Emily says, nudging her sister, who grins. 'Go and say goodbye to her.'

~

When the visitors have left, Josephine suggests that Emily should take a nap before the police come. Emily doesn't feel at all tired, but she likes the idea of spending an hour or so alone, so she goes upstairs with her computer tucked under her arm.

Minutes later, all trace of her earlier bad temper has evaporated and instead she feels overcome with sadness. She finds herself curled up in a ball on her bed, crying uncontrollably into the pillow. From time to time she thumps the bed, punctuating her sobs. She hears her crying rise in a crescendo.

Eventually, Josephine knocks tentatively at the door, but Emily barely registers the sound. Her mother knocks again, then enters the bedroom uninvited. For a moment, she just stands in the doorway. Then she comes over to the bed and perches on the end of it, awkwardly. Finally, she takes Emily in her arms and holds her until she calms down.

'It's so unfair,' Emily says.

'I know.' Josephine rubs her daughter's back. Emily can't remember her mother ever doing this even when she was little.

'I feel so… so empty,' Emily sobs, as much to herself as to her mother, 'and I don't even know if it's my fault he's dead.'

'We're all here for you, Emily,' her mum says.

Emily wishes her mother would say it was an accident – that it was no one's fault. But Josephine doesn't say anything else. *Does she blame me for Greg's death? Am I to blame?* Emily feels her shoulders tense. *Is there any chance he's still alive?*

Emily cries for ages while her mother keeps patting her back to soothe her.

'I'll sleep now,' Emily says at length, sniffing. 'Will you call me when the police come?'

Josephine hands Emily a tissue and promises to tell her as soon as Sergeant Campbell and PC Constable arrive. She leaves the bedroom, closing the door behind her.

But Emily still has no intention of sleeping. She blows her nose, and then flips open the lid of her laptop and enters her password. Next, she logs in to her Facebook account. Many people have posted their condolences on her wall in response to her obituary. The first comment is from Will Huxtable. She hasn't seen him for years – she hasn't even spoken or written to him since that memorable day when he came to visit her. But they are virtual friends on Facebook. As she begins to read through his reply, the notification sound alerts her to a new message.

This time she checks the time and sender. There is no doubt. The sender is Gregory Klein and the message was sent at 14:17. About three minutes ago. Emily is aware her breathing has become shallow.

She reads the message twice. It doesn't make any more sense to her than the first message Greg sent. And yet some intangible memory of a recent event seems to be materialising at the back of her mind. Before Emily can put her finger on what it is, she hears the buzzer. Seconds later, Josephine appears at the bedroom door to announce that the police officers have arrived. Emily closes her eyes and takes a deep breath. She snaps the lid of her laptop shut, gets up slowly and makes her way downstairs.

~

'Good afternoon,' PC Constable says, as Emily sinks into the armchair she vacated just an hour earlier.

Again, Emily can't get comfortable. She tries sitting forwards, but she's afraid of appearing too nervous, so she sits back but she thinks she must look too nonchalant. 'Good afternoon,' she says. She can hear her mother in the kitchen and realises she's making yet more weak tea. Emily resigns herself to having to drink a lot of weak tea while her mother is staying.

'Mrs Klein, we've come to ask you a few questions,' Campbell says in her Glaswegian brogue by way of a greeting. 'We have taken a statement from a member of the public who witnessed your car crash.'

Here, Campbell pauses. Emily wonders if she should say something, but Campbell hasn't asked a question yet. The police officer runs her hand through her spiky red hair. Without taking her eyes off Emily, she unbuttons her breast pocket and slides out her notebook. Then, squinting at something written in it, she clicks her ballpoint pen on and off repeatedly. Emily remembers this habit of hers from the hospital. She wonders if it's an OCD ritual or if she pen clicks absent-mindedly. Either way, it's irritating.

Looking at her pad, Campbell continues: 'This witness was walking his dog, a chocolate Labrador, along a cycle path near the Marston Ferry Road on August the first at approximately fifteen hundred hours. He saw you lose control of your vehicle, a blue Mini soft-top.'

'Nice car. Lightning Blue Metallic?' So it's Constable who has asked the first question. Emily nods. 'Great choice of car and colour. Good taste.'

Emily thinks that if Matt were here, he'd consider Constable to be playing the role of good cop. Campbell is clearly more suitable for the part of bad cop.

'My husband bought me the car for my birthday last year,' Emily tells Constable.

'According to the dog walker,' Campbell resumes, 'you drove your car, for no apparent reason, off the link road at considerable speed straight into a tree at the side of the road. It was this man who rang for the ambulance.'

'Mrs Klein, can you tell us how you came to lose control of your car?' Again, the question has come from Constable, which surprises Emily.

'I honestly don't remember,' she replies. 'I know I was driving. That's all I can tell you about the accident.'

'So you can't tell us if you swerved to avoid someone or something, or if there was a mechanical failure with your car, the brakes, for example?'

'No, I really don't know,' Emily says.

'Do you sometimes lose consciousness?' Constable asks.

'I pass out sometimes,' Emily replies, not immediately under-standing the point of his question. 'If my blood pressure is low, or I feel dizzy, or if I have a shock, for example.' Emily almost mentions that she fainted just the previous day, but she checks herself in time. That would mean having to tell the police about the Facebook messages. She definitely doesn't want to do that. 'It doesn't happen often,' she adds quickly.

'Could you have fainted in the car?'

'It's possible,' Emily says. 'But I don't think so. I wasn't feeling ill.'

She does remember, however, having a shock. Something Greg said had shaken her to the core. Some sort of revelation. What was it? It's somehow connected to the message he sent just a short time ago.

Sergeant Campbell's first question is so unexpected and so extraneous to her introductory comments that it physically winds Emily.

'Mrs Klein, have you been interviewed by the police before?'

Emily doesn't know how to answer that. Is it a trick question? Of course she has been interviewed by the police before. She was interrogated as a teenager when she admitted to killing her father. Is that what Campbell wants to hear? Could Campbell possibly already know that? If she's aware of this, there's no point in Emily denying that she has been questioned by the police in the past.

Emily struggles to recover from Campbell's blow. Her mother helps her unwittingly. With impeccable timing, Josephine enters the living room with her tray of tea and biscuits. When she has gone, Emily takes a deep breath.

'I helped police with their inquiries when my father died,' she says. She realises that the euphemism she has just used probably makes her seem as guilty as if she'd just confessed to the crime all over again.

'How old were you when your father was killed?'

So Campbell does know.

'I'd just turned fifteen,' Emily says in a voice that is barely audible.

'Let's talk about your family,' says the sergeant. 'How many brothers and sisters have you got?'

It strikes Emily that Campbell's questions are probably deliberately haphazard to try and unnerve her. It is working.

'I have a sister, Amanda, who is two and a half years older than me. And a half-brother, Matt, who is seventeen years old.'

'And Matt shares the same biological mother as you?' Campbell's intonation suggests a question, but she's looking down at her notes and Emily isn't sure that an answer is required. It occurs to her that Matt would probably reply: 'Duh!'

Campbell continues: 'Your mother's the lady who just brought us in the cup of tea. Is that correct?' Emily nods as the sergeant bores her emerald eyes into her. 'The other day in the hospital, you mentioned that your mother had been unwell. Could you tell me about her illness?'

Emily glances uncomfortably towards the kitchen door. 'Is this relevant to the car accident?' she asks.

'Mrs Klein, if it's all right with you, I'm the one who usually asks the questions,' Campbell says a little brusquely.

'We're just establishing background,' Constable says, smiling his slanted grin.

'My mother was an alcoholic for several years,' Emily says. 'She had treatment in a rehab clinic in Exeter, initially as a resident and then as an outpatient. She has been teetotal for about three years now.'

'And do any other members of your family have an addiction problem?'

Emily knows that Matt has been in trouble with the police a couple of times for supplying cannabis. That doesn't constitute an addiction, does it?

'No,' she replies categorically.

'Who paid for your mother's treatment, Mrs Klein?'

'My husband and I.'

'Your husband was obviously quite a wealthy man, Mrs Klein. He had a thriving antique business and was able to afford this house on the Woodstock Road. Did he have a life insurance policy?'

'Yes,' Emily says. 'We both did.'

'And can you explain the terms of those policies to me?'

'As far as I know, they're just standard life insurance policies.'

Campbell's gaze remains fixed on Emily and the officer is silent, waiting for her to continue. Emily can see this is part of Campbell's technique, but she feels compelled to add more information anyway.

'I imagine I can claim for the funeral costs. The policy will probably cover the remaining mortgage payments on this house. I haven't checked.'

'Presumably you're the designated beneficiary?'

'Yes, I think so. I believe Greg stipulated spouse, then next of kin for both of us. But I really don't know the terms of the policy.'

'Next of kin,' the sergeant says as she writes down the words in her notebook. Campbell's handwriting is small and neat with pointed letters, Emily notices. 'But you didn't have children with Mr Klein, did you?'

'No.' Emily wants to pinch Campbell hard. Or, better still, slap her pretty face. *She can't possibly know about my child, too. Can she?* Emily suddenly wants to cry.

'Do you know if there is a lump sum to be paid out in the event of your husband's death?'

'I have no idea. I'm not familiar with the terms of the policy,' Emily repeats. She can hear her voice quivering.

'Mrs Klein, is there a clause pertaining to accidental death in your husband's insurance policy?'

Emily feels her heartbeat quicken as she wonders what Campbell is inferring with this. 'Do I need my lawyer present for these questions?' she asks.

49

Campbell must sense her panic because she softens the tone of her voice. 'It's your prerogative, Mrs Klein, if you'd like a lawyer present. But at this stage, it's not really necessary.'

'After a serious road traffic collision, there's always an investigation. It's just routine.'

Emily nods. She finds Constable's words more reassuring.

'As police officers, we're just trying to confirm that this crash was an accident and rule out any prosecutable offence,' the sergeant adds. 'You must bear in mind, Mrs Klein, that your husband lost his life when you crashed the car.'

Emily feels an even stronger aversion towards this woman and a wave of nausea sweeps through her. Tears spring to her eyes. *Greg is gone*, she thinks. *What have I done? Did I kill him? What happened that day?* Each time this alarming thought comes into her head, she tries to push it away. She feels a little spark of anger ignite inside her. She's angry with Campbell, with herself, but also, a little, with Greg. He'd told her something. Something that had come as a bolt from the blue. What was it?

'Mrs Klein, allow me to share our theory with you,' Constable says, interrupting her thoughts. Emily looks at him. He has kind eyes and a nice mouth hidden slightly beneath his moustache. 'We believe that you and your husband were having a disagreement in the car and that something your husband said – or maybe even shouted – caused you to have a moment of inattention, which in turn led you to drive the car off the road and into the tree at the roadside.' He is enunciating slowly as if explaining something complicated to a child. 'Do you think that might be a plausible explanation for this accident?'

Emily shrugs. She doesn't trust herself to speak.

'Mrs Klein do you remember anything about the topic of the conversation you had in the car with your husband?' Evidently, it's Campbell's turn to ask the questions again. 'Can you tell us about your argument?'

'That might help us to complete our report.' Constable says.

'And then no doubt you can sort out your car with your insurance company.'

'Has anything come back to you about your disagreement with Mr Klein? Anything at all?'

'No,' Emily answers.

But that's a lie. Emily has finally remembered what Greg revealed to her in the car. Now she thinks she understands the message he sent her earlier. Part of their row still eludes her. She can't work out what her father has to do with it all, either, and yet she gets the distinct impression that this part is vital. But she recalls the reason why she and Greg were fighting. And she also has an inkling as to why she crashed the car.

Chapter Six

~

Devon, June 1996

Emily had been a resident at Exmoor Secure Children's Centre for a month before William Huxtable came to visit, but he'd written to her several times. Usually, visits were restricted to family members only. Emily's sister and mother came every week, but this weekend Amanda had stayed home to revise hard for her A-Levels. Instead, Will came. He'd told Emily jokingly that he was her cousin for the duration of the visit, but Emily suspected that her care coordinator would have been in favour of the visit anyway. After all, as she often told Emily, socialising with her peers was an important part of her treatment.

'This place is not at all how I imagined it would be,' Will said.

'I know,' Emily agreed, looking around her as they walked through the corridor towards the garden. The home had an institutional feel to it, but at the same time colourful naïve art pictures, in glassless frames, were displayed on the walls, which were themselves decorated in vivid tones.

Emily remembered the day she'd arrived. She'd been escorted through the gates and up the drive in a police car. The building had looked almost welcoming and not at all austere. She wouldn't even have known what it was in different circumstances.

'Were you expecting something resembling a Victorian workhouse?' Emily asked. She certainly had been.

'What?' Will was absent-mindedly sifting through leaflets on contraception and healthy eating on the stand by the door to the garden.

'You know, Oliver Twist?'

'Oh, yeah,' Will said. 'So what's it like here?'

'It's OK. Everything is brand new. My bedroom still smells of paint! This place only opened about a month before I was sentenced... er, sent here. There's a TV room where we all watch *Neighbours* after lunch and *Home and Away* after lessons. There's also a library, although it could do with having a few more books. There's a music room with a piano and a games room with table tennis. But the best bit is that twice a week after lessons I can paint for a couple of hours in the Art and Design workshop.'

'You have lessons?' Will was surprised. 'You didn't mention that in your letters.'

'Didn't I? Probably because I didn't think it was very interesting. Yes, I have to study. I'll be taking my GCSEs next year, you know, whether I'm still in here or not.'

'I'm glad all that's behind me,' Will said. 'That said, A-Levels are worse!' He chuckled. He was eighteen months older than Emily, but a year ahead for his age at school, which put him in the same class as Amanda.

'So, have you chosen a course?'

'Yes, I have,' Will replied. 'My first choice is Veterinary Medicine at the University of Bristol. Dad's still sulking, though.'

'Why? Because you don't want to go to Bicton College?'

'Yeah. He really wanted me to take over the farm.'

'And you definitely won't?'

They sat down side by side on a bench in the Centre's garden. The sun was shining and Will unzipped his jacket. They could see Josephine sitting on a bench a few metres away from them. Her book was open on her lap but her head was bowed low, and Emily assumed she was sleeping rather than reading. The moors rolled out in front of them, green dotted white with sheep, as far as the horizon.

'As you know, Em, I want to be a vet. I got good grades in my mocks. I want to get out of Devon and live in a big city.'

Will was sitting close to her, on her right. Emily noticed him looking at the bandage on her right arm. She tugged down the sleeve of her jumper to cover her wrist. She could see that he wanted to ask her about her wounds, but she didn't want to talk about it.

'I can understand your dad being disappointed, though,' she said quickly. 'You were so helpful to him on the farm. Hey, do you remember lambing together?'

'Of course!' Will smiled. He started humming the melody to Stealers Wheel's *Stuck in the middle with you*. Now it was Emily's turn to smile. Will began to describe their experience of that spring, but Emily tuned out. Closing her eyes and offering her face to the sun, she relived the event for herself.

~

It was a sunny day in March of the previous year when Emily, Will and Amanda stepped off the school bus.

'Em, would you like to come and see the newborn lambs?' Will asked, loosening his school tie.

'Yes, please!'

'Well, go and get changed into some old clothes and put on your wellies. I'll meet you at my dad's farm in ten minutes.'

Will did not extend the invitation to Amanda.

Amanda and Will had been best friends for years, but recently they hadn't so much as said hello to each other. Emily didn't understand why. They'd fallen out on the day Emily's cat, Smokey, had been found dead – run over, her father had said, its head

54

severed from its body. Amanda said Will hadn't been supportive. Maybe that was why they'd rowed.

Later that evening, Will's dad had turned up, rather irate, on their doorstep. Emily remembered him and her own father shouting at each other, but she hadn't been able to make out the words despite their raised voices. Graham stormed into Amanda's bedroom as soon as Mr Huxtable had left. Emily heard him say: 'Explain yourself, young lady!' but then the door slammed shut behind her father and Emily overheard no more of the conversation.

When Emily had asked her about it the next day, Amanda was evasive. She'd muttered something about having to take the rap for Will.

On arriving at the farm, Emily gazed in awe at about a dozen tiny creatures as they suckled from their mothers and wobbled around on unsteady legs. Will told her that many of them had been born only yesterday. He was feeding what seemed to be the smallest lamb in a pen with heating lamps when Emily tiptoed into the barn.

'No need to be scared,' he said. 'Come here and give the bottle to this lamb. It was born earlier today and its mother died. It needs to be fed colostrum.'

'What's colostrum?' Emily asked as Will gently transferred the bottle to her hands.

'It's a mother's first milk. It gives the baby vitamins and antibodies. We keep cow colostrum frozen for orphan lambs. It happens sometimes. We'll find another mother for this little thing later.' The lamb sucked greedily and noisily at the teat, and the liquid soon disappeared. 'Dad has taken the cows for milking,' Will continued. 'I need to go and check on a ewe having a difficult labour.'

Will led the way to another pen. He sucked in his breath when he saw that the ewe's lamb was presenting its head, but his voice was even.

'This lamb is not in the right birthing position, Em,' Will explained. 'I'm going to need your help. There's no time to fetch the vet now. Or my dad for that matter.'

'OK,' said Emily, unsure. 'Tell me what to do.'

'For now, I just want you to hold the ewe and keep her as still and as calm as possible.' He placed his hands on Emily's shoulders and guided her to the front of the sheep, then placed her hands on either side of the ewe. Then she watched Will as he carefully felt and prodded the animal's belly. 'She's expecting twins,' he said.

He poured something that smelt like disinfectant onto his hands followed by a liquid that made his hands glisten. Lubricant, Emily supposed.

'The lamb should come out with its feet under its chin, and that's not the case,' Will said as he carefully knotted a thin piece of cord around the lamb's head, which he then proceeded to push gently.

Emily observed Will. He was frowning and puffing. He was clearly having difficulty.

'This is hard!' he commented unnecessarily. 'The ewe is pushing the lamb to get her out, and I'm trying to push it back in!'

After a few seconds, he grunted in satisfaction and knelt down on one knee. 'Phew!'

Emily kept her eyes on Will. Poking his tongue out in concentration, he repositioned the lamb inside the ewe. His blond hair was quite long at the front and it flopped down over his eyes. He tried unsuccessfully to blow it away. Keeping one of her hands firmly on the sheep's side as Will had shown her, Emily stroked the ewe with her other hand.

A few minutes later, Will said, 'OK, there should be a bit more room to manoeuvre now. Are you all right there, Em?'

Emily nodded. She was amazed at his cool competence.

'Em, I think it would be easier if the ewe was on her back. That way, we'll have gravity on our side. Can you give me a hand?'

Together they laid the ewe on her side, and then rolled her onto her back. Will talked Emily softly through each step. Then his hands disappeared inside the ewe again and finally emerged holding the lamb's two little legs. Its nose and head followed. Will tied another piece of rope around the legs.

'Nearly done,' he said, smiling now. 'This is the easy bit.' He gently pulled as the ewe pushed, and the lamb slipped out in one go. 'Come here, Em,' he said, his smile even wider as he removed the ties. 'Grab some straw and rub the lamb to get her blood circulating properly.'

Emily did as she was instructed. She saw the lamb's belly rising and falling. It was breathing.

'It's going to be fine now,' Will said. His hands felt the second lamb inside the ewe. 'This one's in a good position,' he said. 'We can leave the ewe to get on with it when she's ready.'

Will's high spirits were contagious and Emily found herself mirroring his smile. He started to sing and dance around the pen. 'Stuck in the middle of a ewe.' Then he laughed.

'Is that even a real song?' Emily asked, which only served to make Will laugh more.

'Not quite,' he replied. 'The title is *Stuck in the middle with you.*'

Emily laughed too as she got the pun. 'I hope you don't want to be a singer when you grow up, Will,' she joked. 'I don't know the song, but it sounds terribly out of tune.'

'No,' Will chuckled, 'I want to be a vet. How about you, Em? What do you want to be when you grow up?'

'Happy,' Emily replied.

'That's a good goal,' Will said, his smile slipping slightly. 'Who sings that song anyway?'

'I have no idea. It was part of the soundtrack to the film *Reservoir Dogs.*'

'Have you seen that film?' Emily was incredulous. She knew it had an 18 age certificate. The only film she'd watched that her parents had deemed unsuitable was *Wayne's World*, but she hadn't really understood much of it anyway.

'Yeah. With a friend at the cinema in Barnstaple last summer.'

'Was it any good? Is it really as violent as everyone says?'

'Yeah, it has some pretty horrific scenes,' Will said. 'For example, that song is playing when a character called Mr Blonde tortures a policeman he's holding hostage. He dances along to the radio while he cuts the man's ear off with a razor.'

'That sounds horrible!' Emily exclaimed and Will laughed again. Then he grabbed Emily round the waist and continued to sing *Stuck in the middle of a ewe*.

Their laughter and Will's singing stopped at once when his father erupted into the barn. The reason for Mr Huxtable's foul mood was unclear, but Will was immediately ordered to check on another ewe and Emily was sent home.

~

Will finished reminiscing. 'Do you think there's any chance of you coming home soon?' he asked now.

'I don't know,' Emily said. 'I think at some point I can come home and be monitored there for a few months – follow-up, they call it. In the meantime, I'm getting treatment here, so I don't know whether they'll let me out early or not. I'm here for two years at most, so I may be allowed out after twelve months. You'll have gone to university by the time I get home anyway.'

'I think you might be going away, too,' Will said.

'What do you mean?'

Will hesitated a little before answering. 'Your house is on the market. Didn't your mum tell you?'

'No. She said the stables had burnt down one night. Is that why she's selling? I expect the house and grounds are way too big for her to manage alone anyway.'

'I knew about the fire. My mum was the one who called the fire brigade. But your mum told me today that she's selling because she needs the money to pay for Amanda's studies.'

Amanda wanted to read psychiatry and hoped to get in to Oxford.

'Oh.' All this was news to Emily. 'It's probably just as well she's leaving the Old Manor House. Too many bad memories in that place. It will be good to go somewhere else.'

'I can't wait to get away from home,' Will said. 'It's... stifling. We'll keep in touch though, OK?'

'Definitely,' Emily said.

Will had turned towards her and his knee was touching hers. She saw him glance down again and wondered if he was looking at her bandaged wrist or at her stomach. She used both hands to try and flatten down her tummy. Both the GP at the Centre and her psychiatrist had told her that it was barely showing, though, even after six months. No one had noticed – not even Emily herself. Not really. She'd had stomach pains and nausea and had been feeling very tired, but she'd put that down to stress and her medication.

The doctor had prescribed blood tests, but the results had come as a complete shock to everyone. Dr Irvine, who had continued to treat Emily after the trial, said that Emily was understandably in a state of denial about her condition.

Will didn't know, did he? Her mother certainly wouldn't have told him. According to Amanda, she'd scarcely spoken a word at all since she'd found out the previous week. Amanda didn't talk to Will, and she wouldn't have told a soul, anyway. He couldn't know.

'Are you left-handed?' Will asked.

'Yes,' Emily said.

So it was her arm he'd been scrutinising.

'Did you do that to yourself?' Will gently folded back the cuff of Emily's jumper to reveal the bandage.

'No, of course not.' Emily's voice didn't sound at all convincing, even to her own ears. 'It can get a bit rough in here at times, you know.'

'Can I ask you something else?'

'Yes, all right.' Will could be quite frank and Emily wondered what he was going to say.

'That night, you were lying in bed holding a razor blade. Why?'

'How did you know that?' Emily was taken aback by the question.

'It was in the *North Devon Journal*.'

'Oh, I see.' Emily was silent for a while. 'Well, you know why, Will. You may even be the only one who knows.'

'You were going to cut off his ear?'

'Uh-huh,' Emily replied noncommittally. 'Did they print that in the article, too?'

'No. No, of course not. It was only a short news story. In fact, the reporter didn't even print your name.'

Emily turned to face Will. She had tears in her eyes. She never talked about that night, but she had a sudden urge to tell Will everything.

'So, did you change your mind? You decided to shoot him instead?'

'Something like that, I suppose. I wasn't really thinking clearly.'

'And you shot him with his own gun?'

'Mmmm.' There was a short silence during which both Emily and Will were lost in their thoughts.

'What gun? Not with his clay pigeon shotgun, surely? You couldn't have… Wasn't your father…? How did you—?'

'There's a lot I don't remember about that night.'

She'd used the same answer several times when she was being interrogated by the police a few months ago. That put an end to their conversation. Emily told Will nothing about that night after all.

Suddenly, her tummy tightened painfully. Maybe it was hunger. She'd deliberately made herself sick after lunch. But Emily wondered if it could be a contraction, even though that only made six months.

'I think you should go now,' she said to Will. She resolved not to reply to his letters from now on.

Chapter Seven

~

Oxford, September 2014

Amanda's face turns red. 'He told you he'd had an affair? The bastard!'

Emily is touched by her sister's reaction. Even now, Amanda is protective towards her. Always the big sister. Pippa looks suitably impressed at Amanda's term of abuse.

They're sitting around the table in the window of The Grapes. The pub is conveniently situated a stone's throw away from both The New Theatre and the hall where Amanda and Pippa have been rehearsing that evening with their Amateur Dramatic Society. They are both regulars here.

'Hi, am I interrupting?' A tall, smartly dressed man in his thirties with a rotund face beams at the group. It takes Emily a few seconds to place him.

'No, not at all,' says Pippa, in a tone that implies the exact opposite. 'Have a seat. Matt, this is Richard. Emily, you've met Richard, haven't you? He's performing as Tim in this year's play.'

'Oh, I forgot to ask what the play was this year,' says Emily, as Richard sets his pint down on the table, wriggles out of his waterproof coat and then sits on a stool next to Pippa. He fixes his eyes on Amanda. Emily smiles tightly at Richard, remembering the day he turned up on her doorstep. *It was a long time ago now*, she tells herself, *and that incident is best forgotten. Best to move on.*

'It's *The Sugar Syndrome* by Lucy Prebble,' Pippa says.

'I don't know why the director chose that one. It's not very recent, and there are only really four parts,' Amanda says. Emily hears the whine in her sister's voice.

Emily examines Richard. He hasn't stopped staring at Amanda. He is clearly still besotted with her although their brief relationship ended – badly – seven or eight years ago now. He meets Emily's eyes and she turns away and looks out of the window. It is dismal and grey outside, and the rain is running down the panes. Emily is distracted by this and tunes out of the conversation a little.

'What part are you playing, Mandy?' asks Matt.

'I'm Pippa's understudy,' Amanda replies huffily.

Matt splutters into his lager. 'You're only satisfied if you get to play the role of a murderess anyway,' he teases. 'What was the name of the villain you played last year? Gonorrhoea?'

Everyone laughs except Emily. She's starting to feel disconnected, as though she is removed from the scene. She's thinking about Greg's Facebook messages, of course. She can't get them out of her mind.

'Goneril, you philistine! I did enjoy portraying that character,' Amanda admits, 'even though I had to kill Regan.' She touches Pippa's arm and looks at her apologetically.

'Your own sister,' Pippa jokes. 'Yes, indeed, no sororicide for you this year.' Seeing Matt knit his eyebrows, she explains: 'It's from the Latin. It means killing your own sister.' Matt shrugs. Emily remembers he had dozed off during the performance before Amanda poisoned Pippa.

'That was a good play,' says Amanda. 'How did we go from a

Shakespearean tragedy to a debut play that was written over ten years ago?'

'There were far fewer actors available this year,' Pippa says. 'But it's a good script. It raises important issues. Anyway, you may well get to do it if the baby's late.' She rubs her round tummy.

Emily forces herself to turn away from the window and participate in the conversation. 'What's the play about?' she asks. She thinks Amanda looks a little uncomfortable at her question.

'I'm not sure you'd like it,' Amanda says dismissively. She picks up her glass to sip the wine, but there's none left. Frowning, she puts the glass back down on the table.

It's Pippa who outlines the plot. 'It's about a seventeen-year-old girl who pretends to be a young boy in an Internet chat room. She ends up befriending a thirty-year-old who is struggling against his paedophiliac tendencies.'

'That's me,' Richard says proudly.

'You're not supposed to be the seventeen-year-old girl, are you?' Matt asks Pippa. Richard chuckles at this.

'No, of course not! I'm her mother, Jan.'

'So they become friends because the paedophile thinks he's talking to a young boy?' Matt asks Richard.

'Well, initially, perhaps, but they can relate to each other. You see, Dani, the teenage girl, has spent some time in a clinic because of her eating disorders and Tim has done time in prison. Tim knows his urges are wrong, but he's taken in by Dani's lies, so he becomes a victim, too.'

Emily fights to hide her growing unease. *Amanda's right*, she thinks. *I wouldn't like the play.*

'It's a dangerous world, the Internet,' Matt says. 'Lots of people pretend to be someone they aren't.' He drinks the dregs of his beer.

Emily can feel Matt's eyes on her, but she's looking at Richard. She notices that he repeatedly scratches the back of his neck when he talks. She wonders if his shirt collar is irritating his skin. Or maybe being around Amanda makes him tense.

'It sounds very harrowing,' Emily says.

'Oi, Richard, it's your round, mate.' Emily looks over her shoulder and sees a man standing at the bar waving his empty pint glass.

'Excuse me, please. That's my cue.' Laughing at his own joke, Richard gets up and goes to join his friends.

Once Richard has left the table, Pippa loses no time in getting back to the original topic of conversation. 'So, start at the beginning,' she says to Emily. 'What did the second message say?'

'It said: "*It's me, Em. I'm so sorry.*" I got it just after you left last Saturday.'

'And you think Greg's apologising for cheating on you?'

'I thought that might explain it. The message jogged my memory. I remember now that's what we were arguing about in the car. He told me he'd had an affair and swore it was over.' Emily takes a sip of her mineral water. 'Why else would he say he was sorry?' She sees Amanda's expression. Her sister obviously still thinks there's no way these messages could have been written by Greg.

'For dying?' Emily sees Amanda shoot a warning look at Matt. 'Maybe it's a conspiracy,' he goes on. 'What if someone's trying to push you over the edge, Em? Perhaps you have something that someone needs.'

'Like what?' Emily asks.

'I don't know. Information?'

'Oh, Matt, shut the fuck up,' Pippa says. 'Go and order us some more drinks. An orange juice for me, a Perrier for Emily and a glass of Chardonnay for Amanda.'

Emily suddenly feels like a gin and tonic, even though she has only ever had one before, but she says nothing. She slips Matt a twenty-pound note and he saunters off towards the bar.

'How long is he staying?' Amanda nods towards Matt.

'Just overnight. He's taking Mum back down to Devon tomorrow morning.'

'Had enough of her?' Amanda grins knowingly.

'She means well, but I need to be alone for a while.'

'I still can't believe Greg told you he'd had an affair. Did he say anything else about it? Did he talk about his mistress?' Amanda's smirk has disappeared and her face is serious.

'I don't think so. I don't remember him saying any more than that.'

'Greg's Facebook account may have been hacked,' Pippa says.

'What on earth for?' Amanda argues. 'No one has attempted to extort money from Emily or anything like that.'

'Well, what other explanation can you come up with for her harassment?'

'Harassment? It's only two Facebook messages.'

'Purportedly sent by her late husband.'

'I'm starting to wonder...' Amanda turns to her sister. 'No, perhaps we should talk about it later.' She nods, almost imperceptibly towards Pippa.

'No, it all right,' Emily says. 'You can say it now.'

'Well, you mentioned you were having trouble sleeping. When you were a teenager, you developed a dissociated personality.'

Oh no, here we go, Emily thinks.

'Dissociative disorders can be triggered by trauma, you know,' Amanda continues, placing her hand on Emily's knee. 'And you've just suffered another distressing event with Greg's death. Do you think it could be happening again?'

'You mean, have I been writing these messages to myself?' Emily tries to keep the indignation out of her voice.

'Well, is it possible? It could be a perfectly normal part of the grieving process. You obviously don't want to let Greg go, and so you're acting subconsciously to keep him alive.'

'That doesn't sound very normal to me,' Pippa says.

Amanda adds, 'The message said: "It's me, Em." Think about it. "Me" is "Em" spelt backwards.'

No one speaks for a moment while this sinks in. Matt arrives with the drinks and distributes them around the table. Emily looks out of the window at the rain again. She thinks the weather reflects her mood. She feels like crying.

'That's called a reverse palindrome,' Pippa says eventually. 'A word that spells a different word in reverse.' Matt sighs and rolls his eyes at Emily. She manages to give him a tiny smile.

'You said yourself that you were the only person who knew Greg's password,' Amanda says.

Emily feels the colour slowly drain from her face. Greg's password is 'ecilA0891'. Her middle name followed by her year of birth. Backwards.

Emily chews one of her nails. Is she dissociating? Could there be any truth in what Amanda has said? Or is this the sort of conclusion her sister would naturally make as a psychiatrist? Not for the first time, Emily is frustrated that her sister seems to think this is all the product of her imagination.

A thought suddenly occurs to Emily. A memory from the past. She shivers as if an icy draught has blown over her. She has buried all that. It isn't meant to resurface. *It can't be her.* She tries to push the suspicion out of her head. But it would make sense. It would explain the sleeping problems and the memory gaps. It might even explain the unexpected desire for an alcoholic drink. All this is so unlike Emily. She hasn't been feeling herself, but surely that's normal given the circumstances? *No, it's not her. She doesn't exist.*

Pippa brings Emily out of her reflection. 'It's far more likely that the message didn't come from Greg at all, and it was just someone expressing their condolences,' she says. 'You say "I'm so sorry" to the bereaved when they lose their loved ones. You probably just mistook the sender of the message for Greg. Why don't you have another look when you get home?'

Emily remembers checking when she'd received the message. This time there was no doubt. The sender was definitely Greg. But she nods, grateful to her friend. Pippa is Emily's closest friend even though they met through Amanda. Pippa doesn't know much about Emily's childhood, but she hardly ever asks about it. She doesn't know about the mental health problems Emily had when she was a teenager. Despite that, she has come up with a rational explanation for all of this. How typical of Pippa's unwavering loyalty to reject the idea that Emily might be going mad.

I'm not losing my mind, Emily thinks, *I'm not going insane.*

'Hey, isn't that Charles?' Matt has only met Greg's friend once, but this isn't the first time Emily has been impressed at his ability to remember people's faces and names. Charles Haywood has just entered the pub. He spots them and starts walking towards them, shaking water from his umbrella onto the pub floor.

'I've bumped into him in here before,' says Amanda. 'His office is nearby, just off George Street somewhere.'

It occurs to Emily that it's Saturday and he's unlikely to have been working, but she keeps this thought to herself.

Matt offers to buy Charles a drink, so Charles takes his seat next to Emily. He puts his arm around her shoulders in a friendly manner and asks her how she's coping. Emily is touched – Charles has lost his best friend after all, and yet here he is, showing concern for her without a hint of self-pity.

Greg had been a similar age to Charles, but Emily has always thought of Charles as older. Where Greg's hairline had merely been receding, Charles's head is in an advanced state of baldness. Greg's stomach had been relatively toned whereas Charles's middle-aged spread is losing its battle against gravity. But Charles exudes confidence and charm. His avuncular face examines hers, and she feels that not much would escape his alert blue eyes.

'You will let me know if there's anything I can do, won't you? Anything at all.'

Pippa is quick to try and take up Charles on his offer. 'The other day we were wondering how good you are with computers. We thought you might be able to help Emily out.'

67

'Well, I suppose I'm a little more computer-literate than most people, but I'm no expert. And I don't know much about Macs. You have a Mac, Emily, don't you?' She nods. 'Has your computer crashed?'

'No, I've been getting messages on Facebook. Supposedly sent by Greg.'

'How awful! Are they threatening?' Charles asks.

'No, the second one was apologetic, actually.'

'How many messages have you received?'

'Just those two.' Emily begins toying with a cardboard beer mat.

'The first thing to do, I reckon, would be to contact the Facebook Help Centre,' Charles says. 'You can notify Facebook about abusive or inappropriate content by clicking on the report link. You really ought to do that if you receive another of these messages.'

'But you don't know how to find out who's sending these messages?' Pippa says.

'If someone has hacked into Greg's account, that will be almost impossible,' Charles replies.

Emily has torn up the beer coaster and starts to pile up the pieces on the table.

'Where is Greg's laptop, anyway?' asks Matt, who has come back to the table, armed with a pint for Charles and two bags of crisps. He remains standing as all the seats are taken. No one answers him. Nobody had wondered where Greg's computer was.

'I need a cigarette,' Amanda says.

'I thought you gave up smoking years ago,' Emily says.

Amanda doesn't answer.

'I'll join you,' says Charles, getting up. Matt sits down on the stool Charles has vacated as he follows Amanda outside.

'And I need the toilet,' Pippa says. 'Baby's pushing on my bladder!'

'Too much info, Pippa, brah,' Matt says. She cuffs him gently around his head on her way past.

Greg's computer seems to be forgotten, but Emily determines

to look for it later. She observes Charles and Amanda through the window as she asks Matt about his plans. He left school the previous year with merely a handful of GCSEs and doesn't seem to have landed a permanent job since then.

Ripping open a bag of crisps, he tells her that he's currently looking for building work in Devon, but jobs are scarce at the moment. Emily gets the impression that while the weather stays mild and the surf is up, Matt won't be looking too hard.

The whole time she's talking to Matt, Emily keeps her eyes on Charles and Amanda. They're standing together on the pavement, close to the window, huddled under Charles's umbrella with their backs towards Emily. She watches as Charles lights a second cigarette for Amanda, who touches his arm briefly to thank him.

Emily feels a pang of jealousy. Something about the intimate gesture between Charles and Amanda bothers Emily, who has always been attracted to Charles. He's much older than Emily, as Greg had been, and she loves his striking eyes and beautiful wide smile. She's instantly overcome with remorse at having these thoughts when her husband died only five weeks ago.

'We should go, Matt,' says Emily, leaning towards him and brushing part of a crisp out of his goatee. 'How much have you had to drink?' Matt, who doesn't own a car and has come to Oxford by train, had driven Emily to the pub in Josephine's car.

'Two pints. Do you want to drive?'

'No, I'd rather you did.'

Emily still hasn't taken the wheel since the accident. Her own car is a write-off anyway, but she could have borrowed her mother's car at any time, or used Greg's. Matt has picked the Range Rover up from where it was parked near Greg's shop, and it's now in front of Emily's home. She thinks she'll probably never drive the SUV anyway; it's ridiculously big.

Pippa and Amanda have decided to spend the afternoon at Newbury Racecourse, about half an hour's drive away. The Stuart-Barnes family own several racehorses. Two fillies with unpronounceable names, which belong to Pippa's father, are competing later this afternoon. According to the forecast on Pippa's mobile, the weather will brighten up in an hour or so in time for the event.

To Amanda's obvious delight, Charles accepts Pippa's invitation to go with them. Emily, however, wants to go home, although she can see by the glint in Matt's eyes that he would quite happily try his luck betting some of her money on the horses.

Pippa hugs Emily tightly against her huge bump, and even gives Matt a peck on the cheek. As Emily gives Charles a quick kiss goodbye, she detects a minty smell on his breath from the chewing gum he has put in his mouth to mask the odour of the cigarette. Hugging her sister next, Emily notices that Amanda smells more strongly of tobacco and alcohol. This is partially camouflaged by the powerful aroma of Amanda's perfume. Nonetheless, for Emily, it's a scent that remains disturbingly reminiscent of her father.

When she gets home, Emily checks Greg's study for his laptop. She doesn't find it. She asks Matt if he will drive her back into town so that she can see if Greg's computer is at his place of work. Matt offers to go alone to give his sister a rest, and Emily gratefully hands him the keys to Greg's shop.

Matt is gone for less than an hour. During that time, Emily is constrained to drink two mugs of her mother's weak tea. A cup of tea is Josephine's answer to all of life's ups and downs, now that she can no longer unscrew the cap of the whiskey bottle, Emily reflects bitterly. As she sips the hot drink, Emily tells Josephine about the Facebook messages for which she's hoping to find some clues on Greg's laptop. But Matt comes back without the computer.

'That's odd,' Emily says. 'Where on earth could it be?'

'Shall I check his study for you?' Josephine says.

'By all means, but I've already looked in there.'

Emily follows her mother upstairs to Greg's study. 'I'll have to clear out all this stuff at some point,' Emily says, looking at the papers, files and books scattered everywhere. There's even a stack of chequebooks, most of which contain only the stubs, on Greg's desk. Josephine lifts some papers and finds the small laptop buried underneath. 'It must have been there all the time,' Emily says, feeling stupid.

'What now?' Josephine asks, pushing her glasses up to the bridge of her nose.

'I don't know. I'll have to get someone to take a look at it, I guess.'

'You could tell Sergeant Campbell and that police constable.'

'Amanda advised against going to the police with this,' Emily says. 'She thinks it might reflect badly on me.'

'She may have a point,' Josephine concedes. 'Do you know someone who's good with computers?'

'Yes, Josh. I'm paying him to set up a website for my paintings. I'm seeing him on Monday.'

'Well, maybe he'll be able to help you find some answers.'

'Maybe.'

~

Emily hopes Josh will be able to prove that the messages really have come from Greg. She badly wants to believe that her husband is still alive and that for some reason he can't come to her. But she has to face the facts. Greg wouldn't have written 'Em'. He has never used a diminutive of her first name. He would have called her 'Emily' or 'Alice'.

She thinks over what Amanda said in The Grapes. She wonders again if there could be some truth in it. Amanda's explanation certainly sounds plausible. After their father's death, Emily was diagnosed as having dissociative identity disorder, or, as her psychiatrist, Dr Rosamund Irvine, had sometimes called it, multiple personality disorder.

Emily herself hadn't been able to talk about her pain or describe what had happened to her; she couldn't even remember huge chunks of it. According to Dr Irvine, she'd assumed a secondary identity, or alter. This other personality was stronger, more confident and more assertive. She behaved provocatively, wearing a defiant look on her face and swearing. And she expressed Emily's feelings and memories during therapy.

Her alter seemed to know everything Emily was trying to bury deep inside her, but after the sessions, Emily could never remember anything she'd said. She suspected this was because she'd been in a semi-hypnotic state. The young psychiatrist had been excited to work with Emily because of her so-called personality disorder. But Emily had never really been convinced by Dr Irvine's talk of a secondary identity. She'd always thought that it was just her mind's way of coping. It was the only way she could protect herself from the trauma caused by the sexual abuse and then her father's murder.

Amanda, on the other hand, has always believed in the DID diagnosis. Maybe Amanda is right after all. Maybe Emily's alter is indeed writing these messages and, as a result, Emily herself doesn't consciously realise it. The latest Facebook message read: '*It's me, Em.*' It's phrased ambiguously for a start. On top of that, as Amanda pointed out, 'Me' and 'Em' contain the same letters.

But a terrifying thought had struck Emily earlier when they were in the pub. She hasn't been able to get the idea out of her head all afternoon. It's still scaring the hell out of her. It seems to support Amanda's theory. There's something that very few people know: when Emily was a teenager, her secondary identity – her alter – had a name. It was 'Em'.

Chapter Eight

~

Devon, July 1996

Emily's stomach pain turned out to be Braxton Hicks contractions. Emily was more than twenty-four weeks pregnant, so she was beyond the usual legal limit for a termination. But both the GP at the Centre and Dr Irvine agreed that continuing the pregnancy could seriously affect Emily's mental health. The two doctors also said there was a risk the baby would be born with physical and mental abnormalities due to Emily's anorexia and the medication she'd been taking, not to mention the close blood relation of the father.

The beginning of the pregnancy had been estimated by ultrasound as dating from 26th December 1995. This surprised Emily because her father, who was also genetically her baby's father, had died on the 24th. But the midwife told her this was entirely feasible as the conception depended on the ovulation date. A fortnight after her stomach pains during Will's visit, Emily went into labour. Her blood pressure was very high. She was only at the beginning of her seventh month of pregnancy.

Her abortion had been scheduled for the following day.

Her baby, weighing two pounds and seven ounces and measuring sixteen inches, was born on Thursday 17th July. A ventilator was needed to assist the premature baby's breathing, and an intravenous tube ensured the feeding for the first few days.

Immediately after giving birth, Emily listened out for the baby's crying. When there was none, she felt a wave of relief. But it was short-lived. The wailing began just a few seconds later. Emily didn't want to see her baby. She was afraid that it would be deformed. Even though the midwife had informed Emily of its sex, she couldn't bring herself to attribute a gender to the baby, any more than she could find a first name for it.

But the first time Emily saw her baby, she was amazed. She'd found herself walking slowly towards the nursery in the neonatal unit and, before she knew it, she was peering through the transparent plastic of her baby's incubator. Wearing nothing but a nappy, its little body was perfectly formed. Emily counted ten minuscule fingers, complete with fingernails, and ten small toes. The baby had a beautiful face, and downy hair on a head that was only slightly disproportionate to its body.

As Emily observed her baby, a tiny hand opened out as if reaching towards her. Emily felt overwhelmed by an unexpected surge of love. Unbidden, a first name came into her mind. It would suit her baby very well. And suddenly, Baby Cavendish, as the name on the plastic bracelet read, had an identity after all.

Josephine came to the hospital to visit Emily twice. She was sober on both of these occasions. Emily thought that must have been a considerable effort for her mother, and acknowledged this by tactfully commenting that she was looking very well.

'Yes, well, my doctor has advised me to eat healthily and cut out the alcohol from now on,' Josephine said.

Josephine was being cagey. Emily knew that her mother was hiding something, but she couldn't get any more out of her. She wondered if her mother's liver had finally packed in.

Josephine refused point blank to see the baby. 'You can't keep this baby, Emily,' she said. 'You're still a child, yourself. Apparently, the social worker is coming today. She'll tell you the same thing. You cannot keep this baby.'

Six days after giving birth, Emily left the hospital without her baby. Her breasts swollen needlessly with milk, and her eyes swollen and puffy from crying, she was taken back to Exmoor Secure Children's Centre. For a few weeks she felt moody, sad and irritable. She couldn't sleep. No baby, but she wasn't spared the baby blues.

Six months after giving birth, a year and two weeks after her father's murder, Emily was released from the Centre. Dr Irvine said goodbye and wished Emily good luck.

'I'm so proud of you. You're coping so much better,' the psychiatrist told Emily with tears in her eyes and a smile on her face. Emily suspected that Dr Irvine regretted that her work with Emily's supposed dissociative identity disorder had come to an end.

The director of the Centre also had some encouraging words for Emily. He added jokingly that he hoped they wouldn't see her again at the Home.

Not having made many friends, the only person that Emily knew she would miss was Mr Latimer, her art teacher. He'd had one of her paintings framed as a leaving present for her.

'There is glass in the frame,' Mr Latimer pointed out to Emily. He didn't need to remind her that all of the pictures in the Centre were exhibited in frames with no glass. 'That is a sure sign of the progress you've made!'

'Thank you,' Emily said. She wanted to say something more to express her gratitude towards her teacher, but she had a lump in her throat.

'Please keep up your artwork and art lessons,' Mr Latimer said.

'I will,' she managed.

'This last piece of work shows real promise, Emily.' Mr Latimer indicated her picture in the frame. 'The colours are still a little sombre, but at least your favourite colour is dark blue now. You used an awful lot of black in the beginning.' Emily saw a twinkle in his eye. 'Perhaps one day you'll come out of your Blue Period into a brighter world. That's what I'm wishing for you anyway. I do love the spirals and ripples in your painting. For me, it is reminiscent of Robert Smithson's Earthworks. It suggests infinity and mystery.'

Mr Latimer had mentioned this sculptor before, but Emily wasn't familiar with his work. For Emily, her pictures had nothing to do with infinity and mystery. Rather, they translated her feeling that she was spiralling out of control and hurtling into the unknown or drowning. She didn't share this thought with her teacher.

'Anyway, Emily, all the best to you. I'm glad you're going home.'

'Oh, I'm not going home,' Emily said. 'I'm actually going to my sister's in Oxford.'

'Ah, that's a lovely place.' And with that, he formally shook her hand, turned around and left.

Emily wondered where home was for her now. Josephine had recently sold her daughters' childhood country house and bought a much smaller house in Braunton, a large village near the North Devon coast. She seemed to be drinking much less these days, but she was busy with the move as well as with her new job as a receptionist in a local hotel. There had been no question of Emily moving in with her mother.

As her sister was now an adult, it had been decided that Emily would go to Oxford and live with her. Dr Irvine referred Emily to a good psychiatrist in the city so that she could have her follow-up treatment there.

Amanda was an undergraduate at Christ Church. The College boasted numerous famous alumni, including Charles Lutwidge Dodgson. Better known by his pseudonym, Lewis Carroll, he had written Emily's favourite book, *Alice's Adventures in Wonderland*, for a young girl named Alice Liddell, the daughter of the College Dean.

Emily was both anxious and excited about moving away from Devon. She didn't know Oxford at all, which was the scary part. Lucy, her solicitor, who had visited Emily a few times in the Secure Centre, had family there and assured her it was a wonderful city. Amanda raved about it. Oxford represented a new start for Emily, an adventure. But at the same time, she felt like she was falling down a rabbit hole, and she didn't know if she would sink or swim in the pool of tears.

Chapter Nine

~

Oxford, September 2014

Josh is due to arrive at 9:30 a.m. He turns up at a quarter to eleven, looking sheepish as he stands on Emily's doorstep. She examines him discreetly. He's wearing faded denim jeans and a tight-fitting T-shirt that shows off his biceps and triceps. He's almost irresistible with his dishevelled hair and stubble.

Emily hasn't seen him since the day before the accident when they'd had sex. He attempts to greet her with a kiss on the lips.

'What do you think you're doing?' she demands.

'I thought… I didn't think… I'm sorry.'

'It was a…' Emily avoids using the word 'mistake' just in time. She needs Josh to help her with the computer so she doesn't want to offend him, but he needs to know that it isn't going to happen again. 'It was a one-night stand, Josh. Nothing more.'

'It was during the day.'

'All right. It was a one-off. I'm too old for you.'

'I happen to like cougars.'

'You're too young for me, then,' Emily says, wincing. 'Josh, you're not making this very easy for me.'

'I'm joking. It's OK. I understand.'

An athletic young man in his early twenties, Josh has a wonderfully toned body. He's also fairly intelligent, in Emily's opinion, in a geeky sort of way. She finds him very attractive even though he's ten years younger than her. She feels her face redden as she remembers how she seduced him. *What was I thinking?*

It wasn't the first time she'd behaved like that. Emily often experiences sexual urges. They come from nowhere and with no warning. She used to think she should try harder to suppress them, if only for her husband's sake. Poor Greg. She didn't ever feel anything remotely resembling desire for him. She often wonders if she's capable of associating sex and love.

'Thank you for the card and flowers,' says Emily, anxious to change the subject. 'That was very nice of you.'

Josh had sent her a wreath and some kind words expressing his condolences when he'd heard about her husband's death.

'No problem, Emily.' Josh clears his throat. 'Should I call you Mrs Klein?'

'No, Emily is fine.'

'Shall I show you what I've done so far? And then we'll get the website up and running. If we go through it together, you can tell me exactly what you want.'

Emily had picked up Josh's advert – for designing websites and repairing computers – in a café a few months ago. She's hoping her artwork will sell better once she has her own website. She leads the way to the kitchen where she makes Josh a coffee, hoping that will disperse any awkwardness between them. As the liquid drips noisily from the coffee machine into the cup, Emily sees Josh look up at her print of *The Old Guitarist*.

'It's by Picasso,' she says. 'From his Blue Period.' It's the only print in the house. All the other paintings, including those not created by Emily herself, are originals.

'Is he blind?' Josh asks, still mesmerised by the decrepit musician.

'Yes.'

'Do you play the guitar?'

'I can play. I haven't taken it out of its case for a while though.'

'And do you actually like this picture?' It's clear from Josh's tone that he doesn't care for it much.

'Yes. It's sentimental. It reminds me sometimes that even when I'm feeling down inside, everything seems brighter out there in the world.' She hands Josh his drink and heads into the studio, which is annexed to the main house via the kitchen. Josh follows her.

They sit side by side on the Perspex chairs at the slim Lucite waterfall table. Emily loves this room. It's her haven. She looks around it to avoid looking at Josh. The walls and the large square floor tiles are white. Three sets of sliding patio doors give access to the garden. Emily's paintings – on easels, on the floor and on the walls – add vibrant colours to the room. Everything else in it is either transparent or white.

Emily has booted up her computer, and Josh is hunched over it at the coffee table, which is a bit low for working on. He turns down Emily's offer to work in the kitchen instead.

'I like the light here in the studio,' he says. 'And, anyway, I may need to take more photos of the artwork. It'll be easier if I'm in here.'

Emily tries to banish from her mind images of the two of them making love in this very room the last time Josh called round.

He's keen to show her what progress he has made, but as far as she can see, it doesn't amount to much.

'I've registered a domain name. So, your website address will be emilykleinart.co.uk if you're happy with that.'

Emily nods.

'Now you need a password.' Josh turns the computer towards Emily, just as she gives him a password, so he enters it himself.

'Melody dot Cave, capital M, capital C,' he repeats as he types it in. 'That sounds like a lovely place. Is it?'

'I don't know.' Emily's voice sounds cold to her, but Josh doesn't pick up on this.

'Where is it?'

There is no way she's going to talk about this to Josh. 'In Devon,' she says curtly. 'Look, it was a long time ago. Can we get on with this?'

'Sorry. Sure. I need your credit card now to sign you up with a webhost. It costs around five pounds a month.'

Emily's purse is in her handbag, hanging in its usual place on the newel post in the hall. But she knows her credit card details by heart. She recites them to Josh who types in all the numbers.

'All right. Now I just need to install WordPress, and then you can choose your header image and font. I thought we'd exhibit your paintings with a slider.'

'You do realise I only understand every other word you're saying?' Emily says.

'That's OK. You'll see.'

Less than half an hour later, everything is finished. Josh has uploaded the photos he'd taken of her paintings and Emily is thrilled with the result.

'Nearly there now,' Josh says, as she thanks him profusely. 'Do you have a Twitter or Facebook account?'

'Yes, Facebook,' Emily says. 'That reminds me, I need your help with that.'

'Well, we'll just finish this, and then we'll sort out any other problems,' Josh says. 'We're going to create a Facebook page, and then link it to your website.'

Emily watches silently as Josh works, and a short while later, he has completed this task.

'Now we need to go on to your own Facebook account and invite your friends to like your page,' Josh continues. He angles the computer towards Emily so that she can type her login.

Emily brings up her timeline, and an instant later she gasps. 'That was Greg!'

'Your husband?'

'Yes!'

'Where?'

'A photo of him next to his Range Rover appeared, but it's gone,' Emily says. Her breathing has become shallow.

'In a banner ad?'

'Is that what it's called? It was right here. Beside my timeline.' Emily points at the right of the screen.

'Your husband wasn't a model, was he?'

'God, no!' The idea would have been almost laughable in different circumstances.

'But that's his Range Rover in the driveway, right?'

'Yes.' Emily tries to calm herself down, but her words come out in a rush. 'He bought it about six months ago, although why he needed a four-wheel drive to go from the Woodstock Road to the city centre and back every day I can't imagine.'

'Did he ever look at Range Rovers online before he purchased it?'

'I expect so.'

'Could he have done it from your computer?'

'It's possible, but he's more PC than Mac. He had his own laptop. Why?'

'Banner ads are often tailored to your online habits,' Josh explains. Emily knits her eyebrows. 'When you visit a website, that site remembers you, thanks to the cookies on your hard drive. This information is sometimes shared with other sites via advertising networks.'

Emily feels even more confused, and it must show on her face because Josh attempts to simplify his explanation.

'Basically, if Mr Klein had looked at websites for Range Rovers from your computer, it wouldn't be at all surprising for adverts for four-wheel drive vehicles to crop up on a web page that you're looking at.'

Emily is still reeling from the shock of seeing Greg in the

photo. All of a sudden, she feels like she's drowning. She struggles to make out what Josh is saying. It's as if she is underwater and his words a distorted noise at the surface. She has to remind herself to breathe.

'But why would Greg be in the photograph?'

'Isn't it more likely that it was just someone who looked like him?' Josh says, looking at her with a worried expression on his face. 'There must be loads of men in their late thirties or early forties interested in cars like these. So it could just be a pop-up featuring the type of person that particular car ad would be aimed at.'

Emily doesn't mention that Greg had actually been pushing fifty. *Oh, Greg. Why you?* She misses him so much. Could she be mistaken about seeing him in the advert? Josh's suggestion certainly sounds plausible.

'Are you OK?' He puts his hand lightly on her arm.

Emily nods even as she feels the tension tightening in her shoulders. 'I'm just upset,' she says, 'and a bit paranoid.' She explains about the messages she has received, ostensibly from her dead husband. By the time she has finished telling him about it all, she is feeling almost back to normal. 'Do you think it's possible that someone has…?' She searches for the correct terminology.

Josh supplies it. 'Hacked into your Facebook account?'

'Or Greg's?'

Josh starts to explain how this can be done, but once he has got to the difference between phishing and keylogging, Emily switches off completely. She sighs inwardly, but, again, her exasperation must be palpable because Josh stops mid-sentence and looks at her.

'Do you want me to check your computer? If you fetch Mr Klein's PC, I'll have a look at it as well.'

'Would you, Josh? I'd be so grateful.'

Emily does feel indebted to Josh, but she also feels bored stiff with all the computer jargon he uses. It's second nature to him, but it's a foreign language to her. She'd found it very sexy to listen to his geek-speak last time he was here. But today she finds it downright nerdy. And a complete turn-off.

'It's no problem. But, Emily?'

'Yes?'

'It might just be that someone has got hold of your password. Do you use Melody.Cave for everything?'

'Yes,' Emily admits.

'Well, you shouldn't. So, when I've finished with your computers, change all your passwords, especially your Facebook one. Change Mr Klein's, too. And don't give them to anyone. And that should put a stop to this nonsense.'

Josh is obviously being thorough in his examination of the two computers, as he has been working on them for over two hours. Emily makes them sandwiches when her own tummy starts rumbling, and she paints while he works, bent over the laptops.

Since she always listens to classical music while she paints, she asks Josh if the noise would disturb him. When he says he also listens to music while working, she connects her mobile to the speaker in the corner and puts on Carl Orff's *Carmina Burana*. She thinks Josh might ask her to turn it off, or at the very least turn it down, but to her surprise, he hums along to *Fortuna*. They work companionably without speaking.

In the end, Josh tells her that he hasn't found any evidence of hacking on either computer. He finally leaves, a cheque in his jeans pocket for twice the amount Emily had initially agreed to pay him, and a wide grin on his face. As soon as Emily has closed the front door behind him, she sits down and changes all her passwords as well as the passwords to Greg's and her own Facebook accounts.

She considers what Josh said about the pop-up. She wants to believe that he was right and that it was just an ordinary middle-aged man in the ad. But she can't shake off her belief that it really had been Greg in the photo. She only saw the advert for a second or two on the screen, but she can still see it in her head now. Something else about the photo is troubling Emily. She is convinced she knows where it was taken. Greg was posing by a black Range Rover, just like the one in her driveway.

But it wasn't her house on the Woodstock Road that she saw in the background of the photo. It was the Old Manor House in North Devon. The house she grew up in. Emily knows that doesn't make any sense. She herself hasn't seen the house since she was driven away from it in a police car in the small hours of Christmas Day in 1995. And Greg has never set eyes on her childhood home, much less set foot there.

Emily doesn't know what to do about all this. Her sister, Josh, Matt and Pippa have been trying to explain everything rationally. The truth is: Emily would really like to believe their theories, but she also wants them to believe her. Without her friends and family on her side, she feels powerless to find out what lies behind all this. And deep down, she's terrified of what she might find if she did get to the bottom of this.

Suddenly, Emily is overcome with a feeling of claustrophobia. She has to get out of the house. She used to jog three or four times a week with Greg before her accident, but she hasn't put her trainers on since then, mainly because of her injuries. Amanda and Pippa have both encouraged her to take up an activity, and she has promised them she'll get back into her running.

So, she rushes upstairs and changes into her sports clothes and races back downstairs. She ties up her laces, selects her running playlist on her smartphone and pushes the earphones into her ears. Seconds later, she is concentrating on the beat of her music, her breathing and her pace. It feels so good to be exercising again.

For their runs, Greg and Emily would drive as far as the car park at Godstow and then jog along the Isis Canal at Port Meadow. Emily knows that Charles Lutwidge Dodgson once famously rowed a boat along this part of the Thames with the Dean and his family, including Alice, his muse. It's one of the reasons she likes running there. It's a beautiful place to go to let off steam. It's Emily's wonderland.

She doesn't want to take the car, so she runs southwards along the Woodstock Road in the direction of St Giles. The main road is busy and she soon leaves the cycle path alongside it in favour of smaller roads more or less parallel to the main route.

The sky is blue and it's sunny, and appropriately the song blaring through Emily's ears at the start of her jog is U2's *Beautiful Day*. As she arrives at the entrance to Port Meadow, she notices that nearly everyone is bare-armed. Many people are even barel-egged. She has already been running for a while by the time she reaches the large Nature Reserve, and so she decides to jog along the canal for just five minutes before heading back. She passes walkers, birdwatchers and families on bicycles, all making the most of the weather.

It isn't until she turns round and starts back that she spots him. She's so shocked she doesn't think to call out to him. He's several metres in front of her and he's walking in the same direc-tion as she is now running. She's catching him up. He looks over his shoulder, and – as she gains on him – he breaks into a run. She tries to accelerate, but her legs protest after nearly two months of inactivity.

Still chasing him, but losing ground now, she wonders how she can be so sure it's him. He's the right height and build; he has the same gait and hair colour. But above all, it's the red woollen jumper that has given him away. Everyone else is wearing short-sleeved T-shirts.

As she reaches the car park, Emily sees him leap into a black Range Rover. It's parked at the far end of the car park, which means he has to drive past her to reach the exit. When the vehicle is just a few metres from her, he lifts his arm, and for a split second she thinks he's going to wave, but instead he places his hand on the nape of his neck. The elbow of his raised arm conceals his face so that she can't get a good look at it. Then the car speeds away and Emily is alone.

It takes her a few minutes to catch her breath. She's thirsty. She usually carries a sports water bottle on her runs, but she forgot to strap it around her waist before setting out. She bends forwards with her hands on her knees. '*Damn!*' she says out loud, realising that she didn't think to look at the registration plate.

She half-jogs, half-walks back home. The first thing she notices on arriving is that Greg's Range Rover is in the drive in front of her house.

First in a banner ad, then in Port Meadow. Am I going to imagine seeing Greg and his car everywhere from now on?

In the shower, Emily cries hard. Tears that mingle with the hot water, then swirl down the drain. She steps out of the bathroom into the master bedroom, tightening the cord of her dressing gown. As she removes the towel from around her head and lets her hair fall down, she is reminded of the day she was discharged from hospital.

Coming out of the bathroom that day, she spotted Greg's red jumper. She curled up with it on her bed, holding it to her, and breathing in his scent. Since then, she has deliberately left the pullover on the antique chair next to his side of the bed. She has looked at it a few times, but she has resisted the temptation to pick it up again.

She starts to walk over to the chair, but she can see – even from the other side of the room – that there's no clothing on it. She checks to see if the pullover is under the cushion. *No, it isn't there.* She looks on the floor. *No, it's definitely gone.* She doubted herself earlier, but this time she is sure. Greg's red woollen jumper, the one she saw him wearing at Port Meadow just an hour or so ago, has disappeared.

Chapter Ten

~

Oxford, November 2002

Greg bumped into Emily – literally – in Modern Art Oxford on Pembroke Street. The gallery had just been renamed and the exhibition showing for the reopening was Tracey Emin's *This is Another Place*. Emily was looking at one of the artist's neon creations consisting of blue text framed inside a red heart. Greg was examining a work, which was compellingly entitled *Fuck Off and Die, You Slag*, hanging on the opposite wall. As he took a few steps backwards to get a better perspective, he nearly sent Emily sprawling.

Greg whirled around and reached out to steady Emily in case she lost her balance. He apologised repeatedly for his clumsiness. He guided her to a bench in the middle of the room where they sat down.

Emily studied him as discreetly as she could. He had a nice voice and large hands, a pleasant face with an aquiline nose. He was older than her: at least ten years older. He was quite tall and inspired immediate confidence. In spite of the cold outside, he was wearing a thin raincoat. It was fawn with large buttons and it made Emily think of Columbo. Years later, she suggested that he should donate his coat to a flasher. He gave it to Oxfam and it was in the shop window at a bargain price for several months. It became a joke between them and Emily teased him every time they walked past the charity shop.

'So what do you think of the exhibition?' Greg asked Emily, after formally introducing himself and shaking her hand.

'Eye-catching?' she said, looking at the bright lights of Emin's works. 'Provocative? Controversial.'

'I'd have to agree. Sometimes when I look at contemporary artwork, I wonder if my three-year-old niece could have produced something better, blindfolded and holding a paintbrush between her toes.'

Although it wasn't the first time she'd heard this sort of remark, Emily chuckled politely.

'I find all this –' he waved his arm to encompass the room '– a bit vulgar for my taste, though. I'm not a fan of modern art at all, but I'm trying to understand it.'

'I'm not sure art is about understanding,' Emily said. 'It's your analysis of it that matters. One work of art might evoke different things for different people.' Emily paused. She appreciated that Greg might well be wondering how *Fuck Off and Die, You Slag* could possibly have more than one interpretation. 'I quite admire Emin's candidness. Some of her stuff is very autobiographical. It might be shocking, but it's also very intimate.'

Greg was silent for a while. 'Are you an artist?' he asked at last.

'Not really. I took Art A-level and got an A, but I only got a C in English and I failed History altogether. So I didn't get into the universities I'd applied to. At the moment, I'm working in Alice's Shop and taking two evening classes a week at the Ruskin School of Art.'

'Alice's Shop? The gift shop opposite Christ Church?'

Emily nodded.

'Do you like working there?'

89

'I think I was lucky to get a job there. My sister, Amanda, thinks the grockles must drive me mad…' She stopped when she saw Greg frown. 'Oh, that's Devonian slang. I mean the holiday-makers,' Emily explained.

'Ah, so you're from the West Country. And do they?'

'Sorry?'

'Do the tourists drive you mad?'

'Oh, no, not at all. Alice's Shop wouldn't exist without them. So, yes, I enjoy it, but I don't see myself working there for ever.'

'What would you like to do?'

'Something connected to the art world. I don't really know what.'

Greg's brown eyes never left Emily as he asked his questions. He struck Emily as attentive, but not nosy. They continued their visit together and when they'd finished, Greg asked her, 'Can I buy you a drink in the café to make up for nearly knocking you over earlier?'

Emily hesitated before replying, but only for a fraction of a second. She quite liked this man, and was surprised at how easy she found it to talk to him. She'd already told him a bit about herself, but she hadn't learnt much about him.

'That would be terrific,' she said.

A song by Eiffel 65 – the only song she knew by this Italian group – was playing on the radio and Emily found herself humming along to the chorus while Greg went to the counter to order. *I'm blue da ba dee da ba die.* Emily didn't feel at all blue. In fact, she felt happy for the first time in ages.

Over coffee, Greg asked about her paintings. Even though he wasn't keen on contemporary art, he seemed genuinely interested in her work. He offered to exhibit some of her paintings in his antique shop.

'You never know,' he said. 'You might get a good price for them.'

Emily was sceptical about this. She lifted the mug to her lips and blew on her scalding coffee, keeping her eyes on Greg.

'I do dream of making a living from painting,' she admitted, 'but for most would-be artists like me, that's just a pipe dream.' Emily had never really believed that someone might pay for one of her paintings.

His mouth full of caramel slice, Greg insisted. 'Here take my business card. Come and see me at my shop as soon as possible with some samples of your work. Let's see what happens.'

Emily made price tags for her paintings. She thought if she could get twenty pounds for one of them, she'd be very pleased with herself. Rosie, the girl she sat next to at her art classes, helped her pick out some of her best paintings.

About two weeks after she'd taken three of her works round to Greg's shop, he rang her at home and asked if she would come to the shop and bring some more canvasses. When she arrived the following day, he handed her £400 in cash and a flute of champagne.

'I'm afraid I don't drink,' Emily said, handing back the glass.

'Oh, I'm sorry. I didn't think to ask. Would you like a cup of tea instead?'

'Yes, that would be great.' She looked at the money he'd just given her. 'What's this?' she asked. She vaguely registered that only one of her paintings was displayed on the wall and that it had been framed.

'I've sold two of your paintings,' Greg said, barely containing his satisfaction as he led the way to a box room at the back of his shop. He flicked the switch on the kettle and took a carton of milk out of the fridge.

'But I was selling them for twenty pounds each.'

'Well, I added a zero.'

A slow smile spread across Emily's face. 'And frames, apparently,' she said.

'Yes, and frames.' He beamed back at her, and she noticed the grin stayed on his face as he made her tea.

'Can I pay you for them?'

'Oh, no, that's all right. I had them kicking around. They didn't cost me anything.'

Greg was clearly lying. Emily was touched.

'I'll drink to your success,' Greg said, chinking his champagne glass against her mug.

Emily stayed in the antique shop for two hours, and in between customers, they talked animatedly to each other. Greg told her that he and his wife had lost their son, who was only six, to leukaemia. They'd already been trying for a couple of years to have another baby when little Luke was diagnosed with cancer, and two years after his death, they still hadn't been able to conceive. The strain all of this had put on their marriage had taken its toll. They'd divorced and his wife, who had remarried a year later, was now pregnant.

Emily listened to all of this, her heart aching for Greg. She couldn't help thinking about her own child, but said nothing.

Over the next few months, Greg sold more and more of Emily's paintings, much to her delight. At the age of twenty-two, Emily was still sharing accommodation with her sister and she began to wonder if she could afford to get a flat of her own. Greg enjoyed keeping fit, and Emily started running with him in the evenings when she didn't have art classes.

One day, Greg told Emily that he was head over heels in love with her.

'I'm fifteen years older than you, but there it is. I think about you all the time. You probably already have a boyfriend, don't you?'

Emily shook her head. She'd never had a steady boyfriend. She didn't even have that many friends.

'I don't want children,' Emily blurted out.

'That's fine with me,' Greg said. 'I tried to have children after Luke and it didn't happen for me. I've taken that as a sign that it wasn't meant to be.'

Emily wanted to tell Greg that she was in love with him too, even though she knew it wasn't true. She liked him a lot, and he made her laugh. She felt safe and protected with him. And all that, more than love, was what she needed. The words 'father figure' wormed their evil way into Emily's mind, but she ignored them.

Greg was looking at her with round puppy eyes, waiting for her reaction as though his life hung in the balance. So she opened her mouth to tell him what he wanted to hear, but in the end, instead of lying, she told him the truth about her baby.

Nearly the whole truth.

Chapter Eleven

~

Oxford, October 2014

Emily feels remorseful. Her husband died only two months ago, and here she is removing all trace of him. She looks out of the bedroom window while behind her Amanda and Pippa continue to sort through Greg's clothes. Hugging herself, she tries to swallow down the lump in her throat. It all seems so final, so definitive. *What if he isn't dead?* Emily thinks. *He'll come back and I'll have thrown out all his clothes.*

She wonders why she thinks Greg might still be alive. Is this hope against hope? Gut feeling? Is she in denial so that she doesn't have to fully mourn him yet? So that she doesn't have to accept her role in his death? It would have given her closure if she'd seen his body. But no one did – it was a closed-casket funeral service as his face was badly damaged in the crash. *But if he is dead, then who sent me the messages? And who did I see at Port Meadow?*

A tear rolls down her cheek and she brushes it away with her fingertips. She really doesn't want to get rid of his stuff, but Pippa and Amanda have persuaded her it's the right thing to do.

A magpie hopping across the lawn catches her attention. *One for sorrow*. She automatically scans the garden for another one. She remembers learning a list of collective nouns at school. The term for a group of these birds is a tiding. A tiding of magpies. Is that because they can be the bearers of glad tidings? Or *bad* tidings? You can also say 'murder'. A murder of magpies. Emily shudders. She spots two more magpies, just a few metres away from the first. *One for sorrow. Two for joy. Three for a girl.*

Pippa's posh voice snaps Emily out of her daydream and back to reality. 'Is this the one you thought that fucker was wearing at Port Meadow?'

She turns around to see her friend kneeling by a cardboard box, her rounded tummy resting on her knees. She's holding up Greg's red jumper.

'Yes!' Emily doesn't point out that the 'fucker' in question might have been Greg. 'Where did you find it?'

'It was under the bed,' Pippa says, handing the woollen sweater to Emily as she approaches.

'That's strange!' Emily could have sworn she checked under the bed just the other day. When she came home after the incident at Port Meadow, the jumper wasn't on the chair where she'd left it. She wondered if the pullover had fallen off the chair onto the floor. She did look there, surely?

Pippa goes back to boxing up Greg's clothes. Emily walks towards the window again and surreptitiously holds the jumper to her nose. Her back to her friend, she inhales through her nostrils. This time, though, it seems to smell only faintly of Greg. She can no longer make out the odour of the polish and varnish he used to restore his antique furniture. But the floral scent she detected before seems more pungent somehow. *No, that's impossible.* Maybe a hint of Pippa's perfume is wafting a few metres across the bedroom towards her, or perhaps it's her own face cream she can smell.

Then a thought strikes her. Could Greg have been wearing this jumper when he met up with his mistress for the last time? Is this the smell of *her* perfume?

'Here, Pippa.' Her friend looks up as Emily turns around and tosses her the offending item of clothing. 'You can box this up with the rest of his clothes.'

The jumper falls short of its mark. Pippa crawls a couple of paces on her knees, picks up the sweater, folds it and puts it in the cardboard box.

'Do you want to keep this?' Amanda calls, her arm holding out a briefcase around the door to the walk-in wardrobe.

'Is there anything in it?'

The arm and the briefcase disappear behind the door and Emily can just hear the sound of a clasp being opened. 'Papers and documents, by the looks of it,' comes the reply.

'I'd better make sure there's nothing important in there first.' Emily retrieves the briefcase and takes it along the upstairs landing to Greg's study. It's a mess in here. A lot of Greg's stuff will eventually have to be sorted out in this room as well.

Emily puts the briefcase down and sighs. Not for the first time, she wonders how she would cope without Amanda and Pippa. Her mother-in-law has offered to help her, but every time they speak on the telephone, Emily ends up comforting the older woman. She feels too weak for this role at the moment; she needs moral support herself.

Her sister-in-law, Deborah, has also repeatedly asked what she can do, but with the demands her three daughters make on her time, not to mention her job as an event organiser, Emily knows she only really asks out of politeness.

She thinks about her sister-in-law and her mother-in-law now as she sits on Greg's office chair and swivels slowly around in it. She gets the feeling that, like Josephine, the two women hold her responsible for his death. Obviously, they don't know he'd admitted he'd been having an affair just before Emily crashed the car. Not that that's an excuse for losing control of the car.

Lately, Emily has been wondering why she didn't die in the crash instead of Greg. But it's one thing for Emily to blame herself; it's quite another to feel accused by the very people she needs to reassure her. She sighs again and wipes away a tear with her sleeve, then goes back to the bedroom.

After a well-earned lunch break, Amanda leaves Pippa and Emily to it. She's meeting a friend in Rileys Sports Bar in Oxford. Pippa seems piqued at not being invited, but for Emily, it's her curiosity that's piqued.

'I didn't know you were a sports fan, Amanda.' Emily is holding the front door open for her sister with one hand and the electronic device for the gate in the other. 'Is there a football match or something on?'

'No, it's the Russian Grand Prix.' Amanda fiddles with her car keys.

'I never knew you liked the Formula One! Is it an important race?'

'Look, if you must know, I'm meeting Charles for a drink.'

'Ooooh,' Emily and Pippa chorus.

Amanda blushes. Emily is pleased for her sister even though she feels ever so slightly envious.

'Nothing like that,' Amanda says, a little too hastily, 'I've put a bet on Lewis Hamilton.' And with that, she scurries to her car, waving in the air as she goes. A few of the small gravel stones fly up as she roars out of the drive. Emily and Pippa giggle, then they trudge back upstairs to get on with the task they've set themselves.

It's early evening when they finally load up Greg's Range Rover for Emily to take the boxes to Oxfam the next morning. As Pippa is pregnant, Emily won't let her carry any of the heavy boxes. She feels nervous, knowing she's going to drive for the first time since the accident, but she says nothing about that to her friend. As she shuts the boot of the car, she offers to make some tea.

'As long as you make it less watery than your mum does,' Pippa says cheekily.

Sitting at the kitchen table, Pippa falls silent for a while.

'Is something wrong?' Emily asks.

'Not at all. I've been meaning to ask you a question for some time, but I wanted to be alone with you, and I want you to know that I won't take it badly if you say no,' Pippa begins.

'This sounds intriguing.'

'I hope Amanda won't take this badly...' Pippa continues, twirling a strand of hair around her fingers.

Pippa and Amanda met at their Amateur Dramatic Society when they were both students. The two of them are good friends, and they've known each other for a long time. But Amanda once said to Emily that Pippa seemed to be acting her way through life in her roles of perfect wife and perfect mother, never letting the mask she wore slip. Emily supposes that Amanda sometimes feels she's in Pippa's shadow, especially when Pippa lands the main roles for their plays.

Emily met Pippa thanks to Amanda. Although the three of them often hang out together, Pippa has far more in common with Emily than with Amanda. Pippa describes herself as 'arty-farty' and goes with Emily to art exhibitions and *vernissages*. Emily dotes on Harry, Pippa's four-year-old rambunctious son, whereas Amanda seems to be allergic to children. Emily and Pippa also have eclectic tastes in music while Amanda limits her listening to female singers and pop rock.

'Stop beating around the bush!' Emily urges her friend. 'Spit it out!'

'Andy and I would like to know if you'll be godmother to our baby.' Pippa peers at Emily with her chocolate-coloured eyes through eyelashes so long that they look false.

'I would be honoured.'

'Really?' Pippa is clearly delighted. 'I wasn't sure if that was your thing.'

'Why wouldn't it be my thing? I'm thrilled you asked me.'

'I just thought, you know, maybe you didn't actually like kids.'

'Oh, Pippa, how can you say that? You know how much I love Harry.'

'Yes, I do. But you don't have children of your own, and I don't know the reason, or if it means that you wouldn't want to be a godmother. I'd understand, you know.'

'Greg had a son who died of leukaemia,' Emily offers by way of an explanation. She lowers her gaze and focuses on her mug.

'Yes, I remember him telling me that once a long time ago. That's so tragic.'

'I also had a baby.' Emily's voice is no louder than a whisper. She runs her finger along a scratch in the wooden table. 'I was only a child myself. Neither of us wanted to go through it again.'

Pippa says nothing for a few seconds. Emily imagines questions whirring around in her friend's head, but she knows Pippa is always careful not to ask too much about her past.

Suddenly Pippa gasps loudly. At a loss for words, her mouth remains wide open. Emily looks at her friend and is reminded of *The Scream* by Edvard Munch.

'Fuck!' Pippa has finally mustered her response. 'God, I can't believe I didn't realise it before. You are, aren't you? He is, isn't he?'

Emily stares uncomprehendingly at her friend.

'Matt's your son, isn't he? That's why he's always been closer to you than to Amanda. I'm as thick as pig-shit. I should've known.'

'No, Pippa, Matt's my brother, not my son.' Emily doesn't know whether to be horrified or amused. 'My half-brother. My mother had a drunken one-night stand a few months after my father's death. She says she doesn't know who Matt's father is. She doesn't even remember his name.'

Emily feels slightly guilty at disclosing her mother's secrets when she reveals so few of her own. But she's aware that she's confiding in Pippa at this moment far more than she has opened up to anyone for a long time. Pippa still looks unconvinced.

'But you're not far out on the timing,' Emily says. 'I didn't know it at the time, but my mother was already pregnant when I gave birth.' Pippa's mouth is rounded in the shape of an O again. 'To a baby *girl*,' Emily adds.

'A baby girl?'

'Yes. Melody. Melody Cavendish.'

'Melody Cavendish,' Pippa repeats.

'She was born in July 1996. Matt was born the following year, in February.'

Emily had been released from Exmoor Secure Centre and living in Oxford for just a month when her brother was born, but she doesn't mention this to Pippa.

'February.' Pippa echoes. She seems temporarily incapable of producing speech of her own.

Emily observes Pippa, waiting for her to process all of this. Furrowing her brow, Pippa takes a deep breath. It wouldn't be like Pippa to pry, but Emily braces herself for an awkward question anyway. Pippa is bound to ask what happened to Melody. Emily doesn't want to talk about that. Ever. But she is saved by the bell – literally – as the telephone starts to ring.

I shouldn't answer, she thinks. No one ever rings on the landline except her mother-in-law or telemarketing sales representatives and, more recently, Sergeant Campbell. Emily doesn't want to speak to any of these people. But Pippa, apparently still in shock, jerks her head – causing her shiny black hair to swish from side to side – towards the kitchen door to indicate that Emily should take the call, so she trundles into the hall to pick up the phone.

Emily knows it will be her mother-in-law. In her seventies, Greg's mother is a self-taught expert at new technology and they bought her a smartphone a few years ago for Christmas. But for some reason, she usually calls on the landline from her own home phone.

'Emily, dear. It's me.'

'Oh, hello, Mrs Klein.' It has always seemed strange to Emily to have to address Greg's mother with her own name. She some-times feels like she's talking to herself. 'How nice of you to call.'

Emily grimaces at her reflection in the large round mirror embedded in the 1880s' oak carved hall tree seat. *I'm pulling an ugly face in an ugly piece of furniture.* She immediately feels ashamed for thinking that. *Greg loved this antique*, she reminds herself. He'd had it imported from America at considerable cost.

'How are you?' she asks the older Mrs Klein.

'Oh, Emily, dear, *I* should be the one asking *you* that.'

'Well, I…'

'But since you asked –' Emily rolls her eyes exaggeratedly at herself in the mirror '– I've been thinking about poor Gregory so much; it is truly unbearable for a mother to lose her child.'

Emily feels sorry for her mother-in-law as she hears her first sob. She stops making faces at herself. 'I know,' she says softly.

'I mean, at least Gregory's death has given you a status.'

Emily pictures her mother-in-law standing with her back ramrod straight in the kitchen of her Northampton home, examining an invisible chip in the nail of one of her perfectly manicured hands and holding the receiver to her ear with the other hand. She'll be wearing a beige turtle-necked sweater and perfectly ironed linen trousers.

'A status? What do you mean, Mrs Klein?'

'You were his *second* wife and you're now a *widow.*'

Greg's mother makes it sound like Emily has gone up in the world. She isn't quite thirty-four years old and finds the word 'widow' mildly offensive for someone her age. Emily nearly retorts that Mrs Klein isn't telling her anything she doesn't already know, but she holds her tongue.

'If my darling grandson Luke were still alive, he'd be an *orphan,*' Mrs Klein says. 'But I was Gregory's *mother.* I carried him in my womb for nine whole months. And there is no term for a mother who loses her child. I find that horribly unfair.'

Emily can see her point.

'It's as if there's no recognition of my pain,' Mrs Klein says.

After a few minutes of this, Greg's mother abruptly changes the subject and describes her wonderful new Yorkshire terriers. She adores this breed, and recently she has bought two more dogs to add to her collection, bringing the total up to five. She has always had dogs. Greg and his sister, Deborah, often complained that their mother had cared more for her dogs than she had for her children when they were growing up.

Whenever Emily and Greg had gone to visit Greg's parents, they'd had to drive up and back in the same day or check into a hotel because Mrs Klein's Yorkies sleep on the beds in the two spare rooms of her three-bedroom detached house. They'd suggested on many occasions that it would be easier for Mr and Mrs Klein – and the Yorkies – to come to Oxford to visit them; after all, they had five guest rooms, but Greg's mother was afraid that a weekend away might upset her canine companions.

Emily turns her attention back to the mirror while half-heartedly listening to her mother-in-law's monologue. 'Mirror, mirror on the wall,' she mouths at it. After a while, she tries to interrupt Greg's mother to put an end to their conversation for today, but Mrs Klein is in full flow with her doggy anecdotes.

Emily starts making a cut-throat gesture with her index finger at the Emily in the mirror. Then she gets carried away. *Ha! Amanda isn't the only actress in the family*, she thinks, pretending to brutally stab her mother-in-law with expansive arm movements. It's a terrible reverse impersonation of the famous shower scene from Hitchcock's *Psycho* in which the elderly female figure kills the younger woman.

When Emily has hung up the phone at long last, she realises Pippa is sitting on the stairs behind her, barely suppressing her laughter. The tears start to roll down her friend's face.

'Don't tell me, it was your mother-in-law.'

'Yes.' Emily can feel herself blushing, but she begins to chuckle, too. She sits beside Pippa on the stairs and the two of them laugh until Emily's stomach aches and Pippa starts to wet herself.

When their laughter has subsided, Pippa gets ready to leave. Emily can see that her friend is burning with curiosity, but the mood has changed. Pippa will probably ask about Melody another day. Maybe Emily will even answer her questions. But for now, the moment has passed.

As soon as Pippa has left, the telephone rings again. Assuming her mother-in-law has forgotten to tell her something, Emily hesitates briefly, but thinking it might be important, she picks up the phone.

'Hello?' At first, no one speaks on the other end of the line. 'Hel-lo?' she repeats.

'Can I speak to Emily?' It's a man's voice. A suave voice. It sounds vaguely familiar, but Emily can't place it.

'Yes. Emily Klein speaking. Who is this?'

'I need you, Alice. Can you help me?'

Emily feels as if an invisible hand is squeezing her heart. 'Greg? Is that you? Greg?'

There's no answer, and after two or three seconds' silence, the line goes dead.

'Greg!' Emily shouts. 'Greg!'

Then she replaces the receiver and sinks to the floor. She dials 1471, but the caller's number has been withheld.

Just a few minutes ago, it felt so good to hear the sound of her own laughter, but now Emily bursts into tears.

Chapter Twelve

~

Oxford, July 2004

In the end, Amanda was the one who gave Emily away.

Once Greg had realised how important that was to Emily, he was uncharacteristically firm with Deborah. She'd just set up her own business, registering it under the name *Debbie's Do's*. Greg told Emily he admired his sister's drive and determination, but he didn't think much of the name she'd chosen for her company, mainly because he considered the second apostrophe to be grammatically incorrect. As a newly established event organiser, Debbie had been given more or less free rein to coordinate Emily and Greg's wedding.

Mrs Klein referred to the occasion as either Debbie's first wedding or Gregory's second wedding. Even Emily had come to think of it as Debbie and Greg's Big Day, as she didn't seem to have much say in her own wedding. But she was adamant that she wanted Amanda to give her away.

Emily and her future mother-in-law had shamelessly listened in on the quarrel taking place in the Kleins' living room from the other side of the door, which was ajar. It was a rare moment of complicity between the two women, and Emily savoured it.

'Greg, it's really unconventional for a woman to give away the bride.' Emily could hear the pout in Debbie's voice.

'I know that, Deborah, but traditionally it's the father who gives away the bride, and in Emily's case, there is no father,' Greg retorted.

Emily raised her eyebrows at this. Of course, none of the Kleins knew anything about her father. Greg had told them that Graham Cavendish had died peacefully in bed one night. Greg had lied for her when he didn't even know the full truth himself.

'Well, can't one of her uncles do it?'

'No.' Greg didn't give a reason, but he was categorical. Emily was impressed. She'd always thought Greg was a bit emasculated by his sister and his mother. She wondered if she'd been unfair in her judgement.

'Why not?'

'It's personal.'

'What does that mean?'

'It means it's none of your business, Deborah!'

Emily breathed a quiet sigh of relief. At least he hadn't given the reason. Debbie had insisted on inviting Emily's uncles – her father's brothers. All three of them. Just as Emily had predicted, only one had accepted the invitation; one had declined and the other one hadn't replied at all. Rod, the uncle who was coming to the wedding, had always looked a lot like Emily's father. She was dreading setting eyes on him again. She certainly didn't want to have to ask him to walk her down the aisle.

'Gregory's doing well,' came a voice from behind Emily. Both she and Greg's mother jumped. 'Usually our daughter has more balls than our son.'

This amused Emily, who realised that Mr Klein had been thinking along the same lines as she had. Mrs Klein shushed her husband noisily.

'What about Josephine?' Debbie was relentless. 'Could she walk Emily down the aisle?'

'You just said a woman wouldn't be conventional!'

'Well, yes, but in the absence of the father, perhaps the mother would be passable.'

Greg was silent. Emily imagined him throwing his arms around in exasperation and pacing up and down the carpeted floor.

'What I mean is, Josephine would obviously be a better choice than Amanda.'

'For Christ's sake, Deborah, don't be ridiculous!' Greg never shortened Emily's first name, but she'd never heard him use his sister's full name before this row. 'Depending on how much whiskey she drinks the night before, Josephine might not be able to walk into the church by herself on the day, let alone walk Emily down the aisle!'

Mrs Klein, biting her lower lip, glanced anxiously at Emily upon hearing this. Emily avoided her gaze, shrugging slightly.

Greg's comment had been blunt, but it was true. Josephine hadn't touched a drop of alcohol from the second term of her pregnancy, and then she'd kept her drinking under control until Matt started walking, but she'd gradually reverted to her old habit about five years ago.

'But Amanda can't be the maid of honour at the same time!'

'Why the hell not? The two roles won't clash. She doesn't have to escort her sister on her arm to me at the altar while she's toasting the pair of us with a flute of champagne in her free hand!'

Emily was almost certain that toasting the bride and groom was the best man's job but this last point turned out to be decisive.

'All right. Have it your way. Your sister-in-law can be the father of the bride *and* chief bridesmaid.'

The door flew open into the three eavesdroppers as Debbie stomped out of the living room. She paused briefly to harrumph at them and then stormed off.

~

Amanda complained that the lilac dress made her look fat, but Emily thought she'd never seen her sister look so beautiful and radiant. She'd curled her brown hair, and her brown eyes sparkled.

Emily was wearing an ivory gown, which looked deceptively simple, with lace and tulle detail on the bodice, a sweetheart neckline, a skirt that flared slightly from the hip and a sweep train. She received compliments throughout her special day, and felt happier than she'd ever been.

Debbie had insisted on keeping to tradition. So, inside the church, the groom's family and friends squashed into overcrowded pews on the right whereas the bride's guests were embarrassingly few in number, and were spoilt for choice for seating on the left. Josephine, her sister, her elderly mother, and Uncle Rod sat on the pew at the front. Matt sat next to his mum. The little boy proudly told everyone who asked that he was nearly seven and a half. Emily heard him being complimented on his outfit many times that day, too. He did indeed look smart, she thought, in his black trousers, cream shirt, burgundy waistcoat and matching clip-on bow tie.

Emily's grandmother had survived a stroke, and she didn't really seem to know where she was on this particular day or why she was here. Josephine's sister, Mary, had brought her here from the retirement home in Plymouth for the weekend.

Emily hadn't told Debbie that her paternal grandfather was also still alive, and so he hadn't been invited. He hadn't forgiven Emily for her role in his son's death and he'd made it clear when his son died that he no longer wanted anything to do with her, Josephine or Amanda.

In the second row, Philippa Stuart-Barnes sat between her boyfriend, Andy, and Emily's friend Rosie from her evening classes at the Ruskin School of Art. Since Pippa was Emily's best friend, Emily had wanted her to be a bridesmaid, but Debbie thought that a maid of honour and two flower girls would be enough.

Until just after eleven p.m., everything went according to plan.

Debbie's organisation of the wedding itself was seamless. The reception, too, at an idyllic manor house built in Cotswold stone near the centre of Oxford, also started off smoothly.

In these picturesque surroundings, Greg's sister relaxed more and more as the day went on, in direct proportion to each glass of wine she drank. Debbie's daughters, Chloe, aged five, and Olivia, aged two, faultlessly carried out their duties as flower girls. They both looked sweet and behaved irreproachably.

During the meal, Charles, in his role as best man, delivered a very humorous wedding speech. He confessed afterwards that he'd belonged to a debating society at school in which he was coached for public speaking, and he was thrilled at the opportunity to put those skills to good use again.

Amanda also made a memorable speech, and even Josephine stood up to say a few words. Emily and Amanda cringed when they saw their mother rise to her feet. But Josephine didn't slur her kind words, and their fears turned out to be groundless. In fact, it wasn't until much later that she got drunk, after Aunt Mary had taken their mother and Matt upstairs to their bedrooms. By this stage, so many other guests were inebriated that Josephine would have been conspicuous if she'd been sober.

Debbie's parents-in-law had picked up the two sleepy flower girls and taken them home by the time Emily and Greg started the dancing. Uncle Rod then sang – in a surprisingly good baritone voice – his own acoustic cover of *Bless the Broken Road* by Rascal Flatts while strumming his guitar in honour of the newlyweds. It was the first slow song of the evening and Amanda and Charles, as maid of honour and best man, teamed up and joined the bride and groom on the dance floor. Emily was touched by this gesture from her father's brother, and as the guests applauded Uncle Rod enthusiastically, she felt glad that he'd accepted the wedding invitation.

Everything was perfect. Emily felt happiness like she'd never known. She tried to hold on to it, but somehow it seemed evanescent. She couldn't get rid of the sensation that it was all too good to be true. Too perfect to last. In the end, she was right.

The celebratory mood ended abruptly at about five past eleven. A man appeared out of nowhere, singled out Greg and marched up to him. Emily, who was standing at Greg's side, took a good look at him. He was fairly stout, slightly less than average height and in his late thirties. He had a signet ring on one of his fingers. He was wearing a white shirt, which was partially unbuttoned, revealing dark, thick hair curling around the bottom of his neck.

Emily was pretty sure she'd never seen him before. She wondered at first if this was a practical joke arranged by one of their friends for their wedding. She half expected this man to start taking off his clothes.

But then the man waved his fist in Greg's face and began to shout. He was standing close enough now for Emily to smell the alcohol on his breath. Clearly, he wasn't a strippergram. As Greg took the man's arm to lead him towards the exit, there was a struggle. Greg somehow got elbowed in the face and his nose started to bleed. Emily looked from one man to the other. What was going on?

In a matter of a couple of minutes, most of Greg's friends and relations, following Mr and Mrs Klein's lead, made a hasty exit from the reception hall. Some of them kissed Emily perfunctorily on the cheek as they swooped past; others whispered goodnight. The majority of them were staying in bedrooms upstairs. Emily didn't want them to leave. She wanted someone to take this man away. He was still yelling.

Emily was fuming. *How dare he come in here and hurl accusations at Greg on his wedding day! Who does he think he is? What on earth is the matter with him?* Then another thought struck her: *Is he dangerous? Or violent?*

'You sold me a fake! You bastard! You ripped me off!' the man screamed at Greg.

Instantly, Charles and Emily's friend Rosie pushed past Emily and flanked Greg. Rosie rummaged in her handbag and handed some tissues to Greg, who held them to his nose.

'Let's go out onto the terrace and discuss this calmly,' Charles suggested in a low voice.

That seemed rather unnecessary to Emily, as other than Rosie, Amanda, Pippa, Greg and her, there didn't seem to be anyone else lingering. Amanda and Pippa wouldn't leave and miss a real-life drama, that was for sure. But they made their way out onto the terrace, anyway.

Rosie poured the man a glass of wine as they all trooped through the dining room. Emily wondered if this was meant to calm him down or simply place something in his hand so that he would be less likely to throw a punch.

As soon as they'd set foot on the terrace, the man turned on Greg again. 'You swindled me! That Ming was a fake.'

'Mr Kipling,' Charles addressed the disgruntled customer in a calm voice, no doubt in an attempt to pacify him.

Emily's imagination conjured up mini wedding cakes in foil wrappers, but she wasn't in the mood to find a funny side to this. She noted that Rosie's lip was twitching, though. Then she saw Greg exchange a look with Charles. She realised that they must have been in on some scam together at this man's expense. Her suspicions were soon confirmed.

'You!' Mr Kipling bellowed. He wagged his finger at Charles. His voice was surprisingly deep for his stature. '*You* were in on this!'

'Mr Kipling, how did you know where to find Mr Klein today?'

'His shop assistant told me this afternoon, but I had some errands to run, so I couldn't get here any earlier.'

'Let's sit down and talk about the problem.' Charles gestured to four wicker chairs. The three men sat down and the women remained standing. Emily felt awkward, but Amanda and Pippa looked enthralled. 'I must say I was rather miffed when Greg told me you'd outbid me.'

Mr Kipling stared at Charles in disbelief. 'Are you saying you didn't know it was a fake?'

'Of course I didn't know! Greg didn't know either! Do you really think my best friend would have sold me a fake?' Charles sounded indignant, but Emily could tell it was an act. 'But you examined it. You said yourself that the blue pigments and the borders on the vase were consistent with the Ming dynasty. What makes you think it's not authentic?'

Emily was reminded of evenings when Charles would come round and talk animatedly with Greg about subjects that she found rather tedious. When it wasn't computers, it was often antiques. On occasion, Greg had launched into specialised descriptions of objects from his antique world. Charles had always been able to follow his esotericism.

'The paste.'

'The paste?' Charles and Greg echoed simultaneously.

'Yes, I broke the vase. You really couldn't have known it wasn't an original unless you cracked it open. And who is going to do that with an early Ming vase?'

'So you didn't break it deliberately?' Charles asked.

'No, of course not! I dropped it! I might never have realised if it hadn't smashed. Admittedly, it was a bloody good fake. But the paste gives it away. It's obvious.'

'Have you kept the pieces of the vase?'

Emily was dismayed that Greg was allowing his friend to handle this.

'Yes, of course. You're not seriously going to suggest that we glue it back together are you?'

'No, no, of course not, Mr Kipling. However, I do think that this is neither the time nor the place to sort out this misunderstanding.'

'Perhaps you could bring what remains of the vase to my shop on Monday morning,' Greg said, 'and we'll take it from there.' Emily was relieved that he'd finally found his tongue.

'I want a refund!'

Greg nodded, which Mr Kipling took for consent. He was still visibly upset, but he allowed himself to be led away by Pippa.

Emily hadn't grasped the whole story, but she'd got the gist. Enough to know that the man she'd married just a few hours ago had been involved in some dishonest scheme. She hadn't thought there was a devious side to Greg and she found this troubling. Worse, she felt betrayed, as though she, and not Mr Kipling, was the one who was taken in.

In a way, she *had* been deceived. Did she really know her husband at all? Her *husband*. That word sounded unfamiliar in her mind for the moment. And what about Charles? Had he come up with this plan? Was he a bad influence on Greg? This couldn't have been all Greg's idea, could it? Greg wasn't usually one to show initiative.

'What was that all about?' she asked.

'Don't worry, it's not important.'

Emily was annoyed that Greg was trying to dodge the question. Before she could try to get to the bottom of the incident, Pippa came back out onto the terrace with her boyfriend. Emily realised Andy must have made himself scarce during the confrontation. They were carrying a bottle of wine each and numerous glasses between them and they promptly served everyone a drink. Emily was the only one not drinking.

But Amanda wasn't going to give up. 'Oh, do tell, Greg,' she said.

It was Charles who started to tell the story. 'A few weeks ago, Greg came across what looked like a Ming dragon vase.'

'In Jingdezhen, in China, they make replicas of Ming porcelain and some of them are so well done that they're hard to distinguish from originals,' Greg explained. 'In this particular case, parts of the vase were semi-authentic. The period mark, for example, was probably cut from a shard and embedded in the base—'

'You knew it was a counterfeit?' Emily was appalled.

112

'I didn't sell it as a sixteenth-century vase,' Greg said. 'I told Mr Kipling I thought it must be a later replica but I couldn't see any signs of it having been faked.'

'In other words you led him to believe that it could well be an original,' Emily said.

'To be honest, Em, Kipling was very gullible.' Charles paused to take a big gulp of wine. 'An authentic vase from the Jiajing reign would have cost millions of pounds.'

'How much did you sell it for?' Amanda asked.

'Several thousand pounds,' Greg replied. 'But I never said it was real.'

Emily narrowed her eyes. 'What was your part in this?' she asked Charles.

'Well, Kipling is an antique dealer himself. He's only just opened his business, in Leamington Spa, and he lacks experience.'

'So you took advantage of him!' *They both deliberately led that man on*, Emily thought.

'I asked him to take a look at a vase in Oxford for me. I pretended to be a collector and told him the antique dealer – Greg – was selling a replica that I thought might not actually be a copy.'

'And how did you get the price up?' Amanda was clearly enjoying this.

'He wanted to buy it, but Greg told him I was a valued customer and a friend, and the vase was reserved for me.'

'So he offered a higher price,' Amanda concluded.

'A much higher price in the end,' Greg said.

'You deserve an Oscar, Charles.' Amanda flashed her teeth at him. Emily supposed this was her sister's idea of a winning smile, but her teeth were stained purple from the Cabernet Sauvignon. Emily turned away as Charles clinked his glass against Amanda's.

Pippa and Andy started sniggering behind Emily and soon everyone was laughing. Everyone except Emily. She eventually feigned a smile and felt as much of an impostor as she considered Greg to be.

'It's quite easy to con people in the art world, too,' Rosie piped up when the laughter had died down. 'In fact, Greg, if you want to give it another shot, some of Emily's canvasses are reminiscent of Wassily Kandinsky's prints, especially his circle paintings. Maybe you could arrange for one of the original compositions to show up mysteriously.'

'I don't think—' Emily began.

'That sounds like an ingenious idea, Rosie!' Charles interrupted.

Emily wasn't sure if Charles was joking or not. She glanced at Greg. She could tell he had no idea who Kandinsky was, but he would certainly remember the print in the window of Blackwell's Art and Poster Shop in Broad Street. He accompanied her there regularly.

'Who?' Greg asked.

'A Russian artist,' said Rosie.

'Have some more wine,' Emily said. She grabbed a bottle to top up Greg's glass and wondered how to steer the subject away from fraud.

'Em could be the next Han van Meegeren,' Rosie continued.

'Who?' Greg asked again. He sounded curious.

'He was a Dutch artist, quite a good one in fact, but he is better known for his forgeries than for his own work,' Rosie said.

'Vermeer, right?' Charles asked.

'Exactly,' Rosie confirmed. Emily noticed she had a red wine stain on the skirt of her yellow sundress.

'*Girl with a Pearl Earring?*' asked Greg, sipping his wine. He and Emily had watched the film starring Colin Firth and Scarlett Johansson just a few months ago.

'That is a Vermeer, but van Meegeren didn't do an imitation of that particular work,' Rosie said authoritatively, turning her blonde head from Charles to Greg.

'Did he make lots of money from his forged paintings?' Greg asked. Emily swore under her breath. She noticed that Greg was still holding his bloodied tissues scrunched up in his left hand.

'Yes, he did, actually.'

Rosie proceeded to give a detailed biography of Han van Meegeren. She used her hands a lot when she talked and her voice was silvery. Emily observed Greg and Charles hanging on Rosie's every word as though hypnotised by her. Greg's eyes had a disturbing glint in them.

Emily tuned out, sinking into the empty wicker chair next to Greg. As the conversation went on around her as if nothing had happened, she replayed the evening's events in her head. A feeling of incredulity washed over her. The audacity of Mr Kipling disrupting the wedding reception in that way! But she was even angrier with Greg. Could she trust him after what he'd done to that man?

When Rosie's lengthy account of the Dutch fraudster had ended, Emily hoped that Greg would have forgotten why her friend had brought up Kandinsky and his circle paintings in the first place.

Shortly afterwards, they headed up the Jacobean-style staircase to their wedding suite, and the only trace of the row with Mr Kipling was Greg's swollen nose.

Emily was about to tell Greg how shocked she was at his behaviour, but he spoke first.

'I have a present for you,' Greg said, once they were inside their room.

She couldn't very well give Greg a piece of her mind if he'd bought her a gift. 'As long as it's not a Ming vase,' she said, kicking off her shoes. She threw herself onto the bed, still in her wedding gown.

'No.' Greg chuckled as he handed her a small, wrapped box. 'You married someone old, your wedding dress is new, and I know Debs lent you her garter for the something borrowed. Here is something blue.'

Emily opened the box and gasped with delight at the sapphire and crystal heart-shaped pendant on a white gold chain.

'It's gorgeous, thank you,' she said as Greg did up the clasp behind her neck.

It was some minutes before Greg irresolutely asked her what she made of all this talk of forgeries and fakes. 'Does your work really look like that Russian artist's? What was his name again? Kandinsky?'

'Greg, I hope you'll give Mr Kipling his money back,' Emily said, ignoring his questions, 'and I'd like you to promise me not to try to double-cross anyone like that again.'

'I promise,' Greg said, looking Emily in the eyes. 'It was the first time, but it will be the last. And I'll make it up to Mr Kipling. You have my word.'

Lying on the bed, Emily slid the heart pendant from side to side on its chain around her neck. She watched Greg as he undressed. His eyes were still shining and his cheeks were bright pink. She believed him. After all, Greg was a decent man, and an honest one. Usually. He would keep his promise. She knew he wouldn't lie to her on their wedding night. At least, she certainly hoped he wouldn't.

Chapter Thirteen

~

Oxford, December 2014

Emily knows it wouldn't take much to unhinge her completely, but for now she's holding it together. Just about. The familiar warning signs that she's heading for a depressive episode are there, but no one seems to have noticed them yet. Except Emily herself, of course. She is having uncontrollable mood swings, feeling euphoric at times and irritable at others. And she has boundless energy, which she has been making the most of to try and find some answers.

She has contacted the telephone company to ask them if they can trace the number of the person who called her. She has checked over every inch of Greg's Range Rover inside and out, looking for something – *anything* – that might show it was used in a pop-up ad or driven to Port Meadow. She has even been into every men's clothes shop in town searching for similar red jumpers to Greg's and questioning bewildered shopkeepers about customers who might have bought one.

But every single one of these ideas has led to a dead end. And for a few weeks now, apart from two more phone calls, nothing has happened. Emily refuses to allow herself to be lulled into a false sense of security, though. She knows that this can't last, any more than her hyperactivity.

The depressive phase is on its way; she's sure of that. She hasn't been depressed for about eight years. Last time, it was triggered off by an unfortunate event that she'd had trouble coping with. It was the same incident, in fact, that led to Amanda and Richard's break-up.

No one talks about that now. It's almost as if it never happened. And ever since then, Emily has felt relatively stable. But for the last few days, her stability has felt precarious. She has had the presentiment that something dreadful is just around the corner. She keeps telling herself that it's just her imagination, but the expectation lies heavy in her stomach.

~

It's her birthday, and she has woken up sitting on the floor of her workshop with her head on her arms and pins and needles in her fingers. She can't have slept for more than a couple of hours. She doesn't need much sleep at the moment. She remembers seeing daylight before she finally decided to rest for a while. For now, that's all she can remember. Last night's events are sketchy, at best, in her head. She looks around her. *What was I doing in here?*

Last time Emily was depressed, she didn't have any memory gaps. She sometimes forgot to do things, but that's hardly the same thing. She seems to be blanking things out from her mind. She still hasn't recalled all the details of the accident, for one thing. And now she can't remember what she did last night! She feels as if two entities are fighting inside her head to take control: one of them wants her to get to the truth; the other is trying to protect her from the truth, and maybe even from herself.

Part of her wants to tell Amanda about this, but she knows

she can't. She knows what Amanda will say. The same thing that Dr Irvine, her psychiatrist at the Centre used to say: that Emily's memory gaps were associated with her alter. And Emily doesn't want to admit to herself that her sister might have been right all along. Perhaps 'Em' *was* real. And if that's so, then maybe she's back.

Emily stares at the list in front of her on the table as though seeing it for the first time. Although it isn't as neat as usual, it's unquestionably her handwriting. It looks as if she has scrawled down the ideas chasing each other around in her head before they escaped her altogether. There's no doubt in her mind that this is her work, but she doesn't recall writing these notes at all.

She was very wired last night. *What did I do? What on earth did I get up to?* Nebulous images start to come back to her. *Oh no*, she groans as she remembers ringing Josh at midnight and inviting him round. He didn't need much persuading, as she'd expected. Inevitably they had sex – more than once – and then she asked him to leave.

What happened next? She hasn't slept much, that's for sure; she was far too agitated for that. She has been having difficulty sleeping for some time now, but last night was different. She has also lost her appetite – and consequently, a lot of weight – over the past few months.

Last time he visited, Matt deftly rolled three joints and left them for her. He told her the marijuana would fix her insomnia and make her hungry. She'd kept them in one of the underwear drawers in her walk-in wardrobe. Now she remembers smoking all three of them in bed after Josh left. *Perhaps that's what caused the memory gaps*, she thinks.

The cannabis didn't help her sleep, though. And she's fairly certain she didn't get the munchies, either. She knows she really needs antidepressants and lithium mood stabilisers, not recreational drugs. When this manic period abates, she'll come down with a terrifying thud. It might take anything from a few weeks

119

to several months, but at some stage she will inexorably be swamped in an asphyxiating black fog.

She looks down again at the piece of A4 paper in front of her. There are three columns, apparently drawn up with a ruler, with the paper in landscape orientation. It starts off with relatively even letters, but the writing in the third column is almost illegible. Emily supposes her thoughts must have been racing out of control by this point. The headings are written in capital letters and underlined.

In the column on the left, Emily has noted:

PROOF THAT GREG IS ALIVE:
1) He sent two Facebook messages.
2) He was at Port Meadow.
3) He phoned three times.
3) It was definitely Greg in the photo taken in front of the Old Manor House (banner ad).

In the middle column Emily reads:

WHY HASN'T HE COME HOME?
1) He is being held against his will.
2) He is in hiding because he has swindled a customer who wants revenge.
3) He has faked his death in order to obtain insurance money.
4) He is living with his mistress.

On the right-hand side of her sheet of paper, Emily has jotted down questions she has been asking herself recently. It doesn't look like she has come up with any answers yet.

THINGS THAT DON'T MAKE SENSE:
1) What does my father have to do with this? (He came up in the argument in the car.)

2) Does Sergeant Campbell think the car accident was deliberate? Why?
3) What was Greg doing at my childhood home (photo in pop-up ad)?
4) Why didn't Greg speak to me at Port Meadow?
5) Who is Greg's mistress? Do I know her?
6) If Greg is dead, who is doing this? Why?
7) Chequebook stubs: WTF???

Emily hasn't received any more Facebook messages since she followed Josh's advice and changed all the passwords. She has been contacted three more times, but each time it was by telephone. On one of those occasions, Greg – if indeed the caller was Greg – simply said he needed her. In the other two phone calls, he asked her to speak so that he could hear her voice. Each time she was in floods of tears after the call had ended abruptly.

Emily examines her notes again. She wonders why Greg would need to illegally claim on his life insurance. She's also puzzled by question number seven. The acronym seems less like something Emily would use and more like something Pippa would write in a text message. But more importantly, what chequebook stubs?

Then something comes back to her. She sees an image of herself in the middle of a tidying frenzy in Greg's study during the night. She must have cleared up his study before she came down to her studio to scribble down her thoughts.

Emily makes her way upstairs to Greg's study. Opening the door and setting foot in the office, she gasps at the sight that meets her. Even though she has a vague memory of tidying the room, she somehow expected to see an absolute mess.

The documents, which before were strewn across Greg's desk, are now sorted into three neat piles. On the first document in each stack is a coloured Post-it. Emily walks up to the desk and reads what she has written on each one: 'URGENT', 'TO BE FILED AWAY' and 'MISCELLANEOUS'.

She flicks through a pile of bank statements, colour-coded yellow for 'to be filed away'. She notices that she has organised them according to date. At first glance, Greg's business doesn't seem to have been doing well, but it doesn't appear to have been going under, either. Emily will have to check the accounts more attentively later.

On Greg's corkboard on one of the walls, Emily has taken down the holiday postcards that were displayed there. In their place, she has pinned up a meeting chart sheet. It shows a to-do list written in black marker. She reads the names of customers she has apparently decided she should ring about matters concerning Greg's business. Unpaid bills, for example. She has also written the names of companies she needs to contact, particularly about car and life insurance policies. The phone numbers are noted, too.

Strangely, just as for the piece of paper in her workshop, it's as if Emily has never laid eyes on the chart and the Post-its before. But again, she recognises her handwriting, even though it's messier than usual.

As she scans the room in awe, Emily sees that she has even separated the rubbish into 'recycling' and 'waste bin'. She's stunned that she has been so meticulous and efficient.

Suddenly, she realises the chequebook stubs have slipped her mind. Where could they be? She spots Greg's briefcase against the wall and opens it. Inside is a chequebook, but it's his business one. She thumbs through it but nothing strikes her as out of the ordinary.

Instinctively, she walks back to Greg's desk and opens the drawers. The middle one contains several chequebooks bound with an elastic band with one of her pink Post-its marked URGENT!!! She pulls off the rubber band and sees that she has highlighted the payee on a number of the cheque stubs. She stares incredulously at the name.

Emily's legs buckle from under her and she sinks into Greg's office chair. *I don't get it*, she thinks. She makes herself start at the beginning of the first chequebook and counts the stubs she has highlighted. *What is this?* She wipes her clammy hands on her jeans before taking a sheet of paper from the bottom drawer of the desk and grabbing a pen from the pot. She jots down the dates and the corresponding figures.

The amount of each payment has increased over a period of around a year from June 2013 until July 2014. The first cheque was made out for £2,000 and the last one is for £20,000. She looks at the date of the last cheque again: 4th July 2014. The date of her tenth wedding anniversary. The month before Greg's death.

She finds a calculator in another drawer and works out the total: £50,000. That's a huge amount of money! And Greg has made out all the cheques to the same person! Emily can't imagine why on earth such a large sum of money has changed hands between the two of them. *Why did Greg keep me in the dark about this?* Emily wonders. *It's not as if I don't know the payee.* But she's sure there must have been a good reason. And she is determined to find out what it is.

She needs to talk to someone about this. Now. The obvious choice is Amanda. Emily doesn't have her mobile on her and she has no idea where she has left it. She has no numbers saved in the landline memory, so she uses the telephone in the office to ring her own iPhone. Stepping out onto the landing, she hears her ringtone coming from her bedroom.

But when Emily calls Amanda from her mobile, she gets her sister's voicemail. Sitting on her bed, she leaves a message. She tries to sound casual, although she is desperate to hear what Amanda has to say about this. She's also slightly annoyed that Amanda hasn't rung yet to wish her a happy birthday. It's gone noon, after all.

She toys with the idea of ringing Pippa. She may be able to shed some light on this mystery. But before Emily can make up her mind, her mobile starts simultaneously ringing and vibrating in her hand. The caller ID shows that it's Matt.

Assuming her brother is calling for her birthday, she affects a joyful tone in spite of the shock she has just received in Greg's study.

'Hello, Em.' Matt's voice is funereal. Somehow Emily knows she's in for an even bigger shock.

'What's wrong?' Emily asks.

'I… Mum…' He starts to cry.

'Calm down, Matt.' He hasn't cried in front of her since he was a little boy.

It's a few seconds before Matt can get his words out, but it seems a lot longer to Emily.

'Mum's dead, Em.' He speaks so quietly that Emily isn't sure if she has heard correctly.

'What…? How…? When…?'

'Late last night. We think. I spoke to her… on the phone… around eight o'clock.' Matt is overcome with emotion and Emily waits impatiently but silently for more information. 'I found her… this morning.'

'Oh, God. Oh, Matt.' Emily fights against the lump that has risen in her throat. She knows that Matt's struggling to keep a grip, so she can't go to pieces.

'What happened?'

'She fell off the wagon and down the stairs.'

'What?' Emily can't believe her ears. 'What do you mean?'

'Well, that's the official line, anyway.' There's a hard edge to Matt's voice now and he is more articulate. 'That's what the ambulance crew and the doctors said. The police think so, too. They say she was drunk and lost her footing on the stairs.'

'You don't believe that?'

'Do you?'

'I don't know. I wasn't there.'

'Neither was I. But Mum hadn't touched a drop of alcohol for

124

over three years.' Matt's speech is slow, but still coherent. 'She was fine. She sounded happy on the phone yesterday evening.'

'Matt, I'll pack a bag and drive down immediately.'

'OK. Can you tell Amanda?'

'Yes. I rang her just now actually, but I didn't get through. I'll try again.' Emily thinks she's giving a reasonable impression of being in control, but she can't keep up the pretence much longer. 'It's all right, Matt. I'm on my way.'

Matt is sobbing as Emily ends the call. Her hands shaking, she scrolls down to Amanda's number. She leaves another message, her tone distinctly different from the first one.

As she throws some clothes into a suitcase, barely able to see through her tears, Emily replays the conversation with Matt in her head. Josephine had had a drinking problem on and off through most of Emily's life and all of Matt's. Emily thinks it probably started around the time her father began his visits to her bedroom at night.

Over the years, Josephine made – and broke – numerous promises never to touch alcohol again. Time and time again Emily had seen her go back to the whiskey. They had all been so pleased that Josephine had managed to stay dry for so long this time. But Matt had really believed in their mother. Maybe he'd been too optimistic. Maybe he hadn't seen her fail as many times as Emily had.

It must have been an accident. The alternative doesn't bear thinking about. If Matt's right and Josephine didn't die because she fell drunkenly down the stairs, what could have happened? Surely Matt doesn't really think their mother's death is suspicious, does he?

Chapter Fourteen

~

Oxford, 23rd July 2006

The last time Emily had sunk into to an episode of depression, it had really started on the tenth anniversary. She'd been feeling very low for a few weeks, anyway, but then Richard showed up on her doorstep in tears. The problem between him and Amanda was what finally pushed her over the edge.

Emily had only met Richard twice. The first time was after a play in which he and Amanda had had the leading roles. On the second occasion, she and Greg had gone out to lunch with them at The White Horse in the city centre.

Amanda and Richard had known each other for a while from their Amateur Dramatic Club, but they'd only been dating for about six months. Amanda hadn't told Emily about it until three months ago. Emily had found Richard pleasant, although his flattery of her sister was a bit corny, and his puns were cringe-worthy. He was plainly infatuated with Amanda. But, observing Amanda's attitude and body language towards Richard, Emily was convinced that her sister wasn't nearly so in love with him.

'Richard! What on earth is the matter?' It occurred to Emily that she'd never seen a grown man cry. 'You'd better come in.' She stood back to let Richard pass. She wondered how he'd known where she lived.

'It was an accident,' he said, 'but I didn't want her to kill it!'

'Richard, I'm afraid I have absolutely no idea what you're talking about,' Emily said in what she hoped was a soothing voice. She led him to the sofa in the living room, and waited patiently while he pulled himself together. She pushed a box of tissues towards him along the coffee table. He blew his nose loudly, and then balled up the tissue in his hand.

'The baby,' Richard offered by way of an explanation. 'Where is she? Is she here?'

'What baby?' Emily asked, her heart skipping a beat. Because it was the anniversary and her mind was elsewhere, she didn't immediately grasp what Richard was so distraught about.

'She was pregnant. Didn't you know?'

'No, I didn't,' Emily said quietly, chewing her bottom lip. Her answer seemed to distress Richard all the more, and he cried even harder.

'With my baby,' he eventually added. 'I thought you'd know.'

'No, Amanda didn't say anything.'

'You're so close, the two of you. I just assumed she'd have told you. Actually, I supposed she'd be here.' He looked around him as he said this, as though he expected her to come out of her hiding place.

'No, she's not here.'

'I haven't seen her for about a week. I wanted to get her to change her mind – about the abortion – but she isn't answering my phone calls.'

Emily hadn't spoken to her sister for several days; she just hadn't felt up to ringing her.

'I can't imagine why she didn't tell you,' Richard insisted.

'Neither can I,' Emily lied. She knew full well why her sister had said nothing of this to her.

'That means she must have gone through all that alone.' Richard started sobbing again. 'My poor baby.'

Emily didn't know if Richard was referring to Amanda or to the baby she was carrying, but she didn't ask. She was close to tears herself.

'Maybe I'm not too late. Perhaps I can still talk her out of it. I would support her, you know. I'd do pretty much anything for her. And the baby. Our baby.' He dabbed his eyes with the scrunched-up tissue.

'I'm sure you would, Richard.' Emily was doing her best to come up with comforting words, but, even to her, they sounded like platitudes.

The buzzer rang and made them both jump. Emily opened the front door and was relieved to see Amanda standing at the gate.

'Richard's here,' Emily hissed in warning, as Amanda stepped inside the house.

'I know. He left me a message. That's why I'm here.'

Amanda marched through the hall into the living room. 'Richard,' she said firmly, 'I want you to wait outside for a minute while I speak to Emily, then we'll go somewhere and talk.' As an afterthought, she added, 'I didn't see your car.'

'I came by bus. I was in no fit state to drive.'

'Then wait for me in my car.' Amanda handed him her keys.

Richard nodded, grabbed another tissue, and rose to leave. Emily opened the door for him. He walked past Emily with his head hung low, turning his tear-streaked face away from her.

Amanda and Emily went back into the living room and sank down onto the sofa side by side.

'I'm so sorry, Emily,' Amanda began.

'It's fine. Don't worry about it.'

'What did he say?'

'He told me he was looking for you and that you hadn't returned his calls. He thought maybe you'd be here, although I don't know how he knew where I lived.'

'I showed him once when we were driving past,' Amanda explained. 'What else did he tell you?'

'He said you got pregnant by accident and that you'd decided to have an abortion. He wanted to stop you, I think.'

'Emily, I… I…'

It struck Emily that this might be the first time she'd ever witnessed her sister struggling to find the right thing to say.

'It's all right, Amanda. I'm here if you need me, but it has nothing to do with me.'

As she said those words, she realised that her sister had never come to her with a problem or for advice. It had always been the other way round.

'I didn't tell you because of Melody,' Amanda said. 'I thought you'd be upset.'

'I am, but not because you're planning to have an abortion. It's been ten years, since… you know.'

'I do know. I was aware that this was the date. I just didn't know if you thought about it after all these years.'

'I think about her every day,' Emily admitted.

'I've already had the abortion,' Amanda said. 'On Tuesday. It was early days in the pregnancy and it wasn't very complicated. I told Richard it was over between us. I didn't mean to get pregnant. The condom burst.'

Emily winced. This was definitely too much information. But she didn't interrupt. Amanda was confiding in her. She needed to listen.

'It all made me certain that Richard isn't the person I want to be with for the rest of my life. He's good to me, he loves me, but, well, it's too much. I feel suffocated. I'm not sure if I will ever find "The One", but it's not him. You're rather lucky to have found Greg, you know.'

Emily nodded.

'I don't really want to have children. I'm not very maternal.' Amanda began fiddling with one of her rings.

'Oh, Amanda, you are. You've always looked after me.' Emily placed her hand on Amanda's.

'That's different. You're my sister.' They hugged for a while on the sofa in silence. 'Anyway, I never wanted to get you involved in this,' Amanda continued. 'You shouldn't have been burdened with my problem, especially as I'd already worked out the solution. And I thought you might hate me.'

'I could never hate you! Did you really think I'd judge you because you were getting an abortion?'

'Not judge me, no. Resent me. Because of losing Melody.'

'Amanda, if Melody hadn't been born on 17th July, the pregnancy would have been terminated the following day. How could I possibly judge you when I was to have an abortion myself?'

'Well, that was hardly your decision, was it? Any more than what happened afterwards.'

'It's fine, Amanda. Really. I understand. And I certainly don't hate you. I'm sure, it was all for the best, for you, just as for me.'

Amanda held Emily tightly for a while, and then left to take Richard home.

Emily sat on the sofa for a while, still and pensive. Then she felt hot tears roll silently down her face. She did understand Amanda. She'd carried an unwanted child herself for seven months. At first she'd denied its existence. Then it had felt like a grotesque foreign body inside her own, destroying her and deforming her from within. When she'd given birth, the first emotion she recalled was relief. It was over.

But then her baby had cried. It was alive. The 'it' had gradually become a 'she' and demanded her mother's attention. Emily had held Melody in her arms, she'd fed her, stroked her face, calmed her, loved her. For six days. Then she'd lost her for ever. It was a visceral loss, leaving broken pieces in Emily that could never again be made whole. And yet she would go through it all again, just to be able to hold her daughter in her arms.

Ten years ago to the day. Melody had died of an enterococcus bacterial infection.

Usually the days leading up to the anniversaries of Melody's birth and then of her death almost a week later were far worse than the actual dates when they came round each time. Emily had rituals she carried out and it seemed to keep her going. On the date of Melody's birth, she bought flowers; on the date of her death, she lit a candle. Then she did the same things she did every day. She went for a run or a walk; she worked on her paintings. She arranged to meet Greg or Amanda for lunch.

For some reason, however, this year had been particularly hard. As Greg was away on business, Emily had found herself alone for the past few days. She'd really needed to be surrounded by people close to her, but she'd felt too sad even to call Amanda. She now knew her sister had been dealing with her own problems anyway.

Her mother wouldn't have helped. Melody was a taboo subject between them. Josephine had steadfastly refused to see the baby when she was alive, and hadn't referred to her once in the whole ten years she'd been dead. It was as if she didn't even remember Melody had ever existed.

For Emily, on the other hand, it was essential not to forget. She clung to her memories as tightly as she clung to the pink plastic hospital bracelet in her hand. It was the only tangible link to her daughter she had left. She took her hand out of her pocket and unfurled her fingers. 'Baby Cavendish,' she read. It had been written in blue ballpoint pen on the bracelet the day she was born. Before Emily had named her.

Yes, it was very important to Emily to remember. She worried now, though, that the images in her head were not real recollections, but only memories of memories, mere copies of the originals that were fading over time and losing their quality each time she looked at them. If she saw photos now of newborn baby girls, would she even be able to recognise which one was her own daughter?

Had she lived, Melody would have been adopted. It had been made clear that Emily didn't really have a say in this decision. The social worker had been to see Emily, and both she and Josephine had persuaded Emily that this would be for the best. Those were almost the same words Emily had just spoken to Amanda: *I'm sure, it was all for the best, for you just as for me.*

The hospital chaplain had been to see Emily after Melody had succumbed to her infection, but he hadn't been able to find any better words than those to console her. He had used them, too. *It's probably for the best, Emily.* The nurse had allowed her to say goodbye to her baby, and that was the last time she'd laid eyes on Melody, for no one had raised the possibility of a funeral.

Chapter Fifteen

~

Oxford, December 2014

The sun shines brightly that morning, which doesn't seem right for such a solemn day. The colourful Christmas tree lights in the windows of the houses opposite the church contrast with Emily's sombre mood. It's only the beginning of December, but there are already decorations up all over the village. End of the year celebrations have always been difficult for Emily, and she knows that from now on they will be far worse.

Matt has shaved off his goatee, cut his hair and suited up for the occasion. He is carrying Josephine's coffin with Uncle Rod and two pallbearers from the funeral home. Holding himself up straight, he is focused on getting through his task, and Emily is proud of him.

~

After Matt's phone call just five days ago, Emily eventually managed to get through to Amanda on her mobile. They travelled down to Devon together, although Emily did all the driving as

Amanda was very tired for some reason. They were now staying in Josephine's house in Braunton. Emily sensed she was functioning on autopilot and Amanda had immediately seen through her performance.

'How can I act normally?' Emily snapped when Amanda confronted her about this in the car. 'Mum has just died.'

'You know what I mean,' Amanda said in her big sister voice. 'You're all jittery and wound up, not to mention irritable. Are you OK?'

'Yes. Mmm. No. I don't know. Could you prescribe me some lithium and antidepressants?' Emily didn't really want to take any medication – she knew it would numb her brain – but she also knew that she was going to be spiralling downwards very soon. 'I'm going to need them,' she continued. 'You're absolutely right, of course. You should see what I've done to Greg's study. I've completely transformed it. I've tidied. I sorted all the documents into piles and labelled them with different-coloured Post-its; I've written a list and a chart – I don't remember doing it, but it's definitely my handwriting. My God, I turned thirty-four just a few days ago, and I am both a widow and an orphan. I—'

'Emily, that's enough! You're talking far too much, and too quickly. I can't keep up. I'll write you out a prescription, and you must start as soon as possible. You have to promise me you'll make an appointment with your psychiatrist. You need professional help.' In a softer voice, she added, 'I'm concerned about you.'

Emily had been referred to a good psychiatrist when she left Exmoor Secure Centre. He'd been treating her on and off over the years since then, but she hadn't felt the need to see him for a while. Staff Nurse Peterson had talked her into seeing the hospital bereavement counsellor for one consultation after the accident, but she'd refused any other form of professional help. She certainly had no intention of going to see her therapist now.

'OK. I will. I promise.' Emily was conscious of her own volubility, but she couldn't stop herself. 'Just let me finish telling you—'

'You said you recognised your writing, but didn't remember making out the list?'

'Yes, and the chart. And the Post-its. I did everything last night, but—'

'Emily, do you think "Em" is back?'

That finally shut Emily up. Her sister didn't believe her, and Emily didn't believe in 'Em'. But Emily had had that very thought just the other day. *It's just a coincidence*, she tells herself. *She's not real.*

Amanda hadn't finished. 'How long have you been feeling like this?' She didn't wait for an answer. 'Because, as you know, people with bipolar disorder quite often have delusions. What if you didn't see anyone at all at Port Meadow? Or in the advert on your computer? You might have been hallucinating when you thought you saw Greg.'

'Amanda! My husband died just a few months ago, and now Mum is dead. I'm not insane; I don't have bipolar disorder or dissociative identity disorder or any other psychiatric problem. I'm just not coping very well. That's all. Stop psychoanalysing me! I'm not one of your patients.'

And with that, Emily burst into tears at the wheel. 'I'm just a bit depressed,' she sobbed. Her energy was abandoning her much more quickly than she thought it would. She was suddenly left feeling drained. Amanda put her hand gently on Emily's arm. Emily told herself that her sister was just concerned about her, but it didn't stop the tears coming.

'Look, let me know if there's anything else I can do, OK?' Amanda said after Emily had calmed down. 'I'm worried about you. Mum was, too.'

'Mum? When?' Emily dabbed at her nose with a sleeve.

'The night she died. She said she'd just spoken to you.'

'Really? I don't remember ringing her.'

'She didn't say it was on the phone, now I come to think of it, but I suppose it must have been.' Amanda paused. 'Anyway, when

I called her, she said you were acting strangely. Excited one moment and almost crying the next. She asked me to look out for you.'

'Oh.'

'And I will, all right?'

'OK… Thank you.'

Emily knew she was very forgetful at the moment. But could she really have no memory of talking to her mum the night she died? Why would Josephine tell Amanda they'd talked if they hadn't, though? Perhaps Amanda had misunderstood. Or maybe Josephine had been confused about when the conversation had taken place. Yes, that must be it. 'Em' couldn't possibly be back. She didn't exist. Did she?

~

Josephine's sister, Mary, is at the funeral, of course. She chose not to bring her mother.

'Your granny wouldn't have understood what was going on, my dears,' she tells her nephew and nieces, 'and it's better that way.'

Apart from Uncle Rod and Aunt Mary, Emily and Amanda don't know many other people at Josephine's funeral, although Matt seems to know a few of them from living locally. Emily is touched that everyone who has talked to her has spoken highly of Josephine.

After the service, they invite the mourners to Josephine's home for refreshments. Amanda has ordered lots of food from a local caterer, but Emily busied herself the previous day shopping for ingredients to cook pies and tarts and stayed up most of the night doing just that. It had given her something to do.

In fact, there was relatively little to organise since Josephine, much to Emily's surprise, had had a prepaid funeral plan. Matt had been informed about this long ago, and their mother seemed to have taken care of everything. She'd even left a letter specifying her wishes – she wanted to be cremated and for her ashes to be scattered in the sea at Braunton Burrows or Saunton Sands.

136

For the first time, Emily realises that her mother must have struggled terribly after Graham's death. Perhaps that was why she'd arranged her own funeral plan. There had been extra costs for details not included in the plan, but the funeral home had taken care of most of the preparations.

'It's almost as though she'd intended to do this,' Amanda says.

Emily and Matt don't answer. Emily frowns. Matt isn't convinced that this was an accident, and Amanda seems to think it's a deliberate death wish. Emily doesn't know what to believe.

When she'd moved to Braunton, Josephine had joined a line dancing club for which she'd been the treasurer for a few years. Many of her friends from the club have come to the funeral, some of them with their husbands.

'I'm so sorry for your loss,' a woman says to the three of them. Her voice contains a hint of an Irish accent. She is flanked by two other women, and all three of them are a similar age to Josephine. 'She was a great person. So reliable. Such good fun. We were planning to go for a girlie trip next summer to Scotland, all four of us.'

She remembers her mother mentioning not long ago that she was going to see the Edinburgh Military Tattoo with some of her friends. 'Thank you for coming today,' Emily says.

'I'm Deirdre,' the woman says. 'We all danced together,' her arm makes a sweeping gesture to include the ladies on either side of her.

'It was a terrible shock,' the woman on her right says. 'She seemed so happy the week before her… the last week at line dancing.'

'Yes, we found it hard to believe she would turn to the drink again, without turning to us first,' says the third woman.

Emily sees Deirdre give her a warning nudge. Matt gives Emily a meaningful glance. It seems to say: *Mum's friends haven't really bought the falling-off-the-wagon-and-down-the-stairs version either.*

'Anyway, if there's anything I can do, I wrote my name and

number in the Sympathy Book at the funeral home. It's a lovely wake,' Deirdre says.

The three women all smile sadly at Emily and her siblings. Then they turn around and walk away in a line towards the food table.

It's late evening by the time everyone has left and Emily and Amanda have cleared everything away. Matt is going back to his own place for the night. He has told Emily that he'll come back again the following morning so that they can drive out to the beach and scatter their mother's ashes.

Amanda makes Emily a cup of tea, then opens a bottle of wine and pours herself a glass. The two of them drop onto the couch and sit side by side in silence. Amanda seems exhausted.

Emily takes her phone out of her handbag and switches it on. She has a few text messages from friends and acquaintances offering condolences. Just as when Greg died, she has had relatively few phone calls. Pippa has been great, though. She wasn't able to make it to Josephine's funeral because of juggling the play and a one-month-old baby girl, but she has rung every day since Josephine died.

Everyone else Emily knows seems allergic to her grief, preferring to write a message on Facebook or send a text rather than phoning or giving support with a physical presence. Often they've worded the messages so that it's up to Emily to contact them when she's feeling like it. Charles's text is a prime example: 'I'm so sorry to hear about your mother, Emily. I don't want to get in the way by ringing or showing up, but if/when you want to chat or go out for a drink, I'm here for you.'

She wonders if she would have reacted the same way if one of her friends had lost both their spouse and a parent during the same year. Are people avoiding her in case she jinxes them with her bad luck?

'Did you get a message from Charles?' Emily asks Amanda.

'Well, he rang me, actually,' Amanda says, 'and he sent a wreath. It was at the funeral home.'

'Oh,' Emily replies. Clearly, she's being too harsh in her judge-ment of Charles.

She sees that she has two messages on her voicemail and listens to them. As Emily anticipated, the first is from Pippa. She's pleased to hear from her friend. But Emily wasn't expecting the second caller to ring, and hopes it isn't more bad news. She's aware of an uncomfortable knot tightening in her stomach as she listens to the message.

'Mrs Klein, it's Sergeant Campbell. I'd like to talk to you as soon as possible, if you wouldn't mind giving me a ring. You have my mobile number. Call at any time.'

Emily decides to wait until Campbell rings back. She puts the phone down on her lap and stares at the blank television screen. She looks at Amanda who has finished her wine and fallen asleep on the couch beside her.

Emily has been wondering why the investigation into the car accident is taking so long. She wants it to be over, one way or another. Matt, who by his own admission watches far too many police series on TV, has his own theory about Campbell. He thinks that the sergeant is hounding Emily in the hope of uncovering some pathological serial killer, solving several cold case murders and consequently furthering her own career. Emily supposes that in this scenario, she'd be the serial killer.

Matt seems to think that if the police really did think there had been foul play, CID would have taken over from the Roads Policing Unit before now. He told Emily that if she were considered a suspect, she'd be questioned at the police station with a solicitor. Emily has no idea if any of this is true. She doesn't know much about police procedures, and strongly suspects that Matt doesn't either.

In the end, curiosity gets the better of Emily and she decides to return Campbell's call. She gets up and wanders into the kitchen, closing the door behind her softly so as not to disturb Amanda. She sits on the table and puts her feet on one of the chairs. She hesitates for a second or two, but then she scrolls down to Campbell's mobile number in her phone, and presses the screen to ring her.

Campbell's phone goes to voicemail, and Emily ends the call without leaving a message.

~

The following morning, Emily takes her sister to the railway station in Barnstaple. Amanda is keen to get back to Oxford to see a young patient whose appointment she doesn't want to cancel. As Emily parks in front of Josephine's house, she catches sight of Matt who is sitting on the front step. At first, she thinks that her brother is smoking. But then she realises that he's blowing his breath into the cold air as if exhaling from a drag on a cigarette. Shame. She suddenly felt like having a fag, even though she has never been a smoker.

'Have you been waiting long? You must be freezing,' Emily says as he stands up to hug her.

'No, I'm fine, really. Let's grab Mum and go to the beach.'

Emily arches an eyebrow at Matt as she opens the front door and goes into the house to fetch the urn.

'How are we going to do this?' Emily asks as Matt drives Greg's Range Rover to Saunton Sands.

'I figured we could drive out to Crow Point and scatter Mum's ashes in the Taw Estuary. I've checked the tide times. We're good to go.'

'Is that legal?' Emily asks.

'The funeral home director offered to put me in touch with someone who would take us out to sea in a boat. He was keen to flog me one of his biodegradable urns. But he admitted in the end that it isn't illegal to scatter ashes as long as it's in tidal coastal waters.' Matt takes his hands off the steering wheel briefly in order to make air speech marks with his fingers.

Emily is quiet during the rest of the short car journey to the most southerly tip of Saunton Sands. She gazes out of the window at the agitated sea as she chews on one of her nails.

As she gets out of the car, Emily closes her eyes and breathes in the salty smell of the sea. Matt puts the urn under one arm, clutching it against him with his hand. With the other hand, he takes Emily's elbow and they bow their heads and walk into the onshore wind. The beach stretches out for miles and the hills to their right are hidden by the mist.

Emily and Matt sit on the cold, wet sand. For a while they say nothing and Emily listens to the crashing of the waves. Then they reminisce about some of the good times they had with their mother. Finally they stand up, and with some difficulty, because of his numb hands and the tight seal, Matt opens the urn and slowly tips out the ashes. They remain side by side for a while, Matt's arm around his sister's shoulders.

Finally, Matt breaks the silence. 'The doctor who pronounced Mum dead offered to report her death to a coroner. Maybe I should've accepted.' He looks down at his feet and kicks absent-mindedly at the sand. 'Then there would've been a post-mortem.'

'That wouldn't have changed anything, Matt. Didn't they find an empty bottle of Irish whiskey in her bedroom?'

'Yes. And she smelt of whiskey.'

'Then it does look like she fell down the stairs drunk. What other explanation can there be?'

Emily really isn't sure what to make of Josephine's death. But if Matt tells anyone that he thinks something about it doesn't add up, how long will it be before Campbell comes sniffing around her again? Emily wants to reassure Matt. And anyway, Emily can't think of anyone who would want to hurt Josephine, far less kill her. So, really, as she'd just said to Matt, what else could have happened?

'I'd like to know what pushed her to drink,' Matt says. 'She was fine when I left her that evening. I had dinner with her and she seemed very happy. She had plans, you know. She talked about that trip to Scotland. And we'd agreed on the phone that evening to go for a Sunday roast in Croyde next weekend. It was her idea not mine! She went on and on about how good the sticky toffee pudding was at The Thatch.' Matt gives a sad smile.

Emily is reminded of the phone call Amanda seems to think she had with their mother the evening she died. She still can't remember anything about that. But it has been on her mind. The more she thinks about it, the more certain she is that someone is mistaken. Either Josephine or Amanda. Perhaps Josephine was referring to her conversation with Matt when she mentioned it to Amanda. Either Josephine said the wrong name or Amanda got it wrong.

'It doesn't make any sense,' Matt says.

'I know. I thought about it a lot when I couldn't sleep last night,' Emily says. 'I know Mum was proud that she'd been dry for more than three years. But I think she probably relapsed and fell.' Emily knows this is the most likely explanation. If she can convince Matt, she might even be able to convince herself.

'I just don't understand why she would have relapsed.'

'Christmas must be a hard time for her. She's alone and my dad died at Christmas.' Matt shoots Emily a sideways glance, which makes Emily wonder how much Matt knows about her father's death. They've never talked about it.

'Or, maybe she wasn't sad,' she continues. 'Perhaps she had a drink because she was happy. She might have thought she'd reached the stage where she could just enjoy one glass and stop there.'

'Poor Mum,' Matt sobs. 'Oh, God.' Emily puts her arm around him, too. She watches him stroke his chin where his goatee used to be.

After a few minutes, Emily leads Matt back to the car, holds her hand out for the car keys, and drives him back to Braunton.

~

After Matt has left, Emily decides to try Campbell again. She sits on the kitchen table with her feet on the chair, just as she did the previous evening. Holding her phone in one hand, she supports her chin with the other hand, her elbows on her knees. Campbell answers the phone before Emily even hears it ring.

'Ah, Mrs Klein, thanks for getting back to me.' Sergeant Campbell's Glaswegian brogue is particularly pronounced this afternoon. Emily wonders if she has just come back from Scotland or if she has been on the phone with a member of her family back home. If she still has any family there. She pushes thoughts of her mother's plans to go to Scotland from her mind and waits for Campbell to continue.

'I'd really just called, Mrs Klein, to let you know that the investigation into the road traffic collision has concluded and there's to be no further action taken.'

Emily sighs.

'You're relieved,' Campbell says. It's a statement, not a question.

'I am,' Emily admits. 'I thought it was taking ages, and that it might not be a good sign.'

'Well, when there is a fatality, as in this case, the Serious Collision Investigation Unit has to be involved. There was some evidence to be collected and the RTC booklet had to be completed.'

Emily has no idea what that is, but she doesn't care.

'It can all take some time,' Campbell says. 'In the end, there was a witness statement and CCTV footage, and they both told the same story as you. And that's the end of it.'

'Well, thank you for letting me know.' Emily is keen to end the call, but Campbell hasn't finished.

'Can I just ask you a few questions?'

'Well, is there any point, if the investigation is over? I mean, it was my mother's funeral yesterday…' Emily could have kicked herself for saying that, and regrets it immediately. She can imagine Campbell's ears pricking up at that information.

'Oh, I'm so sorry,' Campbell says. Emily feels her coldness towards this woman thawing until Campbell asks a little too suspiciously, 'What happened to her?'

'She had an accident,' Emily answers curtly.

'A car accident?'

'No, she fell. Look, if you don't mind, I—'

'I just wanted to ask you one thing, really.'

Campbell pauses. Emily supposes she's waiting for her consent, but she stays silent, too.

'It's not really relevant to the investigation, but I wondered if you were aware that your sister has a gambling problem.'

Emily doesn't know if she's more shocked at this woman's rudeness, or the news she has just given her.

'I'm not sure what you mean,' Emily says. 'My sister likes to place bets on horses from time to time.' Emily remembers Amanda betting on the Formula One race the day they packed up Greg's clothes. 'I believe she puts money on the results of other sports competitions occasionally. She may not always win, but I don't think that's what you'd call a problem.'

'When you lose thousands and thousands of pounds, I'd call it a problem,' Campbell says. 'In fact, I'd call it an addiction. As I said, it has nothing to do with our inquiry, but I thought you should know. I believe your husband did.'

There is a pause. Emily wonders if the sergeant is waiting for a reaction. She is certainly not going to thank her.

'Listen, I'm sorry to have bothered you at such a difficult time,' Campbell says, sounding genuinely contrite. 'If you need anything, don't hesitate to—'

But Emily has ended the call. Her head is spinning from the blow she has just been dealt. She hopes she'll never have to speak to that meddlesome police officer again.

Emily realises she's shaking uncontrollably. *What was that all about?* she thinks. *Do routine traffic accident investigations include background checks on the whole family? Or was Matt right about Campbell following a hunch in an attempt to make a name for herself? Thousands and thousands of pounds?*

Emily begins to pace furiously around the kitchen table. She doesn't stop to ask herself why she's so angry. Or who she's angry

144

with. What was it Campbell said? She said that Greg had known about Amanda's gambling problem.

Then it dawns on Emily. She starts to breathe more slowly and sits back down on the kitchen table. *Of course*, she thinks. *That had completely slipped my mind. That explains everything. But why didn't they tell me?* She can feel the tension in her shoulders start to lift.

With the devastating news of her mother's death and the turmoil she'd felt in the days between Matt's phone call and Josephine's funeral, Emily had forgotten that she'd wanted to talk to Amanda about the cheques. She'd thought about it one evening when talking to Pippa on the phone, and she'd contemplated mentioning it to her best friend, but then she'd changed her mind.

She'd reasoned with herself that if she was going to get to the bottom of this, then she had to talk to Amanda about her discovery, not Pippa. After all, the cheques in question had all been made out to her sister. But with Josephine's death, it didn't seem to be the right time to bring up something that might turn out to be a tricky subject.

When she'd found the chequebook stubs in Greg's office, she couldn't work out why Greg would have paid Amanda so much money. But Campbell has just inadvertently shed light on the matter. *Amanda must have run up some gambling debts and Greg bailed her out*, Emily realises. *If neither Greg nor Amanda told me about the payments, it was obviously to avoid embarrassing Amanda any further. Simple as that.*

In the end, Emily resolves not to talk to anyone about the cheques, especially not Amanda. Not right now, anyway. This was between her husband and her sister. It has nothing to do with her. Besides, it's not as if she's going to ask Amanda to pay her the money back.

What's more, Amanda has been very supportive, writing out a prescription for Emily last night before packing her bag and giving her lots of advice and encouragement. *I'll try to help my sister and be equally understanding of her problems from now on*, Emily vows.

Chapter Sixteen

~

Oxford, December 2010

When Emily spotted her, she was coming out of the Clarendon Centre onto Cornmarket Street, weighed down by numerous shopping bags. At first, she wasn't sure if it was her or just someone who looked like her. After all, she hadn't seen her for fourteen years.

Emily had had lunch with Greg and had been wandering aimlessly along Oxford's famous pedestrianised street for the past hour. She was trying to pluck up the courage to start buying her Christmas presents. Her hands were numb as she'd left her gloves in the car, and she'd just decided to leave it until another day and go home. Then she happened to glance up.

'Lucy?' Emily hazarded, just as the woman was about to pass her.

'Emily!' Lucinda Sharpe, Emily's former solicitor, recognised her immediately and, dumping her plastic bags on the ground, engulfed Emily in a big hug. 'I used to wonder if I'd ever bump into you here. My parents live here, you know.'

Emily remembered Lucy telling her that she had family in Oxford. She'd been excited for Emily when she was released from

Exmoor Children's Centre, telling her what a lovely city Oxford was.

'We're all staying at my mum and dad's for Christmas,' Lucy said. 'I've been Christmas shopping.' She pulled a face. 'I hate it!' She picked up her bags.

Emily wrinkled her nose. 'Me, too,' she said. *I hate Christmas altogether*, she thought.

'Every year I resolve to buy all my pressies on the Internet, and every year I leave it too late. Oh, well.' Lucy sighed. 'Have you got time for a cup of tea? It's a bit further along the road, but I love Starbucks.'

'Great idea,' Emily agreed, although secretly she thought the tea in Starbucks was disgusting. She took some of Lucy's bags to help her with her load.

Lucy seemed just as bouncy and hassled as Emily remembered. As the solicitor teetered along next to her, Emily noticed with amusement that Lucy's dress sense hadn't improved since she'd last seen her. She was wearing a medium-length pink duffle coat with multi-coloured toggles. The bottoms of her fake leather trousers were rolled up to reveal red socks poking out of open-toe stilettoes with a zebra design on them.

~

Emily carried the tray upstairs and spotted Lucy sitting at a table she'd found for them by the window. She set the tray down on the table, fetched the jugs of milk, then shrugged out of her thick winter coat. After returning the jugs, she sat down opposite Lucy, whose eyes were lowered as she stirred sugar into her tea.

Emily examined Lucy's face. She'd aged visibly – Emily guessed that she must be in her early fifties by now – but she was still just as beautiful as Emily remembered. She had more wrinkles and laughter lines, and her jet-black hair contained several grey streaks that shone iridescently in the light. She must weigh about a stone more than she did back then, Emily estimated, and her face was rounder, but other than that, she hadn't changed. Emily was surprised now that she'd had any doubt it was Lucy earlier.

Lucy looked up and grinned. Emily tried to find something to say. 'What a coincidence!' she exclaimed at last.

'I didn't know if you'd settled in Oxford or moved somewhere else, but I'm rather amazed now that we've never bumped into each other before,' Lucy said. 'How are your mum and sister?'

'Amanda's fine. She's still in Oxford, too. She has her own private practice and she specialises in adolescent and adult psychiatry. She's very involved in her Amateur Dramatic Club. She's always been a good actress.'

'And your mum?'

'Um… she has her ups and downs.' Emily realised Lucy had never met Matt. 'I have a brother!' she said.

'Really?' Lucy furrowed her brow.

'A half-brother. Mum had a baby the year after…' Emily trailed off. She had been about to say the year after she'd had her own baby. 'The year after I left the Centre,' she said instead. 'His name is Matt. He's thirteen. He's a typical teenager. Spotty, moody, unruly.'

'Tell me about it!' Lucy said, rolling her eyes. 'Does he live in Oxford, too?'

'Oh, no. He lives with Mum in North Devon. He's giving her a hard time of it by all accounts.'

'And what about you? Have you got any children?'

'No,' Emily said.

Lucy slurped her tea, staring over the rim of the mug at Emily, as if waiting for more information.

'My husband had a son from a previous marriage. He didn't want any more kids,' Emily added. 'What about—?'

'So, what's it like being a stepmum?'

'Er, well, you know…' Emily replied evasively. 'How are your children? You had two girls and two boys if I remember correctly.'

'Good memory.' Lucy's smile widened at the mere thought of

her children. 'They're all grown up now. Well, supposedly. One of my boys still brings his washing home! The youngest will be eighteen next February – gosh, that's only two months away – and the oldest is twenty-seven and expecting a baby for next May. I'm going to be a grandmother! Isn't that awful?'

'You don't look old enough,' Emily said, 'but I think that's wonderful!'

'So do I. Can't wait really!'

Lucy took another gulp of tea. Emily marvelled that she could drink it so hot. She blew on hers.

'You know, what you said about this being a coincidence earlier, well, I was talking about you not long ago to someone. I was working with a young client.'

Lucy's mobile started ringing loudly and it startled Emily who spilt some of her tea. As she mopped it up with some paper napkins, she noticed her hands were shaking. Lucy answered the phone and talked briefly to a member of her family. Then she ended the call and made an apologetic face.

'What was I saying?'

'You mentioned a young client.'

'Oh, yes, it was Mrs Justice Taylor QC's last case. She's retired now. Thank God. Oh, Emily, she wasn't a bad judge, but she should never have sent you to Exmoor Secure Children's Home. You were given diminished responsibility. She was just so enthusiastic about this new Centre that she sent you there instead of finding a more appropriate solution.'

'Where else could I have gone?'

'I think you should have been allowed to go home, and failing that into foster care since there was a lack of mental health beds at the time.'

'I think given the choice I would've chosen the Centre,' Emily said. 'I wasn't so badly off there. I got treatment and I continued my sessions with Dr Irvine; I did my GCSEs and had art classes. I wouldn't really have been happy anywhere, but it was all right.'

Lucy nodded.

'So you were talking about me to the judge?'

'Sorry?'

'You said you were talking about me to someone a little while ago.'

'Ah, yes. Not the judge, no. Do you remember DI Hazel Moreleigh?' Lucy asked.

'DC Moreleigh?'

'Well, she's detective inspector now, but yes.'

'Of course,' Emily said, wondering how she could ever forget her.

'After your case, I came into contact with her a few times professionally, and we've socialised on several occasions.'

'Socialised?'

'Yes, you know, gone out for a quick drink after court, that sort of thing.'

'I see,' said Emily, puzzled as to where this was going.

'Recently we were both involved in a case that was similar to yours, and that got us talking about you.'

'I see,' Emily repeated, still failing to see where this was leading, but fearing that Lucy was about to dredge up memories from the past. Memories that were best left forgotten, or at least buried.

'Hazel agrees with me,' Lucy said, locking her large brown eyes onto Emily's. 'The evidence against you just didn't add up. I've always felt bad, Emily, that I didn't do better for you.'

'What do you mean?' Emily heard herself ask.

'I mean, you didn't deserve to have to go through all that – the trial, the sentence, everything.'

Emily didn't know if she should console Lucy; she couldn't really understand what she was feeling sorry about.

'Hazel and I have discussed this many times. Do you know, DS Tomlinson was dismissed a few years after your court case?'

Emily shook her head.

'Gross misconduct. Coerced false confession. Hazel blames him for the outcome of your case, too.'

'Why?'

'He was so pleased to have your confession on tape, but he put words into your mouth, Emily. No, it was worse than that: he force-fed whole stories down your throat. It was an open and shut case for him. He didn't bother delving any deeper.'

'What would have been the point?'

Lucy looked at Emily as if she were looking at a child. There was a mixture of compassion and reprimand in her expression, and it unsettled Emily.

'The point is, Emily, that you know as well as I do, and as well as Hazel does, that you should never have been convicted of that crime.'

Lucy waited for Emily's reaction. Emily sat still and said nothing. She wanted to ask: *why?* But she was afraid of the answer.

'The ballistic report and the bloodstain pattern analysis gave contradictory evidence,' Lucy resumed. 'You'd said initially that you shot your father as you both lay in the bed. 'And you were absolutely covered in your father's blood,' Lucy continued, 'which would tend to suggest you were next to him in the bed when he was shot.'

Under him, I was under him, Emily thought to herself, but she didn't correct Lucy.

'And yet, the gun, which was found placed parallel to your father's body in the bed, had relatively little blood on it.' Lucy was becoming more and more agitated.

'So?'

'So, if you'd fired it from beside him, wouldn't there have been as much blood on the gun as on you?'

'I don't know,' Emily muttered. 'I probably put the gun down before I pushed my father's body off… away from me. Or maybe it was protected by the bedcovers.'

'It was your father's clay pigeon shotgun, Emily, not a pistol. How could you possibly have fired it from that position in the first place?'

Emily didn't answer.

'And why would you need a shotgun as well as a steel-bladed razor?'

Lucy paused, but continued when it became obvious that Emily wasn't going to shed any light on the discrepancies in her case.

'You were sitting on the floor, in your sister's arms, holding the razor in your hand when the police arrived. You said in your statement that you'd taken the razor to bed with you. It had blood on it, but it hadn't been used to injure your father.'

Emily lowered her head to avoid Lucy's penetrating gaze.

'According to the ballistic evidence, the trajectory and spread indicated the rounds were fired from a distance of ten to twelve feet away.'

Lucy paused and let this sink in. Emily had never been told about the ballistic report in any detail.

'Tomlinson suggested your father had fallen asleep and so you got up to fetch the shotgun. You agreed that was indeed what had happened.'

Emily became aware that she was rubbing the scars on her right arm with her left hand inside the woollen sleeve of her knitted jumper. She withdrew her hand and sat on it. But Lucy had noticed.

'You're left-handed. Nowadays, they would be able to tell for sure whether someone was shot by a left-handed or a right-handed person. There would be no case against you if it had taken place in this day and age. Back then, they could have done better, but they didn't bother. It was Christmas, which didn't help. They didn't even think to have your body examined at the hospital to check for a recoil mark.'

Emily looked up and met Lucy's eyes. The kind eyes Emily remembered seemed to see inside her now.

'What happened that night, Emily?' Lucy asked. She sounded harsh, and Emily realised Lucy felt very strongly about all this.

She seemed cross, but Emily wasn't sure if she was angry with her or with herself.

'I don't remember very clearly,' Emily lied. There was no way she was talking about this now, fifteen years after her father's murder, and certainly not to her former solicitor.

'You didn't do it, did you, Emily? *I* think you're innocent.' Lucy started to count using her thumb. 'Hazel Moreleigh has always believed in your innocence –' the index finger '– Rosamund Irvine said you didn't do it –' the middle finger.

'Dr Irvine thinks "*Em*" did it,' Emily scoffed.

'Emily, I know you didn't kill your father, no matter how much harm he caused you.' Lucy's tone had become almost aggressive. 'Not only does the evidence suggest that you couldn't have fired the shotgun, but it's also clear you were incapable of doing something like that.'

Emily put her coat on. She hadn't finished her tea, but it was time to go. Lucy, however, hadn't finished with her.

'I think you're protecting someone. You didn't shoot him, did you? Who did? Who killed your father, Emily?'

Chapter Seventeen

~

Oxford, January 2015

William Huxtable.

The funeral home has sent a list of all the mourners who signed the Sympathy Book or sent wreaths for Josephine's funeral. Will had sent flowers. Emily didn't even notice them, and that makes her feel inexplicably miserable.

She's sitting at the low coffee table in her studio staring at the box of pre-printed Thank You cards, which arrived in the post today. Amanda said that Emily would find it 'comforting and healing' to send the cards out on behalf of the three of them, but Emily finds it depressing and irritating. She takes out a card and reads the message. *Amanda, Emily and Matt would like to thank you for your sympathy at this difficult time. We deeply appreciate your support and kindness.* It reminds Emily of the obituary she posted on Facebook after Greg had passed away. Or disappeared.

Her sister's instructions were to try and personalise each card with a sentence or two. Amanda wouldn't want her to send a card to Will, though. She remembers Amanda's reaction when she discovered that Emily was 'friends' with Will on Facebook.

She'd said he was a compulsive liar. Whatever happened between the two of them all those years ago, Amanda still hasn't forgiven him. Emily knows that. But Will was always kind to Emily, and she wants to thank him.

She tries to spin her ink pen around in her left hand and drops it on the table. What can she possibly write in a card to William Huxtable? *Thanks for the flowers, Will?* No, that won't cut it. *Long time, no see?* Not the type of individual message her sister had in mind, no doubt. *Miss you?* Even worse.

They used to be so close. He'd been part of her daily life and now she'd spent more than half of her life without him. How strange and sad.

Sod this, thinks Emily. *I'm not up to this.* What she really wants to do is swallow a Valium and go to bed early. She looks at her watch. Five o'clock. That certainly would be an early night! She knows, though, if she's going to beat her depression, she needs to get out and be around someone. *Keep going through the motions; keep up the act; keep going.* She decides to ring Pippa.

As she picks up her smartphone, it pings with incoming mail. She has two email accounts and the messages are on the one she uses for business. She opens the first email. It's a short message. Short, but certainly not sweet. As she takes in its meaning, she can feel the colour draining from her face. Then she opens the second message. It is written in a similar tone, although it's not from the same person. Emily doesn't recognise the pseudonyms of either of the senders.

She reads both of the messages again, staring at the screen of her phone. *Is this someone's idea of a sick joke?* She struggles to catch her breath, as if the air has been stolen from her lungs. *Why would anyone write something so malicious?*

Now she definitely needs to go round to Pippa's.

~

Emily doesn't trust herself to drive safely to the Stuart-Barnes' house, partly because her head is still spinning after reading the two emails, and partly because of all the medication she is on. So, she takes the bus. It's a direct line. She gets off at the bus stop right in front of Pippa's house. Andy, a tea towel slung over his shoulder, opens the door as soon as she rings the bell. He gives her a peck on the cheek.

'It's bath time, I'm afraid,' he says, as he makes his way back into the kitchen. 'I'm cooking. Are you staying for dinner?'

'I don't want to intrude…' Emily says, following him.

'I'll be insulted if you don't,' Andy says in a jocular tone. 'Anyway you're all skin and bones; you look like you could do with a decent, good meal.'

'You're confident of your culinary talents.' Emily leans against the door frame and peers into the homely mess of Pippa and Andy's kitchen.

'Yeah, no pressure on me now I've said that, hey?'

Emily forces a grin, and heads upstairs. Pippa is sitting on the closed toilet seat, breastfeeding Imogen while Harry splashes around in the bath. Seeing Emily, he fills up his plastic boat and attempts to throw water across the room at her, but both the boat and the water end up on the floor right beside the bath.

'Behave!' Pippa says. She beams at Emily who grabs Harry's flannel and mops up the water from the floor next to the bathtub.

'I *am* hay-ving,' Harry retorts, and smiles. This was something he'd said as a toddler. At the age of five, he now knows better, but it has become a family joke and Emily is in on it.

Emily kisses Pippa's rosy cheek, and strokes the back of her god-daughter's head, careful not to touch Pippa's breast in the process.

'Time to come out,' Pippa tells Harry.

'Mine is the red one,' Harry points towards the towel rack. Emily fetches his towel and wraps him in it when he stands up, then lifts him out of the bath and pats him dry.

'Where are your pyjamas?' she asks. Harry points to the radiator. 'You can put them on yourself, can't you? You're a big boy.'

As Emily gently combs Harry's hair, Imogen emits an impressive burp for a two-month-old, and Pippa sighs with motherly pride.

'Can you read me my bedtime story, Em'ly?' Harry implores.

'Please,' Pippa automatically prompts her son.

'Plee-ase,' Harry repeats.

So Emily puts Harry to bed and reads *The Gruffalo*, although Harry knows it by heart and 'reads' most of it to her. He coaches her on what each character's voice should sound like. She gets caught up in this lovely moment and breathes in the clean, fruity smell of Harry as he snuggles against her. For a moment, she almost forgets about the emails she has received.

When she has finished the story, Emily can see that Harry's eyes have become heavy. She tucks him in, kisses his head and tiptoes out of his bedroom. To Emily's disappointment, Imogen has already fallen asleep and Pippa has just laid her down in the cot. Emily hasn't held her god-daughter yet. She asks herself if Pippa hasn't given her Immie to hold because she thinks Emily will be reminded of Melody. She held Harry as a baby every time she came round for a visit.

Andy's meal is indeed delicious. Emily hasn't eaten that well for months. She waits until they've all polished off their plates of lasagne to tell Pippa and Andy about receiving the two disturbing emails.

'Are they still on your phone?' Pippa asks.

Emily takes her smartphone out of her handbag, which is hanging on the back of her chair, and opens the first message before handing the mobile to Pippa.

'Murderess! First your father, then your husband! I certainly won't be buying any of your paintings!' Pippa reads aloud. 'That's terrible! And you have no idea who this person is?' Emily wonders if Pippa knows how her father died. She hasn't told her, but

Amanda might have done. She shakes her head. 'I don't even know if that's their usual address, or one they set up just to write to me. It's a Hotmail account.'

'Have you still got the other message?'

'No,' Emily lies, grabbing the phone out of Pippa's hands as her friend starts to fiddle with it. The other email was worse. The sender called her an 'incestuous bitch'. Emily really doesn't want to have to explain that.

'Have you checked your website and your professional Facebook page?' Andy asks, clearing away their empty plates.

'No. Good idea.'

'Come with me.' Andy closes the dishwasher and leads the way out of the kitchen and into his study. He wiggles the mouse until an image appears on his computer screen. Then he steps aside and gestures for Emily to sit down on the leather office chair. She logs in to Facebook.

There's nothing out of place on her professional Facebook page, so she opens a new window and brings up her website. She scrolls down to the posts at the bottom of her page. She's vaguely aware of Andy looking over her shoulder as she finishes reading the insulting post in capital letters: EMILY KLEIN IS A NYMPHOMANIAC AND A MURDERER. HER HUSBAND AND HER FATHER WERE BOTH VICTIMS! STEER CLEAR!

Emily immediately grabs the wastepaper bin and throws up every last mouthful of Andy's lasagne. She feels Andy's hand rubbing her back lightly as she vomits.

'Oh, God, I'm so sorry,' Emily says when she has finally finished retching. 'I need to go home.'

'I'll drive you,' Andy says, taking the wastebasket from Emily's hands.

'No, no, I… I'll take the bus.'

And with that, Emily runs out of the house. Pippa catches up with her at the bus stop, holding the handbag Emily has left behind in her rush to get outside. Pippa also tries to persuade her to let Andy drive her home, but the bus pulls up just then. She gives Emily her bag and a kiss, wishing her good luck as she gets on the bus.

Even though Emily feels more in a daze than ever, her mind seems to be functioning. Admittedly, she'd just forgotten her handbag in her hurry, but she's thinking straight apart from that. It occurs to her that she hasn't logged out of her professional Facebook account, but she knows Andy will take care of that.

She also reasons that she needs Josh to sort out this mess before it gets worse. So, she takes her phone back out of her handbag.

Josh is reluctant to come round to Emily's house.

'It's urgent,' Emily hisses.

'Emily, I'm with someone now; I can't just come round to yours at the drop of a hat. Sorry.'

'This is for work. I can pay you twice the usual amount if that'll help. Someone has written something unthinkably crude in the posts on my website.'

She's still talking to Josh in a hushed voice as she steps off the bus onto the Woodstock Road. Emily can't hear anything, but she gets the distinct impression that someone is walking close behind her. A tingle runs down her spine. She turns round, but she can't see anyone. It's dark except for the dim light of the street lamps. She tells herself that it's just her imagination.

'Did you change the password for your website when I told you to?'

'Yes.'

'Then you can modify it yourself.'

'I don't know how to,' Emily says.

'Then give me your login and password and I'll do it for you.'

Emily is about to give Josh that information when she hears quickening footsteps. She whirls around, and this time sees a tall, dark figure a few metres behind her. A deep wave of fear breaks over her.

'Josh, someone's following me,' Emily whispers into the mobile. 'A man, I think.'

'Where are you?'

'Just a few metres from my house.' Emily has broken into a run.

'Stay on the phone, Em,' Josh says.

Emily feels dizzy, but she runs as fast as she can. She thinks she can hear the person behind her running, too, but she's not sure. When she gets to her front gate, she fumbles for her key ring with one hand, still clutching her phone to the ear with the other. Her hand is shaking and she drops the keys. She can hear the blood humming loudly in her ears as she bends down to pick them up.

She glances quickly to her left as she stands up again. Now there's no doubt. The ground seems to lurch beneath her. She can clearly make out a tall, slim figure in a dark hoodie. He ducks down behind a car in the street when she looks in his direction. There's something familiar about him that disturbs her, but for the moment she can't quite put her finger on what it is.

She opens the front door and deactivates the burglar alarm. The automated voice of the alarm nearly makes her jump out of her skin.

'Intruder at Sensor One at seventeen-thirty.'

'Josh, Josh, did you hear that?' Emily has closed the front door and is leaning with her back against it. She sinks down to the floor as she tries to steady her breathing.

'Emily, stay on the line. I'm coming. Can you call the security company from your landline?'

'I don't know which company it is.'

Emily vaguely recalls seeing some documents about the alarm in Greg's study, but can't remember what she did with them when she tidied up.

'One time when the alarm was triggered, Greg received an alert on his mobile phone. I have no idea how it works. I just know how to activate and deactivate it.' Emily realises she is babbling, and she isn't sure how much of it is comprehensible.

'Have you got Mr Klein's mobile?'

'No. Yes, it's upstairs.' Sergeant Campbell had come round in person to give back some personal effects after the investigation was over. Among those things was Greg's phone, Emily remembers. 'But I don't know the PIN and it's not charged.'

'Does your alarm have video surveillance?'

'No, there's no CCTV.'

'Could it be wrong about there being an intruder?'

'It does happen,' Emily says. 'The sensors are triggered by motion. It could be Mr Mistoffelees, my cat,' she adds. She is still hyperventilating and she forces herself to take deeper breaths. 'Sensor One. That's the front door. It was shut and locked when I got home.' But as she says those words, it also strikes her that any movement by Mr Mistoffelees near the front door would not have been detected by that sensor – the cat would have been too low to trigger off the alarm.

Josh promises her he'll come immediately after all. Emily wonders if she should ring the police. But she supposes that the man who had been following her and the intruder, if there had been one, would be long gone by now.

While she's waiting for Josh, Emily looks around the house, a kitchen knife in her hand. She keeps whispering to Josh over the phone the whole time. True to his word, Josh arrives within twenty minutes, although it seems much longer to Emily. She feels reassured as soon as he arrives, and he instructs her to check the alarm is still working. Then together they check the windows on which the various sensors are trained. There's no sign of forced entry anywhere. After that, Emily boots up her laptop, and Josh not only takes down the comments from her website, but also modifies it so that no posts can be written.

'You need to check your emails and your Facebook page every day,' Josh says. 'Your email address is still on the website. If people continue to harass you, we'll have to rethink that. We may have nipped it all in the bud, though. Only people interested in art would visit your website, really. I don't think that's usually the sort of public who would feel the need to comment on such a libellous post.'

Not for the first time, Emily is impressed by Josh's intelligence. She affects a smile to show him that she's thankful. She can sense that he's keen to leave, but she doesn't want him to, not through any sexual desire on her part – the lithium tends to counteract her libido – but out of sheer desperation. She doesn't want to be alone tonight. Fortunately, she knows which buttons to press to turn Josh on.

~

Afterwards, Josh lies sprawled across the bed, bare, propping up his chin on one arm. Emily senses him watching her as she walks back into the bedroom from the en suite bathroom, putting on her dressing gown. She pauses to look him up and down with an appraising eye – he really does have an amazing body. She knows he runs, cycles, swims and goes to the gym, and it shows. Then she strides towards the bed and dives under the covers.

'Do you want to paint me?' Josh asks, a twinkle in his eye.

'What colour?' Emily asks. 'Black and blue?'

He chuckles. 'I've seen your work, so I know you don't usually paint people, but do you sometimes?'

'Not often, no,' Emily answers. 'When I went to art class, we had to sketch nude models, though, as part of our course.'

'Real live naked people?' Josh asks, sitting up.

'Yes.'

'Did they get paid for that?' He suddenly sounds very interested.

'No, they volunteered to get their kit off for the sake of art,' Emily says, amused.

'Shame. I'll have to keep working for you, then, sorting out your computer problems.'

Josh swings his legs over the bed and picks up his boxer shorts from the heap of clothes next to the bed. He pulls them on, followed by his jeans.

'You don't have to leave,' Emily says softly.

He turns to face her. 'Yes, I do. I have a girlfriend now, Emily. And by the way, this can't go on.' He points his finger at her, then at himself, then back at her. 'This… fling… thing between us.'

'I understand,' Emily says. She thinks it's ironic that last time she threw a sleepy Josh out after they'd had sex whereas this time she's the one who wants him to stay. 'I just felt scared, you know, after all the posts on my website, and being followed home and thinking someone might have broken into my house.'

'Would you like me to have another look around before I leave?'

'Oh, Josh, if you wouldn't mind, that would be very comforting.'

Josh thoroughly checks every room in the house. He looks in the cupboards and behind the doors and curtains; he makes sure all the windows are tightly shut. Emily stays safely behind him. A thud from the kitchen startles them both when they're downstairs. To their relief, it turns out to be Mr Mistoffelees, jumping from the table to the floor.

In the hall, Emily takes her purse out of her handbag and extracts several notes, which Josh shoves into the pocket of his jeans.

'Are you going to be all right?' he asks.

'Yes. Thank you for your help this evening with the computer, and for checking I'm safe.'

'Any time.'

Josh gives Emily a peck on the cheek and leaves. Emily locks the door, and then goes upstairs to get a sleeping tablet. She climbs back into bed, but she isn't tired yet. She is anxious and she can feel the familiar fluttering in her stomach. She's also disgusted with herself. Josh is much younger than her, he's in a relationship, and she seduced him solely in the hope that he'd stay over and protect her.

She gets up again. Her feet are cold, so she pushes them into her slippers and pads back down the stairs. In the kitchen, she puts the kettle on to make a cup of herbal tea. Standing with her back against the worktop, the hot mug warming her hands, she thinks about Will. Her mind feels numb now, but she frantically tries to concentrate on finding the wording for the personalised message on his card.

After a minute or two, she puts down her mug on the draining board and goes into the studio. She switches on the light, sits down at the coffee table and unscrews the top of her fountain pen. She thinks of putting 'Thank Ewe' as a reference to their song all those years ago, but she wouldn't seriously consider writing something so inappropriate. Probably not quite what Amanda meant by customising the message, either. In the end, she simply writes:

Will,

We were all very touched to receive your flowers at Mum's funeral, and I was grateful for your message on Facebook.

Thank you,

Emily

XXX

She seals the envelope and hugs it to her for a moment before sticking the stamp on and copying down Will's address. He lives in Cavendish Crescent in Bath. What a strange coincidence! Her maiden name! Emily remembers going on a school trip to visit the Roman Baths. Afterwards, they'd wandered around. She'd liked the city very much.

As she puts the pen down, she yawns. *Time to count sheep*, she thinks. She's aware that the two sheep jokes she has just made in her mind are really corny. But at the same time, just as earlier when she left Pippa and Andy's, she's surprised that her mind is intermittently sharp along with the haziness. The mood-stabilising drugs make her feel like a brainless zombie most of the time. Perhaps nasty shocks and satisfying sex are the answer.

She thinks about the person she saw behind her earlier. Something has been niggling her about him, but it's just out of reach in her mind. She replays the episode in her head. His gait was familiar. That's it! Could it have been Greg? On reflection, he's about the right height. But then, why didn't he talk to her? She'd been on the phone to Josh. Perhaps that was why he hadn't approached her. *If it happens again, next time, I'll slow down and give him the chance to catch up with me*, she decides. *In both senses of the term.*

But what if it wasn't Greg? Maybe this person wants to hurt her. She might be in real danger. She shudders, but tries to keep calm. There is no way she's going to give in to paranoia. On her way back through the kitchen, though, she takes a carving knife from its drawer. She'll keep it under her pillow tonight. Just in case. Before heading upstairs to bed, she checks the front door is locked.

Chapter Eighteen

~

Oxford, February 2015

'Emily Klein, you're under arrest!' Sergeant Campbell said, making no attempt to conceal her relish. She wrenched Emily's arms behind her back with unnecessary violence and snapped on the handcuffs.

'You can't arrest me,' Emily said. 'I didn't even know you when I committed that…'

'Crime?' Campbell suggested.

'I was going to say "error". I need a lawyer.' Emily caught sight of Pippa standing at the window, her dark hair shining in the light. 'Pippa! Pippa! Can you call my solicitor?'

'I'm already here,' she said, turning around. Emily could see now that it was Lucinda Sharpe, not Pippa. Lucy was looking considerably younger than the last time Emily had seen her when she'd bumped into her on Cornmarket. She was wearing an eye-catching chunky necklace, which made the word 'bling' pop into Emily's mind.

'Perhaps you could tell us your version of what happened?' Police Constable Constable suggested, flashing his strange smile.

Emily deduced that he must have just scoffed a doughnut or a pastry since he had some sugary food stuck in his moustache. The stereotypical cop. The morsel of food and the moustache both moved up and down when he spoke, which Emily found rather hypnotic. Lucy nodded encouragingly at Emily.

She replayed the events of that particular morning over in her mind, and obediently described them to her attentive audience.

~

It was a beautiful day and after lunch they'd gone to Hinksey Park for a walk. It had been Greg's idea, but Emily drove because he'd drunk two glasses of wine with his meal. Evidently, a lot of other people had had the same idea, and the park was full of families with young children and couples holding hands while they ambled along the paths. Afterwards, they sat down side by side on a bench by the lake and enjoyed the sun on their faces.

While they watched two little boys kicking a football to each other, they chatted, although Emily couldn't remember now what they'd been talking about. After a while, Emily got her Kindle out of her handbag and Greg went off to buy them some ice cream.

A woman was sitting on the grass nearby, trying to persuade her recalcitrant toddler to sit down on the picnic rug she'd laid down on the ground. The woman had a pram parked next to her. Emily realised that she'd been so distracted by the boy and his mother that she'd read the same paragraph several times without taking anything in. She switched off her Kindle and continued to observe the woman with her son.

'Fergus! Sit down! Calm down! Shut up and eat up!' the mother yelled, holding out a squashed sandwich to the little boy.

Fergus, however, had other ideas. He snatched the sandwich and ran off towards the lake. Instead of running after him, the woman took a packet of Marlboro out of her handbag, extracted a cigarette, lit it and inhaled deeply.

Emily tutted. She used her hand to shield the sun from her eyes while she watched the little boy in case he fell into the lake. She was ready to jump into the water and fish him out if need be. She watched as Fergus lobbed his sandwich in the general direction of a duck. The bread fell very short of its mark, but the little boy was delighted to see the duck swim towards it and start to peck at it. To Emily's shock, his mother lit another cigarette from the stub of the first. Then she threw the butt behind her.

A few minutes later, seemingly bored, Fergus tottered back to his mother and declared, 'I'm hungry!'

'You should have eaten your sandwich, then,' his mother said.

'I wanna sandwich!'

'You fed yours to the duck.'

Fergus started to wail.

'Oh, why can't you be like your baby sister? She's as good as gold and she never cries. *She* is a dream baby. *You* are a pain in the arse.'

'Wee wee,' Fergus sniffed, his head bowed in shame.

'Oh, Fergus, not again. You're supposed to tell me when you need to go for a wee. Come on!'

The woman stood up and grabbed the boy by the wrist. She looked around her, spotted Emily and headed over to her. 'I need to take my son to the loo,' she said. 'He's had an accident so I'll have to clean him up – *again*.' She rolled her eyes conspiratorially at Emily. 'Would you mind awfully looking after my daughter for a moment?'

'Er, no, not at all.'

The woman returned to the picnic rug and hoisted her large handbag up onto her shoulders. Then she wheeled the pram over to the bench on which Emily was sitting. Next, she headed off towards the public toilets situated a few metres up the slope from the bench.

What sort of woman leaves her baby girl with a complete stranger?

What a loud, chain-smoking cow! She's not fit to be a mother! Emily thought to herself. Without pausing to consider what she was about to do next, Emily got up from the bench and started pushing the pram towards the exit from the park.

It took Emily a few seconds to spot the car – she was looking for her Mini, but of course Greg hadn't bought it for her yet and she still had her VW Beetle. The baby started crying before she could get the carrycot strapped into the back seat of the car. The seat belt only just stretched around it. She struggled to work out how to fold down the chassis, and sighed with relief when she was finally able to close the boot of the car and get in behind the wheel. She kept looking around her, but there was no sign of the baby's mother.

The baby cried all the way home. She was still crying over two hours later when Greg arrived home from the park.

'Emily what the devil is going on? Where did you go? Why did you come home without me? And WHOSE BABY IS THAT?!' Greg rarely shouted, but he seemed pretty mad.

Emily wondered how he'd got home. Hinksey Park was a short ten-minute drive away from their home, but it was a bit far to walk. Maybe he'd hitched or caught the bus. 'She's our baby now. Her mother said that she was a dream baby. She said she never cried, but I can't stop her crying.' Emily was close to tears herself.

'Where did you get it?' It was almost as if Greg was enquiring about where Emily had bought a new T-shirt.

'At the park. It's a she.'

'We can't keep it.'

'Her.'

'Maybe we should change her,' he suggested. Of course! Greg had been through this before, with Luke. He knew what to do. The baby would be in good hands. Emily thrust the tot into her husband's arms.

'We should definitely *ex*change her,' Emily muttered just as the buzzer went.

169

'That'll be Mum,' Greg said.

Emily swore loudly, and then heard herself sob. She went to let Greg's mother in.

Mrs Klein waltzed into the living room and stopped dead when she saw the baby. 'Ooh, this must be my granddaughter,' she cooed. 'What's her name?'

'Er...' *Quick, think of a name...* 'We named her after you.' Emily couldn't remember her mother-in-law's first name. 'She's called... Mrs Klein.'

'You named the baby Mrs Klein?' Greg's mother and Sergeant Campbell asked simultaneously in disbelief. Emily had been so immersed in her own story that she'd completely forgotten the two police officers were there.

'Er, no, I mean we called her Henrietta.' Emily frowned. 'That is your name, isn't it?'

'No, it's Harriette!' Mrs Klein's raised voice made the baby screech even more loudly. This in turn made Greg jump and he dropped Henrietta/Harriette on the floor.

~

Emily wakes up from her nightmare, screaming. She is drenched in sweat. She's drowsy, and it takes her a while to realise she was dreaming. She rolls over to cuddle up to Greg. It's only when she finds his side of the bed empty that she feels fully awake. She's sobbing uncontrollably, and it sounds to her like the noise she's making is echoing in another part of the house.

For a moment, she stays sitting up in bed, hugging her knees to her chest. Then her mobile rings. It's on her bedside table. She'd left it on last night when she went to bed in case there really had been an intruder and he came back during the night. She sees Pippa's name and photo on the screen of her phone and answers the call.

'Emily! Andy and I have been so worried about you since last night. I read what was posted on your website, by the way. I hope you don't mind,' Pippa gushes. 'I think it's a horribly vindictive thing to have written. How are you this morning? Are you all right?'

'I'm OK,' Emily croaks. Her mouth is dry. She clears her throat. 'I've just had a bad dream.'

'Oh, I'm so sorry. Did I wake you? We get up so early with the kids. It's ten o'clock though.'

'No, I was awake. I'm still in bed, that's all.' Emily has stopped sobbing, but she can still hear wailing. 'Pippa, is that Imogen in the background?'

'No, Andy has taken Harry and Immie out to give me a break. Isn't that sweet of him?'

'Can you hear a baby crying?'

'No.'

'Shhh,' Emily says into the phone. It seems to her that the noise is coming from her own house. 'What about now?' She holds the phone away from her. 'Well?' she asks, pressing the phone to her ear again.

'Nope. Nothing,' Pippa says.

'Pippa, I have to go.'

Emily ends the call and gets out of bed. From underneath her pillow, she takes the knife she put there the previous night.

'*What are you going to do?*' asks a voice in her head. '*Knife the baby?*'

'What baby?' Emily whispers aloud. She shakes her head as if to clear it, and walks along the corridor. The squalling is coming from the guest room. She turns the doorknob, but as she opens the door, the noise stops abruptly.

She stands still on the threshold and listens. Then she takes a step inside the room. At first she can only hear the sound of her own breathing. But then she hears a dull noise. It came from downstairs. *There is someone in the house.*

Still clutching the knife, she races to the staircase. Just as she reaches the top of it, she distinctly hears the front door slam shut. She almost falls down the stairs in her haste, her heart pounding in her ears. She pulls the front door open. She looks outside, but can see no one. She hears a car start up and speed away. She runs down the drive to the gate, but she can't see the car.

Emily comes back inside the house, closes the door and walks to the staircase. She sits down on the bottom step. Her head is spinning and she holds it in her hands. *Did this really just happen? Or is it a figment of my imagination? How can I possibly have heard a baby crying in my own home? Was someone following me last night or did I get spooked? Was there even an intruder?*

Just as Emily is wondering if her imagination is running wild, she looks down at the knife in her hand. She clearly remembers taking *two* precautions last night as she was going to bed: she took the knife from the kitchen and she checked the front door before heading upstairs.

A few minutes ago, when she thought someone had just fled from her home, banging the door behind them, she ran down the stairs and yanked the front door handle. The door opened. It wasn't locked. But she is absolutely certain she locked it last night.

Until now, Emily has vacillated between believing her own eyes and ears and wondering if all this is in her head. *I haven't lost touch with reality*, she thinks now. *I need to trust my gut instinct.* She wishes she were hallucinating, though. All this would be a lot less frightening if it wasn't real. *If my mind isn't playing tricks on me, then* someone *is playing tricks on me. Someone with evil intent is determined to scare me. This has to stop. I need to figure out who is doing this and why. Urgently.*

~ Part Two ~

Chapter Nineteen

~

Oxford, February 2015

The pleading and screams of the paedophile's young victim still ringing in her ears, Emily walks along George Street between Pippa and Charles. They're heading for The Grapes. Amanda will join them when she has changed her clothes and removed her stage make-up.

'It's a very controversial play,' Emily says to Pippa. 'That's the second time I've seen it and I still find it distressing.' Matt, who ordinarily is no theatregoer, is also coming to see it, if only out of a sense of duty towards one half-sister and as an excuse to come and visit the other, as he told Emily. That means she'll have to sit through the play at least one more time.

'It is rather provocative,' Pippa agrees. 'Your sister was good as the mother.'

'Yes, she was.' Seeing the expression on Pippa's face, Emily adds, 'You both played that role very well.'

The Sugar Syndrome is still running, although only on Thursday evenings now. Pippa asked Amanda to take over her part so that she could spend more time with Harry and Imogen. This evening, however, Andy volunteered to look after the kids to allow Pippa to go to the play with Emily.

Throughout the performance, Emily observed Pippa mouthing the lines of the character Jan, as Amanda delivered them on the stage. It made her wonder if her friend really needed more time with her children, or if she just generously let a delighted Amanda act in her place.

Charles leaves the girls at their favourite table in the alcove by the window and goes to place the orders at the bar. When Amanda arrives, looking rosy-cheeked and beautiful, Charles and Emily are flirting harmlessly. Emily picks up on her sister's tetchiness, and in case it's out of jealousy, she practically ignores Charles and lavishes praise on Amanda for her acting skills.

Amanda scratches her head and complains about being made to wear a wig. 'He wants me to look like you in the poster for the play,' she moans to Pippa. 'My head itches like hell now.'

'Put your foot down!' Pippa says.

'Keep your hair on.'

Emily had spotted Richard sauntering towards them out of the corner of her eye.

'Ah, it's Pun Man,' says Amanda, her voice dripping with sarcasm. Emily knows Amanda is teasing him, although it seems to have come out sounding a little unkind. But Richard seems flattered by the attention, his smile widening as he greets Amanda.

They all exchange pleasantries, then Richard wishes everyone a nice evening. Just before he makes his way back to his friends at the bar, Emily catches his eye. He's looking at her with a strange expression on his face, but Emily can't decide what it is. *Pity? No. Concern? No, that's not it, either.*

She forgets about Richard as the conversation turns to the post on her website and the resulting emails the previous week. She runs a finger absent-mindedly around the rim of her glass.

'Have there been any more comments or emails?' Pippa asks.

'No, not since Josh took the post down.'

'Josh?' Charles asks.

Emily sees Amanda glowering at him and feels guilty for hogging the limelight after her sister's performance in the play.

'He's a young chap I'm paying to help out with my computer problems,' Emily says. 'Well, I *was* employing him. He's… busy now. I think he might be less available in the future.'

'Well, if you need any help, just let me know,' Charles says. Emily notices her sister nudge Charles.

'Can we go? I'm really tired,' Amanda whines.

'Of course. I'll just finish my pint,' Charles says, picking up his beer.

'Josh came out straight away when I realised I was being followed home,' Emily says.

'You were followed?!' Pippa exclaims. 'What? When you left our place?'

Emily nods. 'There was someone behind me on my road when I walked home from the bus stop.'

'Shit! You didn't tell me that when I rang you the next morning.'

'I was distracted by the noise of the baby crying.'

'Whose baby?' Amanda says. Emily remembers Greg asking that very question in her dream after she'd stolen the girl in the pram.

'I don't know. It was coming from the guest room, but the crying stopped as soon as I opened the door and walked inside.'

'Emily, you must have been dreaming,' Amanda says, scratching her head again. She lowers her voice and leans towards Emily. 'You were prone to somnambulism when you were younger, you know.'

Emily gets the unpleasant impression she's being analysed, as she always does when Amanda uses technical terms. She doesn't remember anyone ever mentioning to her that she'd been a sleep-walker as a child.

'You did tell me you'd just had a nightmare,' Pippa says.

'And as for being followed, perhaps in the dark there were shadows and you heard a cat or a dog,' Amanda suggests.

'I saw a man duck down behind a car,' Emily protests half-heartedly. She is determined not to start doubting herself again. She thinks better of telling them about the hypothetical burglar who didn't actually steal anything.

'Are you sure it was a man following you?' Charles asks.

'No,' Emily concedes.

'Will you be all right?' Pippa asks. 'You know you can always stay over at our house if you want to.'

'Thank you, that's very kind of you. But I'm fine.'

Emily sees Amanda shoot Charles a meaningful look. Charles hasn't quite finished his beer, but at Amanda's insistence he stands up and helps her into her coat.

'Are you sure *you* are all right?' Emily asks, giving her sister a kiss goodbye.

'Yes, I'm OK. Really. The play tonight has left me exhausted, that's all.'

'You were excellent,' Emily says. 'Well done again!'

Charles offers Pippa a lift, so she leaves with them. Emily drove into town this evening and the car is parked nearby.

'I'll just pop to the ladies', then I'll be off, too,' Emily says as the other three make for the door.

On her way out from the toilets, she is collared by Richard. He has a glass of sparkling water complete with a twist of lemon waiting for her on the bar. Emily is surprised that he knows what she drinks.

'I enjoyed the play immensely,' Emily lies. She compliments Richard on his interpretation of the paedophile, Tim.

They briefly discuss some of issues the young playwright had aimed to raise, such as eating disorders and paedophilia and whether society and the media are partly to blame for these phenomena. But Emily is uncomfortable with these topics. She deftly steers the subject onto smoother terrain and they end up talking about her artwork and her goal of holding another exhibition before the end of the year. It has been a few years now since her last one.

Although she doesn't mention it, Emily's mind is on the post on her website and the emails she received.

Emily notices that Richard is holding her gaze for longer and longer. She, in turn, starts to get more tactile, touching his hand as she laughs at his puns. *Perhaps I won't have to be alone tonight*, she thinks.

Richard walks her back to her car. He has desperation written all over him. It's almost too easy. When they get to her car, she turns towards him, and he's the one who makes the first move. He pushes her against the Range Rover and begins kissing her. His tongue is a little bit too far down her throat for her liking, but she likes the taste of the beer on him. Although she doesn't feel aroused, she decides to ask him to come home with her. As he ardently squashes his body against hers, she can sense he's up for it, in more ways than one.

As she drives, Richard rides his hand up and down her leg, and leans over to kiss her every time she has to stop at a red light. They talk very little.

Once inside the house, Emily fumbles with her keys to lock the door behind them while Richard, whose hands have found their way inside her jumper, fumbles with her bra clasp. When he finally manages to unhook her underwear, his hands work their way round to fondle Emily's breasts. Despite Richard's clumsiness, Emily feels a sudden, unexpected surge of desire, and it takes all the willpower she can muster to push Richard's face off her own and stop this before it really begins.

'This is wrong, Richard. We can't do this.'

Richard sighs and removes his hands from Emily's breasts. He scratches the back of his neck. With a pang of guilt, Emily remembers Amanda scratching her head because the wig had made it itchy. Right now she hates herself.

'It's not right. You used to date Amanda.' Emily can hear that her voice sounds too high-pitched.

'I know, I know. I nearly had a baby with your sister,' Richard says, bowing his head.

Emily thinks that's a bit of an exaggeration, but she keeps her thoughts to herself.

'You're right. It would be wonderful, but so wrong for us to make love,' Richard says.

So, instead of making love to Richard, Emily makes him a cup of tea. She adds cold water to her own herbal tea and discreetly takes a gulp of water straight from the tap to swallow a Valium.

They sit down at the kitchen table. Emily uses her mobile to call Richard a taxi. While she waits impatiently, he keeps up a monotonous monologue about all his problems. He certainly seems to have his fair share of them: nasty neighbours, a family feud, financial troubles, girlfriend worries (he's worried he'll never find one).

Although the sleeping tablet can't possibly have kicked in yet, Emily's eyelids feel heavy. She strives to concentrate on what Richard is saying. She was prepared to sleep with him so as not to be alone, and now she's struggling to listen to a single word he's saying. She is deeply ashamed of herself.

'You're a good person, Emily,' Richard says.

Yeah, right, Emily thinks. *I was going to seduce my sister's ex-boyfriend. That doesn't make me a good person by any stretch of the imagination.*

'I think I've made a dreadful mistake,' he continues.

'No, you haven't,' Emily says. 'We nearly did something we would both have regretted, but we controlled ourselves. There's no harm done.' *Although it might be better if Amanda doesn't find out about what nearly happened*, she adds to herself.

'That's not what I meant,' Richard says. 'I was referring to something else. I've done something bad. And I've promised to… I think I should tell you about it. I don't know the full repercussions of my acts, but…'

The taxi horn sounding from outside saves Emily, who breathes a quiet sigh of relief.

'We'll discuss this another time, Richard,' she says, bundling him out of the kitchen and through the front door, despising herself all the while for her callousness.

She escorts Richard down the drive and watches the tail lights of the taxi until they disappear round the corner.

As she walks back towards the house, a voice calls out to her, startling her: 'Hello, dear.' It's Mrs Wickens.

'Hello, Mrs Wickens,' Emily says, cringing inside.

'Speak up, dear,' Mrs Wickens says.

'Hello, Mrs Wickens,' Emily repeats loudly.

Josephine had once joked that Emily's garrulous neighbour could talk the hind legs off a donkey. She'd nicknamed Mrs Wickens 'The Donkey's Enemy' because of this. Emily had meant to ask Pippa if she knew where that expression came from. She thinks Pippa will probably know as she's fascinated by language and etymology. But she has never asked her. Thinking of her mum, Emily sighs wistfully.

Mrs Wickens lives up to her nickname and talks about the weather, her pansies and forget-me-nots, her grandchildren and the young man she has just seen leaving. *She might be hard of hearing, but there's certainly nothing wrong with her eyesight*, Emily thinks, zoning out as the elderly lady rattles on. Emily waits for her to pause for breath so that she can make her excuses and get back inside the house. Stifling a yawn, she wonders what the old woman is doing outside in the cold at this time of night. Perhaps she's looking for her cat.

At long last, Mrs Wickens says something that grabs Emily's attention.

'Was there a problem the other night?' she asks.

'When?'

'I'm fairly sure it was last Thursday evening.'

'What sort of problem?'

'Well, your security alarm went off. You weren't burgled, were you? I watched the house for a while, but I didn't see anyone come out, or go in, for that matter.'

'No, I wasn't burgled. I don't know what set the security system off. How long did the noise of the alarm go on for?' Emily has forgotten to speak up and has to repeat her question.

'Not long. Not even a minute, I'd have said,' Mrs Wickens replies.

'Did you notice any cars in the street that aren't usually parked there?'

'No, I'll tell you what I did see though, but it was a bit later on in the evening.'

Emily wonders if The Donkey's Enemy spends all her evenings curtain twitching. 'Yes?' she prompts.

'I saw someone skulking about in the street.' Mrs Wickens points an accusatory, bony finger in the direction of the Woodstock Road beyond their driveways.

'A man or a woman?'

'That I couldn't say. It's so hard to tell these days, dear, isn't it? Women hardly wear skirts any more.'

'Can you describe this person?'

'He or she was wearing black clothing. Or maybe navy blue. The hood of their jacket was pulled up, so I couldn't see their hair. That struck me as peculiar because it wasn't raining.'

'I saw the same person! It was a man, I'm sure of it. I think he followed me. What was he doing exactly?'

'Nothing much.' The elderly woman pauses. 'Just lurking and lying in wait,' she adds ominously.

Emily is amazed that Mrs Wickens seems excited by what she has witnessed rather than feeling afraid or threatened by a suspicious stranger hanging around in front of their homes.

'Mrs Wickens, do you think this man could possibly have been Greg?'

Her neighbour looks at her as if she's mad. 'Do you mean your late husband Mr Klein?'

Emily immediately regrets asking her question. After all, Mrs Wickens said she wasn't able to tell whether the loiterer was male or female. 'Yes,' she admits.

'That's highly unlikely, my dear. Your husband has been dead for six months now, hasn't he? I don't believe in ghosts.'

And with those words, Mrs Wickens turns and disappears inside her house, shaking her head in bewilderment. The cat makes it through the door just before it closes.

'Goodnight,' Emily calls after her, but there's no reply.

Emily shivers, but she lingers outside for a moment, lost in her thoughts. She mulls over what Mrs Wickens said. So, the elderly woman saw the man in the hoodie, too. But maybe she's right. There's very little chance it was Greg. Emily wonders if she has been clinging to that hope in desperation. Maybe it's time to let go. She has allowed herself to think that there's a chance Greg could still be alive, and in so doing she has avoided having to fully accept that she is responsible for his death. She suddenly feels weighed down with guilt.

All the same, Emily is relieved. Her neighbour saw someone fitting the description of the man who followed her that night when she got off the bus. But she's dismayed that Amanda didn't believe there had been anyone there. Her sister is convinced she's psychotic and delusional. Even Pippa seemed sceptical this evening.

Emily looks at her neighbour's closed front door and realises she has never been so alone. Her husband is dead – it's time to face facts. Her mother is dead. And her sister and best friend think she's imagining things. She walks back inside her house and closes her front door behind her.

As she turns the key in the lock, the Calypso tone sounds faintly from her mobile. She realises she's jumpy. Even that familiar noise scared her. She fishes her iPhone out of her handbag, which is in its usual place hanging from the newel post. She swipes the screen and taps on the bubble icon to read the text message.

Can you meet me 2moro? Modern Art Oxford at 5 p.m. Don't tell anyone. Come alone. Please. It's a matter of life and death. G. X

At the top of the screen is the name Greg Klein. The message has been sent from his mobile phone. *How is that possible?* She runs upstairs to check among the belongings impounded after the car crash. Campbell had recently returned them to her. She'd charged Greg's phone just the other day after the burglar alarm had gone off and guessed his PIN correctly (it was his year of birth backwards), but there had been no message about an intruder from the security company.

The door bangs against the wall as Emily bursts into the office. She opens the bottom drawer of Greg's desk where she put his personal effects. She can't believe what she's seeing. Or rather, what she's not seeing. The drawer is empty. She opens all the desk drawers. She rummages around in some of them; she pulls other drawers out completely and tips the contents onto the floor. Then she stops, suddenly unable to move and unable to breathe. There is no mistake. Greg's mobile phone has gone.

Chapter Twenty

~

Oxford, February 2015

Despite the sedative she took the previous evening, Emily sleeps fitfully, and gets up at six o'clock. She has only been taking small doses of her medication, and she really needs to double the quantity. Instead, she decides to stop taking the tablets altogether. She doesn't want to sleep through anything that might happen during the night.

If she'd woken up instantly the other morning instead of emerging hazily from her zombie-like state, she might have seen who had left her house, slamming the front door on the way out. She needs to have a sharp mind and keep her wits about her, and her medicine is making her dim and lethargic.

By half past six, Emily has already looked at the clock or her watch or the time on her smartphone at least a dozen times. She was told in the text message to come to Modern Art Oxford at five o'clock in the afternoon. She has a lot of time to kill. On top of that, time is not going to go quickly today, so she decides to go for a long run.

The air is cool and it's peaceful at this time of morning. She heads towards the Oxford University Parks, but turns around before she gets there, realising it's too early for them to be open yet. It will be too far for her if she gets there and runs around the park before jogging back, anyway. She loses herself in her music, the beat dictating her pace as her feet pound the ground. She tries to block everything else out of her head while she runs. When she gets back home, she feels a lot better for letting off steam.

After her shower, Emily sits down to eat breakfast. She finally allows herself to think about the text message. Last night, she'd convinced herself that it couldn't have been Greg following her. She'd told herself it was time to let him go. But now this message has confused her again. It was sent from his mobile and it was signed off the same way he'd always signed off his messages to her: with the initial 'G' for Greg and a single kiss in the form of a capital 'X'.

But that doesn't prove it was from Greg. Anyone who had taken the phone from her house could have read through the text messages he'd sent her in the past and signed off that way. And if Greg did send her the text, then he must have taken his phone from their home at some point between the security alarm going off and last night when she realised it was missing. If he was alive and wanted to talk to her, why hadn't he spoken to her then?

The more Emily thinks about it, the less doubt there is in her mind. *Greg can't possibly have written this message*, she reasons with herself. *So who did? Who can it have been?* Obviously the same person who wrote the Facebook messages and followed her. If she tells someone about this or doesn't go to the art gallery alone, will she scare off this person and never find out who it is? Or worse, will she run the risk of never putting an end to this harassment or stalking, or whatever it is? And who could she tell anyway?

She's still very reluctant to call the police. She's sure Campbell would jump at a chance to snoop around and find any grounds at all on which to convict Emily herself; she wouldn't be looking for any other villain. Amanda still doesn't believe her, and even Pippa isn't sure what to believe any more. Emily would ring Matt if he didn't live so far away.

She and Greg had first met in Modern Art Oxford. She went there recently to see a William Morris and Andy Warhol exhibition. It's still on. She'd planned to return with Pippa, but she has changed her mind. She'd found the comparisons drawn between the two artists rather far-fetched, and hadn't rated the show very highly.

This afternoon, there will be lots of people there to see the exhibition for themselves, she imagines, in spite of some poor reviews. She won't be in any danger in a public art gallery surrounded by a crowd, will she?

She has no appetite, but she has just been for a run. She has to eat. She gets up from the table to put more bread in the toaster. Then she notices something. *That's very odd*, she thinks, standing by the worktop and scowling. The kitchen knife and the bread knife are missing from the block set. She doesn't remember taking a knife up to bed with her again last night, but her memory is so unreliable at the moment she can't be certain. She rushes upstairs and checks under her pillow, but there are no knives there. Sighing, she puts the mislaid knives down to absent-mindedness. *They'll turn up soon*, she tells herself.

Emily looks at her watch again. It's now a quarter to ten. She has some work to do as she's going to be exhibiting some of her pictures in a few months' time in a local art gallery. Painting is the last thing she wants to do right now, but perhaps she can organise her canvasses to try and visualise how she'll display them. With this in mind, she downs the dregs of her coffee and makes her way to the studio.

At first, Emily observes the scene that meets her in silence. She scans the room to assess the damage.

'Nooooo!' she screams.

She swears; she cries loudly; she throws herself down on all fours and beats her fists against the floor until she can physically feel the pain.

'No! No! No!'

She raises her head and stares incredulously at the vandalism of her studio, the violation of her sanctuary. The paintings she has been working on over the past months, which are on the floor and propped up against the wall, have all been splattered with blood-red paint. Her works are completely ruined.

If the colour itself wasn't a clear enough threat, the two missing knives from the kitchen certainly send an unequivocal message. They have been thrust into a large blob of red paint on two different paintings; the paint has trickled down from under each knife as though to show someone bleeding out from a stab wound.

For several minutes, Emily sobs and screams. Then it takes her several more minutes to catch her breath. Finally, she goes back into the kitchen and rings Amanda from her mobile. The phone goes to voicemail. Her sister always turns her phone off when she's in a session with a patient. Next Emily tries Pippa, who says that she'll organise childcare for her kids and come straight round.

While Emily is waiting for her friend, she calls Sergeant Campbell's direct line, as Pippa advised. The two women arrive at Emily's house at the same time.

Pippa makes tea while Emily tells Campbell about nearly everything: the messages on Facebook, the phone calls on her landline, being followed in the street, the automated voice of the security system alerting her to a possible intruder and the fact that she'd locked her front door but that it had been unlocked the following morning.

Emily even says that Greg's mobile phone has disappeared, but she doesn't tell the police officer about the text she received asking her to meet him that afternoon. She also fails to mention that she thought she'd seen Greg at Port Meadow and heard a baby crying in her guest room. She isn't sure if she should leave out the part about the malicious comment on her website, but in the end Pippa fills Campbell in on the recent post and the spiteful emails.

'All this has been going on for some time,' Campbell notes wryly. 'Why haven't you reported this before?'

Emily gives her a hard stare, but doesn't answer the question.

Campbell clears her throat and looks Emily in the eye. 'There was a routine investigation, Mrs Klein, after the car crash. There were some circumstances that appeared suspicious to begin with. Certain incidents that required my attention. I know some of that was unpleasant for you.'

Emily suspects that Campbell had gone way beyond the call of duty to rake up the dirt from her past in the course of her routine investigation, but she supposes that she'll get no closer to an apology from Campbell than that.

'This isn't really my domain,' Campbell continues. 'We're going to have to call in forensics. And a senior officer from the Criminal Investigation Department. But if you'd like me to, I'll see what I can do to help.'

'Thank you, Sergeant,' Emily mutters.

'It's Inspector now, actually,' Campbell says, combing her fingers through her spiky red hair, 'and my colleague is now a sergeant.'

Despite the horror of the morning's events so far, Emily feels pleased for Constable, although she thinks that 'Sergeant Constable' still sounds rather incompatible.

While Campbell is busy making phone calls and Pippa is making more tea, Emily wonders if this will all be over by 5 o'clock.

Within two hours, Emily's house is bustling with people. Two CID officers question her again in the presence of Inspector Campbell. One of the officers seems particularly interested in where the blood-red paint has come from, but Emily is sure it's her own paint that has been used. The other one explains what the scenes of crime officers are looking for in the studio. After photographing everything, they'll check the knives for fingerprints and try to find the vandal's DNA thanks to something left unwittingly at the scene.

Campbell, Pippa and Emily watch from the doorway as the team work methodically in the studio.

'We'll get forensic evidence, don't worry,' Campbell says. 'There's a theory – it's called Locard's exchange principle – that the culprit always brings something to the crime scene and leaves with something from it. It's nearly always true.' The police officer is upbeat and is no doubt trying to be reassuring. But Emily is despondent, and doesn't feel at all buoyed up by her words.

Outside the studio, the security alarm is also checked and the control panel is dusted for fingerprints. All possible entry points into Emily's home are thoroughly examined. The two CID officers, two SOCO officers, Inspector Campbell, Emily and Pippa check outside along the pavement and between the cars for any clues left by the person who followed Emily home. The SOCOs pick up some cigarette butts for analysis.

At ten past five, everything that hasn't been dealt with yet is left for the day. Emily is ordered not to go into the studio until the SOCOs have finished off their work in there the following day. Emily listens to the CID officers' instructions, her eye on the clock. *I'm already late.* She can't wait to get rid of everyone. Fortunately, once the decision has been made to wrap it up for the day, everyone leaves fairly hastily, including Pippa who has to pick up her children.

It's ten minutes to six when Emily finally arrives at Modern Art Oxford. The lady at the front desk isn't letting anyone else in, but Emily spins her a story about being very late to meet up with someone. It's not a complete lie although Emily can see the lady doesn't believe a word of it. But she recognises her – some of Emily's paintings had been exhibited there a couple of years ago and she's often a visitor – and the woman allows her to enter the art gallery.

Emily doesn't know where to look, or for whom. She races through the exhibition but there are few people there now. *I'm too late*, she thinks. *I've missed him.*

On her way past the café, she looks in. There is hardly anyone there now. She is tempted to buy a hot drink and something to eat. She hasn't had a bite to eat since breakfast, she realises. She pushes the door open and makes her way to the counter to read the blackboard on the red brick wall behind it. But then she changes her mind. She'll have a snack and a cup of tea at home instead. She wants to get out of here. She has had more than enough for one day.

As she turns away from the counter, she spots him. He's sitting alone at a table in the far corner behind the door. He must have been there when she came in, but she hadn't seen him. He has his back to her, but she recognises his clothes. She'd been with him when he bought that green, waxed Barbour coat in Mole Valley Farmers in South Molton. She's sure other men wear similar coats in the agricultural or equestrian communities of North Devon, but this is the centre of the city of Oxford.

She remembers the rip in the jacket from when he'd caught it on a barbed wire fence one day as he bent down to pick up the cat. *I can't see from here. I need to get a closer look.* She walks forwards on tiptoe, as if afraid that he'll hear her approaching from the other side of the café. As she approaches, he gets up and, keeping his back to her, he disappears through the door. For a split second, she is rooted to the spot, but then she breaks into a run and chases after him.

As the café door closes behind her, Emily stands still, looking around her. She has lost him. But there's only one way he can go. She races through the gift shop and catches sight of him again. As she pursues him out into the yard, she has gained enough ground on him to see the back of his jacket clearly. The coat has a tear across the back! Emily gasps and stumbles. The gap between them increases and when Emily comes out onto St Ebbe's Street, he is nowhere to be seen.

Bent over with her hands on her knees, Emily tries to catch her breath. She can't even begin to process what she has seen. *My eyes must have been playing tricks on me. It can't possibly have been him. How could it be him?* He is the last person in the world she ever wants to see again; the last person it is possible to see again.

She walks slowly in a daze to where she has parked the car. She only realises that tears are streaming down her face when she notices people staring at her. She concentrates on her breathing, trying to calm herself down.

Afterwards, she remembers nothing of the drive home, only that her heart was racing the whole way.

Chapter Twenty-One

~

Oxford, 20th March 2015

Emily isn't sure she believes Will, but she's excited, as well as very nervous, about seeing him again after all this time. He'd written her a message via Facebook, explaining that he was at a symposium on veterinary medicine at Oxford University and asking if they could meet up for dinner.

He'd given her his mobile number, so Emily rang him. They only spoke for a few minutes, but Emily's heart thumped the whole time. Will was a bit vague about the conference and Emily still doesn't know whether he's attending one, or giving the talk. She got the impression he wasn't telling her the full story. But the main thing is that he's coming to Oxford, and after all these years, she's going to see him again.

Will left it up to her to make reservations for dinner, but promised – in another Facebook message, this time with a winking smiley – to pay. She spent at least two hours on the Internet trying to find a place where she hadn't already eaten with Greg. She wanted somewhere reasonably classy, but not too expensive, since Will was footing the bill.

Pippa came up with the solution. She suggested a nice Thai restaurant called The Green Papaya, which opened recently in St Clement's Street. Emily has booked a table for half past seven.

At ten to seven, she is still clad in only her underwear, desperately looking in her walk-in wardrobe at the few clothes remaining on hangers. She has tried on numerous shirts, blouses, trousers, dresses and skirts and rejected them all. There are clothes strewn all over the floor.

This is ridiculous, Emily thinks. *Will has seen me in my school uniform and Wellington boots – not together, and it was a long time ago, but all the same! He probably won't even notice what I'm wearing.* At seven o'clock, she finally decides on a green and blue long-sleeved T-shirt and a pair of tight-fitting green jeans, which is in fact the very first outfit she pulled on that evening.

She walks into the bathroom and stands for a few seconds, staring at the gaunt face in the mirror while she tries to work out why she came into this room in the first place. Then she remembers. Accordingly, she gets out her make-up bag and starts to apply foundation. She grimaces as she notices her crow's feet have multiplied. It also strikes her that her laughter lines are looking more and more like scars. She mentioned to Amanda just the other day that she thought she'd aged noticeably over the last six or seven months.

'Nonsense. You'd look a bit less drained if you put some weight on,' was Amanda's response, 'and the lines you have on your face are rather charming.' *Easy for her to say*, Emily thinks now as she recalls this conversation. *She hardly has any wrinkles, and she doesn't have any laughter lines at all.*

'Now for some damage limitation,' she says aloud to her reflection. And when she has finished painstakingly applying her make-up, she's pleased with the result.

Emily received substantial payments both from Greg's life insurance policy and for her car late last month and, with Matt's help, she promptly bought a new car and put an advertisement on eBay to sell Greg's Range Rover.

She drives into town carefully in her white three-door Audi A1. Matt's choice, in fact, but she likes the car very much. It's comfortable and a lot smaller than Greg's Range Rover, more practical altogether for driving around in the city. But despite its compact size, it takes her far longer to find a parking space this Friday evening than it has taken to drive into town.

Predictably, Emily arrives late at the restaurant, and is stressed at the thought of keeping Will waiting. She needn't have worried; he isn't there yet. She sits down at their table to wait, and takes out her phone to text him. Then she remembers that she can't.

She noticed something very strange that morning: all the contacts in her mobile had disappeared. She's reluctant to try and sync her iPhone on her computer, as the last time she tried that, she lost not only her contacts, but also her most recent photos. She has decided to ask Charles if he can help, and, failing that, maybe she'll call Josh.

Briefly, she panics. She won't be able to send a message to Will. *What if he's lost? He probably doesn't know Oxford.* But then she calms herself down. If he can't find the restaurant, or is going to be very late, he can contact her. He has her mobile number. As for the problem with her phone, she'll sort that out tomorrow.

'Would you like a drink while you're waiting, madam?' the waiter asks Emily, interrupting her thoughts.

She orders her usual soft drink and chews on one of her nails. *Is Will going to stand me up? Will I even recognise him after all this time? Will he recognise me?* After she'd received his Facebook message, Emily had a good look through all his photo albums on Facebook. To her frustration, most of the pictures were of two blond boys, landscapes, or a Border Collie puppy. Will didn't appear in any of them. She supposed that Will was usually the family photographer and that these boys were his sons. He hadn't filled in anything for his relationship status, but she assumed he was married. *Still, there's nothing wrong with having dinner with an old friend, is there?* Emily thinks now.

After half an hour, Emily wonders how much longer she should wait. She has no way of getting in touch with him. Or does she? She takes her phone out for the umpteenth time and looks at the screen. Her text messages have disappeared and her call log is empty. She thinks of messaging him on Facebook. If he has a smartphone, he might receive it, or at least an email notifying him about it, immediately. Then she remembers that he'd given her his mobile number in a Facebook message in the first place, so she can call him after all.

'Emily, hi.' She looks up and feels a contraction somewhere between her heart and her stomach. His hair is still light blond, but it's short and no longer flops over his tanned face. He has a few wrinkles – more than she has – but in spite of them, he looks young for his age. 'I'm so sorry I'm late. I'm afraid there were lots of questions after the talk and I couldn't get away. Did you get my text message?'

'Hi, Will.' It sounds wonderfully strange to hear herself say his name aloud after so long. 'Er, no, I didn't. My phone is playing up. But you're not that late.' Emily gets to her feet, and for a fleeting moment they stand awkwardly, then Will holds her elbows in the palms of his hands as he leans in to peck her cheek. She catches the scent of him as he does so. He smells amazing.

There's no more unease after that. They sit down at the table, smile at each other and chat animatedly. Will is a good listener, Emily soon discovers. With his elbows on the table, he places his left hand on top of his right one, providing an adequate chin rest. He maintains eye contact, but doesn't say a word while Emily speaks.

When it's his turn to talk, he unclasps his hands and uses them energetically to emphasise what he has to say. Emily studies his hands. They're strong, as tanned as his face, and his fingers are long and slim. There's no wedding ring, she notices.

At first, they talk about mundane things, then more intimately about their lives. It's as if they've never lost touch, but at the same time, they have almost two decades to catch up on.

Will has two boys aged eight and ten. He's divorced, his wife having left him for one of his best friends. While Emily listens to every detail, she surprises herself by eating voraciously. The food is delicious, but she has such an appetite that she thinks she could wolf everything down even if it was nearly inedible.

'A cliché,' he says, shrugging, referring to the breakdown of his marriage. 'Anyway, what about you? What have you been up to all this time?'

Emily starts by telling Will about leaving Exmoor Secure Children's Centre and moving to Oxford; about meeting Greg and about her art. She mentions her late husband's work and outlines their life together.

When she has finished, he gently prompts her. 'Didn't you want children?'

Emily sighs. Will might consider that his life has been common-place; her life has always lacked normality. She has always felt the need to tell Will the truth, the whole truth. That's why she stopped writing to him all those years ago. She couldn't answer his questions dishonestly, so she'd chosen not to answer them at all. She puts down her spoon on her empty dessert plate, takes a deep breath, and tells Will firstly about Greg's son, Luke, then about her own daughter, Melody.

Will stays silent while she confides in him. His eyes betray neither revulsion nor judgement.

'I dreamt recently that I stole a baby girl,' Emily says, lowering her voice. 'I've been over that nightmare a lot in my head, and I know deep down that I would've liked children, or a child. I just didn't want to have children with Greg, and I was scared that I wouldn't be a good mother. It's too late now. Amanda doesn't seem to want children either, but I'll probably be an aunt one day when Matt has kids. And I'm a godmother. That's enough for me.' She smiles a little sadly.

Emily thinks she sees Will's face cloud over at the mention of her sister, but he quickly recovers his countenance. For a long time, Will doesn't speak. Then he reaches across the table and takes Emily's hand. He holds it for just a second, and then lets it go.

'It's not too late, Em. You'd be a great mother. You may get your chance yet.'

Will asks Emily a lot of questions concerning Greg's death. Emily feels like she's unburdening herself by telling Will about the police interrogation and the suspicion that had hung over her for months. She describes the guilt she still feels now, knowing that she was driving, even though she recalls the accident more clearly now than when she'd made her statement to Campbell and Constable.

'We were going to Headington to see an antique wardrobe Greg was interested in buying. I was driving. On the way, Greg told me that he'd had…' Emily feels ashamed at telling Will this, as though it's somehow her fault that Greg had been seeing someone else. 'He'd had a mistress. For quite some time, apparently. He said it was over. She was threatening to tell me about their affair, so he told me instead, I guess.'

Will says nothing. He just keeps his eyes on Emily and waits for her to continue.

'Then we got into a fight. I'm still not quite sure what we were arguing about. He asked me a question: "Who was it, Emily?" And the answer I gave him was: "My father," but I have no idea what my father had to do with it. I was looking at Greg and I'd veered into the middle of the road, so Greg leaned across me and grabbed the wheel suddenly and pulled it down hard to the left. And that's wh… when I crashed the car into a tree. Greg was killed instantly. His funeral was held while I was still in hospital.'

'Were you injured badly?'

'No, just concussion and a few broken ribs.'

'How are you coping with your loss now?' Will asks, sounding concerned.

'I'm all right. Pippa and Amanda have been my rocks. I couldn't have made it through this without them.'

Again Emily fancies she sees a flicker of annoyance in Will's eyes at the mention of Amanda's name. *He's still hurt that they fell out*, she thinks, *even after all this time.*

'And how are you surviving financially? That's often a big problem after the death of a spouse. I mean, you have the upkeep of a large house to cover on your income alone now.'

Emily's eyes widen in surprise at the same time as Will covers his mouth with his hands, realising his gaffe.

'How did you know I had a large house?'

'I looked up your address and then checked it out on Google Earth,' comes the reply. Emily admires Will for continuing to look her in the eye as he admits this instead of lowering his gaze.

That's called cyberstalking, a voice in her head points out.

You did it, too, Emily, you googled him and trawled through his Facebook photos, another voice reminds her. The second voice sounds spookily like Josephine's. Emily shakes her head as if to force out the unwelcome opinions.

'I'm so sorry,' Will says.

'No, that's fine,' Emily says. 'I tried to find out about your conference on the Internet, and I searched for images of Cavendish Crescent. That's just as bad.'

Will grins. 'What a coincidence! My address and your surname.'

'Maiden name,' Emily corrects.

Will nods. There is a brief silence. Emily breaks it by answering his question.

'Greg's life insurance money came through. The mortgage was paid off in full according to the terms of his policy. Financially, I have nothing to worry about. Not for a while, anyway. And you're right; it's very comforting to know that. I'm so glad I don't have to deal with money problems on top of everything else. I have a small income from my painting and I was due to exhibit my work soon, but it wouldn't have been enough to continue the mortgage payments on the house.'

Emily doesn't mention that she's planning to sell the house. It's far too big for her alone – it had been too big for the two of them as well – and she wants to get away from everything that reminds her of what she has lost. She's even contemplating leaving Oxford. After all, apart from Pippa and Amanda – and she'll never lose touch with them anyway – what is there for her in this city?

'Have you cancelled your exhibition? What happened?'

This is the cue Emily needs to fill Will in about all the strange events that have occurred since Greg's death. Contrary to the account she gave Inspector Campbell, this time Emily leaves nothing out. Again, Will listens attentively without interrupting, although his facial expressions show his surprise, shock or anger at Emily's ordeal.

She pauses after telling Will about the destruction of her paintings. Seeing the look on Will's face, she attempts to adopt a more flippant tone.

'Matt says I'll probably be able to sell them for a fortune, especially if the knives are included,' she jokes. 'He says they're reminiscent of the portrait of Dorian Gray.' What Matt actually said was: 'You can name your paintings after that bloke who fancied himself and stabbed his portrait and grew old and decrepit in the book by that Irish guy we had to read at school.'

Despite Emily's attempt to make light of the vandalism, Will's not amused.

'Emily, this is very serious, and very violent. Knifing your paintings and making them appear as if they're bleeding is unspeakably intimidating. Someone's trying to cause you pain. Sending a few messages from beyond the grave over Facebook is one thing – that could just be a very sick practical joke. The same goes for the phone calls. And the torment from that is psychological. It's another thing entirely to break into your home and

200

carefully stage this… this sabotage to threaten you like this. And with knives and blood-red paint, it seems to me that the message is clear.'

'You think my life is in danger?'

'Maybe, yes. But if you haven't been attacked yet, then there must be something that someone wants first.'

'Revenge?'

'Can you imagine what for? Have you any idea who could be doing this to you? Or why?'

'No,' Emily says, 'I've been racking my brains over those very questions. But I think it's somehow connected to my past.'

'What do you mean?'

'The only thing I haven't told you about yet is the text message I got on the day before my paintings were destroyed. It was sent from Greg's mobile. It said to come to the local art gallery alone – that's where I first met Greg – without telling anyone. When I got there, I saw a familiar figure in the café. He had his back to me, but I ran after him to get a better look. I saw the rip in the back of his Barbour jacket. I recognised him from the coat.' She pauses. 'This is going to make me sound like I'm insane.'

'Go on. Tell me who you saw.'

Emily hides her face in her hands. 'My father.' A different question to the one Greg had asked in the car, it occurs to Emily, but the same answer.

'Em, you know that's impossible, don't you?'

'Yes, I do. But—'

'It was his jacket.' Will finishes her sentence.

'Exactly.' Emily looks up and her eyes lock onto Will's.

'Someone's playing horrible tricks on you, Em.'

'Yes, but, Will… the point is… it must be someone who knows me very well and who knows about my past. The text message was supposedly from Greg, but I didn't see my husband; I saw my father. This links what happened all those years ago with what's happening now.'

'It connects Greg's death to your father's.'

'Yes. Precisely. Perhaps someone thinks I should be punished for killing both my father and my husband.'

'If that's the case, the person doing this to you doesn't know you as well as you think. The car crash was an accident. And you certainly can't be held responsible for your father's death. That means your stalker, or whatever he is, can't know what really happened that Christmas Eve.'

Emily is pensive for a few moments. She can see Will is making an effort to refrain from probing deeper into the events of that night. He had never asked her if she'd killed her father – he'd never needed to. He already knew the answer. But there are details about that night that he still doesn't know.

Will pays the bill and they leave the restaurant. Side by side, they walk along the pavement outside, their arms touching at times. He tells her that he's driving home straight away as he's working tomorrow. He walks her back to her car. They hug each other, and the moment fills Emily with warmth. Then Will kisses her cheek close to her mouth.

'Promise you'll keep in touch this time?' These are the last words he says to her on this first day of spring.

'I promise.'

As she watches her childhood friend walk away, a memory comes to Emily. She was sitting next to him on a bale of hay in his father's barn. He'd put his arm around her and he whispered something in her ear. She can't remember now what he said, but she does recall the electric shock she felt when his leg touched hers. The picture is so vivid that she imagines she can smell the straw.

She realises for the first time that it's possible for her to desire and love the same person. She can only describe to herself the sensations of happiness and safety she experiences in Will's presence as feeling like she's at home. Home, but without all the negative thoughts she associates with that single, complicated word.

Emily's warm feelings of happiness last only as long as the drive home. As she gets out of the car in the driveway, she spots Mr Mistoffelees on her front doorstep. He isn't moving. Emily realises immediately that he isn't breathing, either. Her hand in front of her mouth, she forces herself to walk towards her front door. She can see blood all around her cat. She retches, but stops herself from throwing up. Then she screams so loudly and for so long that Mrs Wickens comes out of her house next door.

'I'm so sorry, Mrs Wickens,' Emily says, seeing her neighbour appear in her dressing gown. She moves a few steps forwards to shield the elderly woman from the view of the dead cat. 'My cat's dead,' Emily offers by way of an explanation, somehow remembering to speak loudly.

Mrs Wickens's cat had come outside when the old lady opened the door. She scoops it up, and holds it tightly to her, as if she's afraid that Mr Mistoffelees has died of a contagious illness. Sensing this, Emily tries to reassure her neighbour: 'He seems to have been run over, Mrs Wickens.' Emily only realises she has been holding her breath when she goes to speak. She makes herself breathe in and out slowly.

'Anything I can do, dear?'

'No, thank you. Goodnight.' Emily tries to keep her voice even, but she's close to screaming again.

Hearing Mrs Wickens's door close behind her neighbour and her cat, Emily looks down again at what remains of Mr Mistoffelees. She feels another wave of nausea come over her, and this time she doesn't manage to keep her dinner down. When there's nothing left inside her, she sinks down onto the step, taking care to sit as far away from the cat as possible. She can smell and taste her own vomit. She starts to cry, and she tries to think.

She remembers the suspicion she voiced earlier to Will that what was happening in the past was somehow connected to the events in the present. The gruesome sight lying at her feet has just confirmed that. It reminds her of Smokey, the cat she'd had when she was a child. *This is no coincidence.* Emily's thoughts are lucid in spite of the shock she's in. *This is obviously supposed to make me think of Smokey. It's deliberate.*

'Poor Smokey. Poor Mr Mistoffelees,' she sobs out loud.

My two cats have met the same end, Emily thinks. *If they were killed in the same way, they may have been killed by the same person.* She looks at Mr Mistoffelees again. She feels another wave of nausea. It's such a horrifying sight. Just like Smokey, Mr Mistoffelees's head has been severed from his body.

Chapter Twenty-Two

~

Oxford, 2nd – 4th April 2015

Nearly two weeks later, Emily still hasn't sorted out the problem with her phone. At first, without the phone numbers of her friends and family, she felt cut off from everyone. She felt scared of being on her own; at the same time, she needed a few days alone to think about everything that had happened. Really, she has been feeling far too exhausted to do anything about her mobile. At least, that's what she has told herself. But then she scolds herself for her inertia. So, when she stumbles upon Josh's advert – with his number on it – in a drawer in the coffee table, she decides to ring him.

When she was younger, she reflects, she knew several phone numbers by heart: her grandparents' and Uncle Rod's; the number for her father's mobile, which was huge and heavy compared with today's models; Will's landline – incredibly, she can still remember that three-digit number to this day, although she has long since forgotten the one for the Old Manor House.

Now she doesn't even know her sister's and Pippa's landline or mobile numbers. She knows her own, but that's of no use to her. Greg bought Emily her first mobile phone about twelve years ago and since then she has made no effort to memorise contact details herself.

The previous day, Emily received a bizarre text message. It read: 'Please tell Lenny his granny wishes him many happy returns. Love, Mum.' On reading the word 'Mum', Emily's eyes welled up with tears. Just after the message had come through, Emily received a selfie of a black lady from the same mobile number.

She zoomed in to examine the photo in as much detail as possible. The woman looked to be in her sixties, but Emily found it hard to tell. She had a beautiful, wide smile and very white teeth, and she was holding a present, gift-wrapped in childish paper, next to her cheek with one hand. Emily could make out the name 'Lenny' on the envelope sellotaped to the present.

She'd dismissed the message and the photo as a wrong number until that very morning when she received an alert for a calendar event. It was a reminder for Lenny's sixth birthday on 1st April. Emily now wonders if this might all be significant. Somehow.

When she calls Josh, he suggests that Emily's mobile is somehow synced to another phone of the same make via iTunes.

'Can we find out whose phone mine is synced to?' Emily asks.

'I don't know,' Josh says. 'If it was done on your computer, maybe there's a way. If it was done on someone else's computer, that might not be possible.'

'But how does that even happen in the first place?' Emily asks.

'It happens quite often. My uncle and aunt had that problem, too. They both have iPhones and they synchronise them using the same computer, but my uncle once accidentally used my aunt's iTunes account.'

Emily wonders if her phone has been *deliberately* synced to someone else's phone. Could someone be keeping a close eye on her through her phone? She puts this to Josh.

'It sounds a bit far-fetched,' he says. 'But I suppose your move-ments could be monitored to a certain extent via a synced phone.'

'That might explain how this… vandal knew when it was safe

to come round and destroy my paintings. And kill my cat. He knew I was out.'

'Mmm. Do you know if a location app has been installed? Find My iPhone, for example? That would be the easiest way to spy on you.'

'No. What's that, exactly?'

'It's an app that helps you find your phone if you've lost it. But it could also enable someone to see exactly where you are if you've got your phone on you and you're sharing your location with their device.' Emily shivers. 'I'll have a look, but at the moment, I've got a few deadlines to meet,' Josh continues. 'If you just want to get your phone back to normal, I can talk you through that now if you like. It's not difficult.'

'No, it's all right, Josh. I really need to find out whose phone mine is synced to. When you have a spare moment, will you let me know?'

'Of course.'

Immediately after Emily's telephone conversation with Josh, Pippa calls her. Then Matt rings to say he's coming to stay. Thanks to them, she now has Amanda's number. Emily knows she must get in touch with Amanda soon. Her sister will be worried about her as they rarely go for more than a few days without talking or texting.

Emily is starting to feel more connected to her loved ones again, and it's a relief. She resolves to take matters into her own hands. Lately, she has been too passive, too inactive. She needs to get herself and her life sorted out. Starting with the phone. It may just be a silly idea she can't get out of her head. Perhaps no one is tracking her movements and she's just being paranoid. But she should check it out.

The next day, Matt arrives. He has been working on a building site, but he's taking some time off, although he's evasive as to why this is. While he's staying with Emily, they'll be going to see Amanda's play, which is still running one evening a week, much to Matt and Emily's dismay. Emily finds Matt's presence in the house comforting, especially after finding Mr Mistoffelees dead on her doorstep.

Emily tells Matt about the phone problem. Matt spends some time checking the settings on Emily's mobile.

'Is this your number?' he asks after a while, showing Emily the screen.

She examines the details concerning her mobile on the screen. 'Yes,' she says.

Emily watches over his shoulder.

'The text from Lenny's granny!' he says after a while. 'We have a phone number for "Mum".' Matt does the air quotes with his fingers. 'Let's give "Mum" a call and see what we can find out.'

'Clever. But it's not much of a clue. We just know thanks to the selfie that the person whose phone mine is synced to is likely to be of African descent or of mixed heritage.'

'Oh, Em. When did you get all politically correct?' Matt says. 'Give her a ring. Ask her questions about her son or daughter.' He hands Emily the mobile.

'Which?' Emily asks her brother. 'Son or daughter?'

'Just give it a go.'

Emily holds the phone in her hands for a while, biting her nail pensively. Then she smiles. 'I've got an idea,' she says. She presses the phone number of the sender of the text message and selfie, and activates the speaker mode so that Matt can hear both sides of the conversation.

'Hello. You don't know me,' Emily begins when 'Mum' answers the call, 'but I've just found a mobile, an iPhone, in the street and I have no idea who it belongs to. Your number was in there, listed under "Mum" in the contacts. Do you have a son or daughter who has an iPhone? I'd very much like to be able to give it back to its owner.'

'Oh, it's so reassuring that there are some honest people left in the world,' comes a smooth, deep feminine voice in reply. 'That would be my Frank's phone. He was so proud of his new mobile. He showed me lots of things it could do, but I don't understand smartphones. It's so typical of him to lose it. He's always losing his stuff. Ever since he was a little—'

'Do you think you could give me Frank's home number or address so I can get in touch with him? Or does he live with you?' Emily is slouched in her armchair in the sitting room with Matt perched on its arm. She uncrosses her legs, moves so she's sitting on the edge of the chair, leans over to the coffee table and grabs a pen and the pad.

'No, he lives with his girlfriend. I know his home number, but I'd have to look up his address. He's just moved.' She reels off the number and Emily writes it down. Next, Frank's mum launches herself into a description of his new house. Emily politely brings the conversation to a close and ends the call.

'Not just a pretty face, Em,' Matt says, stroking his chin. Emily realises with amusement that although he hasn't let his goatee grow back after the funeral, he has kept this idiosyncratic gesture.

'Your turn,' she says, handing him the phone.

'Perhaps we should hide your caller ID.'

Emily nods, so Matt does it. He taps in the landline number they've just been given. Emily holds her breath in anticipation.

The telephone sounds for several rings, and finally Matt is invited by an automated voice to leave a message.

He swears, using a word Emily doesn't recognise. He doesn't leave a message.

Matt and Emily try the number many times during the day, but no one answers the phone. Then they try to find the name and address for that number by using an online reverse directory. That doesn't yield any results, either.

It's only the following evening, once they've arrived home from Amanda's play and the traditional drink afterwards in The Grapes, that they get through to Frank. It comes as such a surprise when he answers that Emily is rendered temporarily speechless.

'Hello? Hello?'

'Er, um, yes, g-good evening.' There's a slight pause. 'Is that Frank?'

'Yes.' He has a gruff voice.

'Er, I'm ringing you about your iPhone. I was wondering if… Could you tell me how…? Um… My phone seems to be synced to yours… Have you had any problems with your mobile?'

There's silence from the other end. Emily and Matt look at each other. Frank has ended the call.

'Shall I call back?' Emily asks Matt.

'No. What's the point? He won't answer.'

'This is a dead end.' Emily can hear the disappointment in her voice.

'Maybe Frank bought the phone second-hand. Or stole it,' Matt says. 'Either way, we need to find out where he got the phone and who he got it from. We could send him a text message. But he's not likely to reply. Let's sleep on it. See if we come up with any other ideas.'

But before bedtime, Emily receives another alert for an event in Frank's calendar. She shows Matt.

'Crocodile Zoo. Brize Norton. Lenny. Saturday 4th April,' Matt reads aloud. He looks at Emily, a mischievous gleam in his eyes. 'That's tomorrow. Fancy going to the zoo, Em?'

'Are you sure? I haven't really got any proof that someone has tampered with my phone. This might turn out to be a wild goose chase.'

'It doesn't matter. This is fun. And I like crocodiles. We haven't got anything better to do, have we?'

Emily manages a weak smile. She is disturbed by the children's song that has wormed its way into her head. *Going to the Zoo*. She remembers singing it in the car with Amanda when they were little. Their father was driving, and their mother, in the passenger seat, turned round frequently to grin at her daughters in the back seat.

They were on their way to Paignton Zoo. *Daddy's taking us to the zoo tomorrow, zoo tomorrow, zoo tomorrow...* That may well have been one of the last outings they'd had as a normal family. Two daughters who sang and played together, bickered together. A mother who didn't often drink excessively, but who smiled a lot, and a father who protected his daughters instead of abusing the younger one. Em knows the song will be playing on an annoying loop in her head for several days now.

'Em? Em?'

'Sorry, Matt, I was miles away.'

'I was saying, we'll check every black or dark-skinned man with an iPhone who comes into the zoo until closing time if need be. We'll find him,' Matt says confidently.

'Frank has a girlfriend, remember? His mum said he lived with her. He may be with her, and he'll be with Lenny, who's obviously his son. He's just turned six.'

'Good. That will make him easier to find. A man and a woman with a child at the zoo. On a Saturday.'

Emily isn't sure if Matt is poking fun at her or not.

'Well, I think we've hatched a cunning plan, Matt.' Emily doesn't feel nearly as jovial as she sounds, but she's grateful for her brother's help and support.

'Yeah, it's off the hook.'

'If you say so,' Emily says.

~

Matt is overjoyed at the opportunity to drive Emily's Audi to Brize Norton. They aim to arrive for opening at ten o'clock, but an overturned lorry has shed its load on the A40, so they're held up for over half an hour. They arrive at twenty to eleven. Emily pays for the tickets and they hang around the entrance for a while, looking out for a man who could feasibly be Frank.

After around twenty minutes, Emily sees a familiar figure

paying for tickets for herself and two children around the age of seven. For some reason, her throat constricts.

'Matt.' Emily points her finger. 'I know her.' It comes out as a half-whisper, half-croak. It doesn't occur to Emily that the woman is too far away to have heard her even if she'd spoken loudly.

But as the woman comes through the entrance turnstile, Emily sees that it's not Lucinda Sharpe, as she'd thought. She reminds herself that her former solicitor's children are all grown up. Lucinda would be a granny by now, and her grandchild would only be a baby.

'Let's go for a wander,' Matt says.

They spend the next hour walking around the zoo, examining not the reptiles, but the visitors.

By midday, Matt is hungry and Emily is downhearted. She takes out her mobile and wonders if the icon for a location app such as Find My iPhone would appear on the screen. None of the icons seem unfamiliar to her.

'Maybe Josh can find Frank using the location app if there's one on my phone,' she says.

'Maybe,' Matt says.

The two of them go to the café and eat lunch. Emily spends the whole time observing other people who come and go. Matt eats ravenously, but Emily picks at her food. By the time they've finished their coffees after lunch, Emily is fidgety.

They leave the café and walk around the Crocodile House again.

'There!' Matt says jubilantly to Emily, pointing at a man with black skin who is carrying a little girl in his arms. A woman next to him, who is also dark-skinned, is holding a young boy by the hand.

But as they walk up to the couple, they hear the woman say, 'Steve, it's the crocs' feeding time. Let's watch this before we take the kids to see the lizards.'

Emily shakes her head at Matt. His first name is Steve, not Frank. And the couple both had American accents.

'False alarm,' Matt mutters.

Emily looks at her watch. It's one o'clock. 'Let's give it another hour and then get out of here,' she says.

Emily reads one of the signs aloud:

'DO NOT STAND, SIT, CLIMB OR LEAN ON THE ENCLOSURES. IF YOU FALL, CROCODILES WILL EAT YOU AND THAT MIGHT MAKE THEM SICK.'

Matt chuckles, then reads out another one:

'**ZOO RULES**: THOSE WHO THROW OBJECTS AT THE CROCODILES WILL BE ASKED TO RETRIEVE THEM.'

Emily is suddenly reminded of a poster in the café she glanced at while they were eating lunch. It was an advertisement for children's birthday parties.

'It's Lenny's birthday party!' she exclaims. 'We've been looking for a family of three. We passed a group of kids earlier. Let's try the café again, Matt.'

They head back to the café. In the corner is a group of children. They have coloured beakers with straws on the table in front of them. They watch a handsome young boy with tight black curls blow out the candles on his birthday cake once the other children have finished singing *Happy Birthday*. Emily counts six candles. The boy smiles, revealing a few gaps where milk teeth have fallen out. Emily points at a man who is using his phone to take photos. He has to be the birthday boy's father.

'Is that an iPhone?' she asks Matt.

'I can't tell from here.' Striding across the café, Matt calls out: 'Frank?'

The photographer whirls round.

Bingo, thinks Emily, following Matt.

'Result!' Matt whispers as Emily catches up with him.

'Hi. Are you Frank?'

'Ye-es. And you are…?' It's the same gruff voice she heard on the phone.

Emily doesn't give her name. Instead she gets straight to the point. 'I think my phone is synced with yours and I—'

213

'You're the lady who rang me.' Emily sees his eyes flicker from right to left.

'Yes.'

'Listen, I'm not sure what this is all about, but this is my son's birthday party.' Frank gestures towards the group of children. A petite blonde woman, presumably his girlfriend, glances over at him anxiously as she cuts the birthday cake into slices and hands around the plastic plates to Lenny and his friends.

'We don't want to take up too much of your time,' Emily says.

'It's just we believe the mobile might have some clues to um… an act of vandalism,' Matt adds.

'We were hoping you could help us.' Emily can hear her pleading tone.

Frank hesitates.

'You OK for a sec, Sarah?' Frank asks the blonde woman. She nods.

Frank leads Emily and Matt a few metres away from the kids' party. Emily doesn't know if this is because of the noise the children are making, despite having their mouths full of chocolate cake, or so as not to be overheard.

'Are you Greg?' Frank asks Matt.

His question takes Emily's breath away.

'What makes you think that?' Matt asks, recovering his composure before Emily.

'When I connected the mobile to my computer, that's what it came up as: Greg's iPhone.'

Emily turns towards her brother. Her eyebrows shoot up. So this is the phone that was stolen from her house. This is the phone that was used to send her a text telling her to meet Greg in the art gallery. This is Greg's mobile.

'Er… no, it's not my phone,' Matt says.

'We think this phone was deliberately synced to mine and that it may have been used to keep tabs on me,' Emily says.

'How?' Frank asks.

214

'Maybe with a tracking app?' Emily's intonation suggests a question.

Frank has become a little jumpy. He seems to know something, but isn't sure if he should trust them.

'I've been threatened recently,' Emily says, hoping to persuade him to give them what information he has.

'We believe her life is in danger,' Matt chimes in.

Sarah has joined them. She slips her hand into Frank's.

'Frank found the phone. It was left on a park bench,' she says. She turns to Frank. 'This sounds serious, Frank. Perhaps you should help them if you can.'

Emily smiles at her, studying her. Sarah is dainty. Her eyes are a little too close together and her nose is a bit too large for her face, but she is undeniably attractive.

'There were two tracking apps installed in the mobile phone,' Frank says. 'Find My Friends and Connect.'

'I've never heard of either of them,' Emily says.

Frank shrugs. 'Find My Friends just means you can see where your friends are on a map on your phone, providing they agree to share their location with you.'

'And Connect?'

'That's quite a new app. People use it to track their spouses and check they're not cheating on them, that sort of thing.'

'So you can track someone without their consent?'

'Probably not legally,' Frank says. 'But, yes, you can.' He offers Emily the phone. 'Look, I don't want any trouble. This is my kid's birthday party, for goodness' sake. There was nothing in the phone that I could use to work out who it belonged to.'

'We didn't come to take it back,' Emily tells him. 'We simply want some clues as to who has been harassing me. Can you think of anything?'

'There were some text messages and emails from a chick called Emily. Emily... I can't remember her surname.'

'Really?' Emily can feel her heartbeat quicken. 'They appeared on your phone?' It occurs to her that Frank can't have tried try that hard to find out who the mobile belonged to.

'Yes.'

'Right. That's interesting. Where exactly did you find the phone? Which park?'

'Did you happen to see the person who left the phone on the bench?' Matt adds.

'Christchurch Meadows. There was a couple sitting on a bench. They were eating pastries by the river. They were long gone by the time I discovered they'd left the iPhone.'

'When was this?' Matt asks.

'It was a weekday, about a fortnight ago. I'd just picked up Lenny from school. It was sunny, so I took him to the play area.'

'Can you describe the couple?' Emily asks.

'They had their backs to me. I didn't see their faces. The guy had long legs stretched out in front of him. Brown hair. A round bald patch. That I remember because I saw him scratching his hair under it. I wondered if he'd been bitten by midges or mosquitoes or if it was too early in the year for that sort of insect. The woman sitting next to him threw the crust of her tart or something into the river for the ducks or swans or whatever. She was about average height. Longish hair. Dark, maybe. Not light anyway. She had darker hair than you.' He waves his hand towards Emily's curly, chestnut head. 'She wasn't thin, but not really fat either.

'Any idea how old they were?'

Frank whistles through his teeth. 'Thirties? Forties?'

'Is there any information in the phone itself that could help us to identify them? A call log or emails or text messages?' Emily asks. 'Anything?'

'I've deleted everything, I'm afraid. There were only emails and text messages from this Emily chick. Klein, that was it. Emily Klein. I remember thinking the phone didn't seem to have been used for much. There wasn't much music in it, and there were only a few apps apart from the two tracking apps – I've deleted

216

them, too – and the ones that are already installed when you buy an iPhone…'

'Or take it,' Matt mutters. Emily nudges him, but luckily Frank and Sarah don't seem to have heard.

'There were no contacts whatsoever. In the Notes there were times and dates,' Frank continues, 'but I couldn't work out what for. If I'd known it was going to be important, I'd have paid more attention. Sorry.'

~

On the drive home, Emily is absorbed in her thoughts. She is alarmed at the idea that someone stole that phone from her house and then used it to stalk her. She tries to push this thought away and instead replays in her mind the conversation they'd had with Frank.

Matt concentrates on the road. From the corner of her eye, Emily sees him glance at her from time to time. After a while, his curiosity apparently gets the better of him. 'OK, out with it. You're not going to tell me you recognise the bloke from that sketchy description, are you?'

'No, but something he said has got me thinking. He said the man scratched under his bald patch.'

'Yes. How many men do you know with bald patches?'

'I don't know. I'm not sure I ever notice that sort of thing, really. But that's not what got me thinking. Do you remember Richard?'

'The actor guy? The one I've met a couple of times in The Grapes?'

'Yes.'

'Is he going bald?'

'Will you forget about the baldness? He has a habit of scratching his neck.'

'O-Kaaay?'

Emily is silent for a few seconds. Something about this mannerism disturbs her, but she can't quite pinpoint it. It's a vital clue, though, she feels sure of that, an essential piece in the alarming puzzle that her life has become. But for the moment, she can't work out how it fits in.

'I think I need to talk to him,' she says at last. 'It might be important.'

And without revealing any more, to Matt's obvious frustration, Emily takes her mobile out of her handbag and rings Pippa. They chat amiably for several minutes while Matt drums his fingers on the steering wheel impatiently. Before ending the call, Emily asks Pippa for Richard's mobile number.

'He wasn't in The Grapes on Thursday evening after the play,' Emily says, 'I just wanted to send him a text to congratulate him on his performance.' She feels a pang of guilt for lying to her best friend.

'I don't know how to look up the number in my phone without ending the call, so I'll send you a text with his number in a mo,' Pippa says. 'How did Matt enjoy the play?' Emily and Pippa both chuckle.

'I don't know. We're in the car. He's driving. I'll ask him. Matt, what did you think of the play?'

Matt rolls his eyes skywards at Emily as a reply, then turns his head back to look at the traffic in front of him.

'So-so,' Emily translates, and Pippa laughs again.

The text message arrives a few seconds after Emily has finished talking to Pippa. She immediately calls Richard.

'Hi, Richard, it's Emily Klein, Amanda's sister.' She activates the speaker mode for Matt's benefit.

'Oh, Emily. I've been in two minds as to whether to contact you. I'm so glad you rang me.'

Emily instantly regrets putting the conversation on the speaker, dreading that Richard is about to mention their kiss – which, of course, she hasn't told Matt about. But her fears are unfounded.

'Can I come round and see you, Emily?' Richard asks.

'Yes, I was going to invite you round, actually. I wanted to ask you a few questions about something.' Emily tries to sound a little stern so as not to give Richard the wrong idea. She doesn't want him to think she's coming on to him again.

'I'm going away on business next week. Shall I pop round to your place one evening when I get back?'

Emily has no idea what Richard does for a living, and she doesn't ask. She remembers Amanda telling her a long time ago that he didn't earn very much, but that's all she knows. 'Yes, that would be fine.'

'Are you calling me from your mobile?'

'Yes.'

'In that case I'll save your number and give you a ring before I come.' He pauses, then adds, 'I'm afraid I've got a bit of a confession to make, Emily.'

Chapter Twenty-Three

~

Oxford, April 2015

'When Inspector Campbell and Sergeant Constable found me, I was digging the hole with a spade in the back garden.' Emily says. She sees Pippa and Amanda exchange a bewildered look, just as the two police officers had done. 'Constable asked if I was burying someone or something. He was joking, of course. It's not at all funny, though, is it? Poor Mr Mistoffelees.'

It's a sunny day, and despite the cool breeze, the three women are sitting in Emily's back garden. Pippa is admiring the crab-apple tree Emily has planted over the grave she dug for Mr Mistoffelees. Matt comes out of the house carrying a tray with a teapot, mugs and biscuits.

'Nice mugs,' Pippa says. 'There's only three of them, though.'

'I'm having apple juice' Matt says. 'Same as wee Harry here.'

'I've had the mugs for ages,' Emily tells her friend. 'I was given them as a present when I stopped working in Alice's Shop – you know the tourist shop opposite Christ Church.' She doesn't use these mugs often, but Matt has obviously found them at the back of the cupboard.

Matt pours the tea and Pippa examines the mugs. They all have illustrations and quotes from *Alice's Adventures in Wonderland* as well as handles in the shape of keys.

'Did you tell them about your cat?' Pippa asks, her eyes still on her mug.

'Yes, of course. Constable even took some photos. He said he didn't think it looked much like an accident to him.'

'How could he tell that?' Amanda asks.

'I don't know. He didn't really examine the cat. He just looked closely at where his neck had been… separated… from…'

'So he thinks someone deliberately decapitated your cat.'

'What's wrong, Amanda?' Emily asks, picking up on her tone. 'You sound a little irritable.'

'It's just that I've been worried sick about you. I left messages, sent texts. I called round a couple of times, but both times you were out. I couldn't understand why you hadn't called me before now, to be honest.' Amanda gives her a weak smile. Emily hasn't seen her sister for a while and feels a stab of guilt for not contacting her earlier. 'And I'm furious that someone would do this to you,' Amanda continues. 'You shouldn't have had to go through that on your own. I wish you'd told me.'

'I know. I'm sorry. I've been meaning to call but I had some problems with my phone. Matt arrived a few days afterwards, so I wasn't alone.' Matt only arrived two weeks after Emily had come home to find her cat dead, but she thinks it wise not to be too precise. The image of Mr Mistoffelees lying in a pool of blood on her doorstep pushes its way into her mind, and she feels sick all over again.

'What did they want, anyway?' Amanda asks, her eyes narrowing.

Emily has lost the thread of their conversation. She knits her eyebrows.

'Tweedledum and Tweedledee.'

'Ah. Constable and Campbell. They wanted to let me know that not everything from my studio has been forensically tested yet. But they've found a black hair. They're hoping it might be turn out to be significant.'

Pippa's mouth opens wide.

'Probably not yours, Pippa,' Matt says. 'Well, on second thoughts, it might be. They don't know if it's a human hair.'

Pippa sticks her tongue out at Matt.

'Mr Mistoffelees'?' Amanda asks.

Emily shrugs.

'Did they take a sample?'

'What? Of fur from the cat? No-o!' Emily is rather surprised at her sister's question.

'What would they do that for, Mandy?' Matt asks, chuckling.

'Well, to eliminate him.'

'You think the cat stabbed the paintings?! You want him eliminated from the inquiries?'

'No, that's not what I meant by "eliminate", Matthew!'

'I see. Well in that case, he has been eliminated, hasn't he?'

'Matt!'

'Sorry, Em.'

Emily turns to Pippa. 'Can I hold her?' she asks.

'Of course.' Pippa looks delighted and Emily wishes she'd asked before now. She takes Imogen onto her lap. The five-month-old baby grabs the large wooden beads of Emily's necklace and starts to chew on them.

'She's holding herself up well now, isn't she?' Emily says.

'Yes, she is. She can just about sit up now,' Pippa says proudly.

Harry has finished eating his chocolate digestive and he has chocolate around his mouth. Pippa takes a wet wipe out of her handbag to clean him up. He steps back before she can wipe his hands.

'Careful, that's hot,' Pippa warns as Harry brushes the tray on the little wooden table.

'What does it say on your cup, Mummy?' Harry asks, as Pippa picks up her mug again from the tray.

'It says: "Drink Me!" You could have read that yourself,' she replies.

'What does it say on your cup, Em'ly?' Harry asks. 'Is that a caterpillar?'

'Yes, it is.' Emily turns round her mug and obliges Harry by reading the quote: '"I can't explain myself, I'm afraid, sir," said Alice, "because I'm not myself you see."'

Harry looks confused and Emily thinks he's going to ask her to explain what that means, but he turns instead to Amanda.

'Come on, mate,' Matt says before Harry can ask what's written on Amanda's mug. 'We'll go and wash your hands.' He holds out a large hand for Pippa's son to place his sticky little hand in. 'Then we'll see if Em has a ball we can kick around, shall we?'

'I don't think I have,' Emily says. 'I don't have any children's games at all.' She feels saddened at this thought. 'That will have to change, won't it, Immie, with you as my god-daughter?' Imogen has given up on the beads and is now gnawing away on her mother's car keys.

'That's all right. We'll walk down the road to the newsagent's, Harry. He sells tiny bouncy balls and big footballs.' Matt leads the boy into the house, and Emily overhears him as he whispers in Harry's ear: 'and sweets.'

'Thanks, Matt,' Pippa calls after him.

'No problem. You three can talk about knitting and babies or literature or whatever it is you women natter about while we men are gone.'

'How long is he staying with you?' Amanda asks when Matt has left.

'He says he wants to stay until the police catch the person responsible for harassing me,' Emily answers.

'Do they have any clues?' Pippa asks.

'I don't think so, but the forensic tests from my studio may reveal something. I think it takes a while to get the results back, though.'

223

'And what have you two been up to since he's been here?' Amanda asks in her big sister voice.

'Oh, we went to the zoo! I forgot to tell you about the stolen phone!'

'What zoo?' Pippa asks at the same time as Amanda asks: 'What stolen phone?'

Emily tells them about locating the iPhone hers had been synced to. She fills them in on their outing to the Crocodile Zoo and on finding Frank.

'Is that what you meant when you said you were having problems with your phone?' Pippa asks.

'Yes.'

'You're turning into a proper Miss Nancy Drew,' Amanda says. 'Did this guy Frank tell you anything useful?'

'Only that he got the phone from a couple who left it on a bench in Christchurch Meadows. It was Greg's mobile. It was stolen from my house.'

'Have you reported this?' Pippa asks.

'No. There's nothing to go on,' Emily says. It's an excuse. She really doesn't want the police involved in this.

'Do you believe this bloke?' Pippa looks at Emily, narrowing her eyes.

'Yes, I do. His story sounds unlikely, I know, but I think he was telling the truth. More or less.'

'Did he describe the couple?' Amanda asks.

'He said the man had a bald patch. He was sitting next to a woman with longish, dark hair. That was all he could say.'

'Is your phone fixed now?' This time the question comes from Pippa.

'Yes,' Emily says. 'Josh restored the phone using my computer just a couple of days ago. He deleted a location app. I only lost a few recent photos, that's all. I'd lost all my contacts, but I got nearly all of them back.'

The only one she hasn't got back is Will's, as it wasn't saved in her iTunes account. But she found it in her Facebook messages. In the end, he got in touch with her before she'd got round to ringing him. They've been talking on the phone and emailing every day for nearly two weeks now. In fact, he's supposed to be ringing her this evening. Emily doesn't mention any of this to Amanda. She's certain her sister won't approve of her being in touch with Will. But she realises that she has been smiling to herself just thinking about him.

'Em, why don't you fetch your guitar?' Pippa says after a while.

'I haven't played for ages,' Emily says. 'I must be very rusty by now.'

'Oh, go on. I'll sing if you strum.'

Pippa has a lovely voice. How can Emily refuse? She hands Imogen back to her mother, fetches her guitar and tunes it. Pippa sings with Emily as she plays *Closer* by Dido, *Run* by Snow Patrol, *Wish You Were Here* by Pink Floyd and *More Than Words* by Extreme.

Then Pippa requests Anna Nalick's *Breathe (2 AM)* for which Emily has to look up the guitar tabs on the Internet on her laptop. Pippa urges Amanda to join in the singing, but she refuses, insisting that she can't carry a tune. Amanda watches Emily and Pippa with a peculiar expression on her face. Emily interprets it as a mixture of envy and admiration. Anyone hearing Pippa sing would be jealous.

Once Harry and Matt have finished playing football, Harry demands *The Wheels on the Bus*, which Emily does her best to improvise. Before she reaches the end of the first verse, however, Imogen starts to cry. Emily suddenly stops playing, much to Harry's indignation.

'She needs changing,' Pippa says. 'Keep going. I'll get her sorted out.' She disappears into the house with Imogen on her hip and her bag slung over the other shoulder.

Emily's hands are shaking as she continues the song, Harry prompting her with the keywords before the beginning of each verse: 'Wipers!' he shouts, and: 'Horn!' The verse about the babies crying unsettles Emily again. Her voice starts wavering and she can hardly sing. If Harry and Amanda notice, they don't say anything. But Emily can feel Matt's concerned eyes on her.

It is getting late, and it's time for Pippa and Amanda to get ready to go. Matt asks Amanda if he can have a word with her and the two of them walk to the end of the garden for more privacy.

'Pippa, can I ask you something?' Emily says as Pippa starts to pack up the keys and toys in her bag.

'Of course. Anything. This sounds ominous.'

'Do babies have different cries?'

'Yes, they do. People say mothers always recognise the cries of their babies. They sound very different from other babies when they cry. Like our voices, I suppose.'

'Would you say Imogen's crying voice has changed much over the last –' Emily reflects quickly: *When was it?* '– three months or so?'

'No, not really. I haven't noticed if it has, anyway. What are you driving at?'

Emily doesn't reply straight away. She looks around her, and then her gaze focuses momentarily on Matt and Amanda. Their body language suggests to Emily that they're arguing. She can't make out their words from where she's sitting, even with their raised voices, but something in the way they're standing – Amanda with her hands on her hips, and Matt, with his back to Emily and his arms flailing around – catches Emily's attention.

She turns back to Pippa. 'Do you remember when I heard a baby crying in one of my guest rooms?'

'Yes.'

'I could swear it was Imogen.'

If Pippa thinks Emily has finally gone round the bend, she doesn't say so. 'When was that?'

'Back in February, I think.'

Pippa is silent for a few seconds. Then she takes out her phone from her handbag. She scrolls through her photos and videos until she finds what she's looking for. She selects a video and hands the phone to Emily. It shows Harry playing with his little sister. Imogen is giggling as he moves a wooden toy into her view and then takes it away again.

'That was in February. She'd just started to laugh.'

Emily nods, keeping her eyes on the video. She sees Harry drop the toy accidentally on Imogen's nose. Andy must have been the one filming because Pippa swoops in to pick up and console her daughter, whose wailing rises in a crescendo. Emily's eyes widen.

'I'm sure it was Imogen I heard, Pippa.'

'You know, when it's not your child, one baby's cry is very like another's,' Pippa reasons.

Emily is unconvinced.

'If I remember correctly, Imogen was with Andy the morning I rang you. He'd taken the kids out so I could have a lie-in. Immie couldn't have been in your guest room.'

Just then, Amanda strolls back to the group, followed by Matt who helps Harry into his cardigan as Pippa zips up her baby bag.

'I've just thought of something, Emily,' Amanda says. 'Do you remember that cat you had when we were kids? Smokey? He was found with his head detached from his body, just like Mr Mistoffelees.'

'I know, I was struck by the similarity, too,' Emily says. 'There was something strange about that, wasn't there?' She wonders if he'd also been left dead on the doorstep. 'Where was he found? Who found him?'

'I don't remember all the details,' Amanda replies. 'Daddy found your friend, William Huxtable, with Smokey's body in one hand, and his head in the other.'

Emily's head starts to spin. 'Didn't Mr Huxtable have a huge row with our father about that?'

'Yes. Dad wanted to call the police.'

'Why?'

'Well, he thought William had killed Smokey deliberately. Strange coincidence, don't you think?'

'Yes, it is,' Emily manages. Her heart is racing so fast it feels like there is just one continuous beat.

It can't have been Will, she reasons. *He was with me the evening Mr Mistoffelees was killed.*

Yes, but he arrived at the restaurant late, another voice pipes up inside Emily's head. *Over half an hour late. And he knew you lived in a big house.*

After Pippa and Amanda have left, Emily walks back through the house and out to the garden in a daze. She feels like she's sleepwalking through a nightmare she'll never wake up from. She carries the tray into the kitchen and starts to stack the mugs in the dishwasher. Her movements are slow and robotic.

'Are you all right, Em?' Matt sounds worried.

'Yes. No. I just can't reconcile the image of Will killing a cat with the caring teenager I saw lambing. He's a vet, Matt. That's what he always wanted to be. He saves animals; he doesn't kill them.'

'I take it Amanda doesn't know you're seeing him again.'

'I'm not seeing him, exactly, but no, she doesn't know.'

'Perhaps you should ask him for his side of the story.'

'I will, Matt, thanks. He's ringing me this evening.'

Emily picks up the last mug to load it into the dishwasher. It's Amanda's mug, the only one no one read out to Harry. Emily knows what it says, but reads the quote silently anyway: *It would be nice if something would make sense for a change.*

'Indeed it would!' she mutters aloud.

Chapter Twenty-Four

~

Oxford, April 2015

Emily wakes up in a filthy mood. Will rang yesterday evening, as planned, but it was only to tell Emily that he couldn't chat as there was an emergency at the veterinary surgery. He has promised to ring her today for a chat instead. When he does, she wants to ask him about the incident with her cat, Smokey, although the very idea of this fills her with trepidation. Last night, she had difficulty sleeping, and she still doesn't know exactly how she'll broach the subject.

Matt seems to have made it his morning's mission to snap Emily out of her glumness, but his chirpiness is trying her patience.

'When are you going to start painting again?' Matt asks.

'I don't know, Matt.'

He makes fresh coffee and tops up their mugs, then sits down opposite her at the kitchen table. She catches his sympathetic look as she glances up. Her chin in her hand, she sighs.

'I can't get motivated to start all over again.'

'I'll help you.'

'How can you help me?' Emily knows she's being curt.

'I don't know. How difficult can it be to flick a few blobs of paint onto a canvas?'

'Well…' Emily doesn't know how to react to that.

'I'm joking, Em. I don't know. I can take photos, go out and buy your materials, take care of the advertising; I have no idea how you prepare for an exhibition. What I do know is that you haven't got much time. And I have lots of time on my hands. If I can help, I will.'

'I've managed to postpone the exhibition until December, which gives me a bit more time. But, OK. Thank you.' Emily feels her mood slowly lifting. She thinks she should try to get back into her work. Matt's right. And it will be easier with his support. She wonders what he's planning to do. He doesn't seem keen to look for work, either in Oxford or in Devon. 'Matt?'

'Yes?'

'I can't employ you officially. I don't earn enough with my painting to be self-sufficient. I've got some insurance money, so I can pay you for this job, no problem, but I can't offer you a steady income. Not long-term, anyway.'

'That's not what I'm after, Em. I just wanted to help out while I'm here. I'm worried about you.'

This seems like the opening Emily has been waiting for to bring up the topic of Matt's future. 'I'm worried about you, too. What is it you want to do? You weren't happy with your situation in Devon, were you?'

'I don't want to be doing odd jobs. I need something more stable. I'd like to do a course to be a classroom assistant in a primary school. I could do that in Barnstaple.'

'Matt, that's a really good idea! You're so good with kids.'

'Mmm.'

Emily isn't sure what that means. 'What's the problem?' she asks.

'Well, I was hoping to live in Mum's house in Braunton while I did that.'

'So, why can't you?'

230

'Amanda said as it was going on the market, I had to move. I gave up my flat when Mum died. There didn't seem much point in paying rent when there was an empty house just up the road.'

'Amanda didn't discuss that with me.' Emily resolves to talk to Amanda at the earliest opportunity. She thinks that it would be a great help to Matt if he could live at their mum's house, at least while he gets the qualifications he needs. *Does Amanda need money again?* Emily wonders. *I'll have to ask her now. I can give her some money if necessary.* 'Is that what the two of you were arguing about yesterday?'

'Yes, it is.'

'Can I help you out? You know, until you've finished the course?'

'Financially, you mean?'

'Yes.'

'If I need help, I'll ask you for a loan, Em, if that's all right. But it's time I stood on my own two feet and got myself sorted out.'

'OK.'

They sip their coffees. Matt burns his tongue and pulls a face.

Then Emily asks, 'Isn't it strange, living in Mum's house?'

'Sometimes. Sad more than strange, really. I've cleared out some of her stuff, and that's hard. You know, clothes and things.' Emily nods. 'There were also a few men's clothes.'

'Really? Perhaps Mum had a boyfriend.'

'That's what I thought at first. But some of them looked horribly old and unfashionable. And they smelt… well, I imagine that's how mothballs smell. I wondered if those clothes could have belonged to… er… Graham.'

Emily has a sudden flash of her father's Barbour jacket with the rip.

'If Mum kept hold of some of my father's clothes, someone might have stolen his jacket to stage that sighting at the art gallery,' she says.

'That's what I thought,' Matt says again. 'Em, do you think it could have been your uncle Rod you saw there?'

'Uncle Rod? But why on earth would he be playing tricks on me like this?'

'I don't know. Revenge? If he thought you should've been punished more for Graham's death? After all, that seemed to be what both their brothers – your other two uncles – believed. Mum said that's why they haven't spoken to you since your father died.'

'I didn't see the face of the man in the art gallery. He might not have looked like either my father or my uncle Rod.'

They finish their drinks in silence while Emily ponders over Matt's idea. Uncle Rod? Could he be behind all this?

Then she showers and forces herself to go into her studio. She hasn't set foot in there since finding the vandalised paintings even though the police no longer consider it a crime scene. With Matt's help, she starts by cleaning it. Emily puts on classical music while they work, and in her head, she visualises what she wants to create.

Over a year ago, she abandoned an idea she'd had because she was commissioned to do some work for an art collector instead. Now she decides to go back to those ideas. Inspired, lots of images and colours suddenly start to swirl around in her head.

She has some of the materials in the studio, and other necessary paraphernalia in the shed in the garden. She'll spray semi-translucent paints onto wood panels and coat them with epoxy resin. The paintings will be eye-catching, vibrant and full of movement, and above all, she'll be able to produce several works along similar themes within a relatively short space of time. If she works hard, perhaps she'll be ready for her exhibition at the end of the year.

Matt helps her carry everything into the studio and they set up the first rectangular panel on the trestles. She is deep in thought, and Matt, no doubt sensing this, makes himself scarce.

To begin with, Emily concentrates only on her work, but as the first painting starts to take shape in her head as well as on the wood panel, her mind wanders and she finds her attention returning to Uncle Rod. Could the person in Modern Art Oxford have been her uncle? Surely if he wanted to avenge his brother's death, he'd had ample opportunity over the years. Why would he have waited so long? On reflection, Matt's idea simply doesn't seem plausible.

By lunchtime, Emily is making headway with her first painting. She's delighted with the effect so far, and she's famished. When she stops for a break at one o'clock, Matt has already prepared a ploughman's lunch for them both. Her mouth full of bread and Cheddar, she describes the six paintings she has envisaged in her head to Matt. Then she tells him about the aluminium wall stands she wants for one of her triptychs and the black wrought iron floor stands she'll use for the other one.

After lunch, she sketches exactly what she wants, marks the dimensions clearly, and gives Matt the name and address of someone who will make these for her. She also needs a precision blowtorch, and she tells Matt where he can buy that, too. Apparently pleased to have something to do to help his sister, Matt takes the keys to her Audi, and leaves as soon as he has drunk his coffee.

When Emily has finished for the evening, she leaves the windows and doors in her studio open to ventilate and dry the paint. She makes her way into the kitchen. She notices that on her mobile, which she'd left on the table, she has four missed calls from Will. She decides to freshen up and change her clothes before sending him a text to see if he's busy. She takes her phone upstairs to her bedroom, leaves it on her bedside table and heads into the bathroom.

As Emily is pulling a cotton jumper over her head, the phone rings again. Pushing her arms frenetically through the sleeves, she runs out of her walk-in wardrobe, throws herself onto the bed and grabs her mobile.

'Hi,' she says.

'Hello. You sound out of breath.'

The sound of Will's voice makes Emily's heart beat wildly. She has been longing to hear from him despite the fact she's now harbouring suspicions about his role in her cats' deaths.

Emily tells Will about her painting that day. She describes the materials she's using and what she wants to achieve with the colours she has selected. Will is full of praise and encouragement; he seems genuinely delighted that she has taken up her artwork again.

Then they talk about the puppy Will tried to save the previous night. He'd been brought in just before the surgery was due to close. Will diagnosed him as having canine parvovirus, a contagious illness that is fatal for most puppies. Although Will stayed up most of the night with him, this puppy didn't survive.

All the while Will is telling her about the puppy, Emily is thinking about her cats: Mr Mistoffelees and Smokey. Something doesn't add up. *Will can't be involved in this,* she thinks. *What was done to my cats was vicious and cruel. Will is devastated that he couldn't save that puppy.* Then a voice in her head says: *Maybe he's just pretending to care.*

'Do you remember me telling you about my cat, Mr Mistoffelees, a few weeks ago?' Emily hears herself asking.

'Yes, of course,' Will says. 'The death of a pet is really horr—'

'I didn't tell you everything.'

Will is silent. Emily briefly wonders if the communication has been cut off, but then she remembers he usually listens without interrupting.

'Well, as I told you, I found my cat dead that night when I got back from the restaurant we went to. At first I assumed he'd been run over and that someone had put him there. But that was impossible. The front gate was closed and locked for a start. I think that's just what I wanted to believe. Anyway, it can't have been an accident. Someone deliberately killed my cat. As if that's not bad enough, he was decapitated.'

Emily stops here and waits for Will's reaction. This time there is a long silence. Emily is determined not to break it.

'That was a vile, malicious thing to do, Emily. I'm so sorry about your cat,' Will says eventually. 'And I'm sorry you had to find him like that on your doorstep.'

Emily waits for Will to add something. She has a lump in her throat and doesn't trust herself to speak straight away.

'It seems too similar to be a coincidence, doesn't it? You said you thought the person responsible for all this harassment and intimidation might know about your past?'

'What do you mean?' Emily knows he's alluding to Smokey, but she wants to hear him say it clearly.

As if reading her mind, Will says, 'I think this was to remind you of how your cat died when you were a little girl.'

Emily hadn't been that little then, but she doesn't correct Will. 'I don't know what really happened to Smokey,' she says, quietly. She is on the verge of tears. She can't decide if Will is putting on an act or not. She so badly wants to trust him.

'I don't really know, either,' Will says. That sentence sounds flat to Emily's ears. She's not sure that she believes him. 'I just know that your cat's head had been cut off. Just as you've described for Mr Mistoffelees.'

'Who found Smokey?' Emily asks.

There's a pause. 'I'm not sure of the details,' Will says. Now Emily knows without a shadow of a doubt that he is lying to her. The hesitation has just given him away. 'I got into a lot of trouble over your cat. But I'm not sure exactly why. My father didn't explain.' His voice hardens. 'Actions spoke louder than words for him.'

Emily imagines Mr Huxtable beating Will. She wonders if he said that to make her feel sorry for him, or if that was supposed to put an end to her interrogation. Emily isn't going to be deterred.

'Will, why did you fall out with Amanda? Did it have something to do with Smokey's death? The two of you were as thick as thieves until that day.'

'Emily, it was such a long time ago. I really don't remember now.'

'At the time, Amanda said you weren't very sympathetic when Smokey was killed,' Emily recalls. 'She also said something about having to take the rap for you. What did she mean by that?'

'I have no idea,' Will answers. He sounds hurt and angry now. 'Why did *you* take the rap, Emily?'

She feels as if she has been punched. A whimper escapes, and she immediately feels ashamed.

'I'm sorry, Em. I didn't mean to upset you,' Will says. 'Listen, I could ask my father about your cat if you like. He knows what happened.'

'There's something you're not telling me,' Emily says.

She hears Will sigh. 'Em, I was the one who found Smokey. He was by the side of the road in front of your house.'

'But I was told that my father found you with Smokey's body in one hand and his head in the other.'

Will sighs again. This time he sounds disappointed, perhaps because he realises Emily doesn't believe a word he's saying. 'I knew you'd have to be told about your cat, and I was afraid you'd want to see him. I sat down on the grass bank against the wall to your garden, and tried to work out how to put Smokey's head back on so the sight of your dead cat would be slightly less... traumatic for you.' Will's voice has become almost inaudible. 'Stupid of me, I know.'

This time Emily thinks he's telling the truth. She's afraid she has probably caused irreparable damage to their friendship now. He must have realised she didn't believe him. But then again, he lied to her. First, he told her that he didn't know who had found her cat, and then he admitted he'd been the one to discover Smokey at the roadside.

'I'll ask my father for the whole story,' Will promises. He sounds brusque.

Emily feels hollow when he ends the call. She tries to write a text to apologise, but she struggles to explain what for. After changing the wording three times, she taps 'cancel' and tosses her phone onto the bed.

After a minute or two, she picks it up and writes: 'I'm sorry.' This time she leaves it at that. She presses on 'send' with her index finger and hears the sent text sound. She waits for a few more minutes, but there's no reply.

Chapter Twenty-Five

~

Oxford, May 2015

Richard doesn't call round to see Emily until a month after she had spoken to him on the phone on the way back from the Crocodile Zoo. She's curious about the confession he said he had to make. So curious that she has considered ringing him a few times. But in the end she always decides against it. This is partly because she cringes inwardly with embarrassment every time she remembers almost seducing her sister's ex-boyfriend. But it's also because she wonders if Richard's confession might turn out to be some sort of declaration of his feelings for her, and she wants to avoid leading him on at all costs.

Matt has gone back to Devon for a few days, although he was reluctant to leave Emily on her own. A friend of his had informed him of some cash-in-hand work. The same friend also informed him that the surf was up. Emily suspects that he needed some more weed, too.

Richard doesn't phone beforehand, as he said he would. He just shows up one evening unannounced. As she isn't expecting anyone, Emily is startled when the buzzer goes. He's at the front gate. She wishes Matt were here. She is suddenly wary and mistrustful of Richard, but she doesn't know why. She notices her hand trembling slightly as she presses the button to open the gate.

Richard strides up to the front door and stands on Emily's doorstep, the light of day fading behind him. He unzips a smile, which she supposes he intends as disarming, but it appears more like an inane grin. At first, Emily avoids his intense gaze, and looks down as if her doorstep has suddenly become fascinating. But then she catches sight of a small red stripe illuminated by the outside spotlight above the door. The stain didn't quite disappear when she'd scrubbed the step.

The image of Mr Mistoffelees lying there, decapitated, flashes before her eyes. She glances up. *How come I haven't noticed before how strange Richard is? He's staring at me as if he can see straight through me.* She can feel her hairs bristle on her arms. *I shouldn't have answered the door.* Emily briefly studies his face. She thinks that Richard might be considered vaguely attractive from a distance or in poor lighting. But the way he is gaping at her is giving her the creeps.

She steps back to let him in, trying to examine the back of his head as he passes her to see if he has a bald patch. He's too tall. She stands on tiptoe to try and get a better look, but he turns around too quickly.

She offers him a drink and goes to fetch him a beer from the fridge.

'I didn't think you drank alcohol,' he says as she returns with a bottle and a glass. She hands both of them to him, and gestures for him to go into the sitting room. As he passes, she tries to get a better look at the back of his head. *Damn! I still can't see if he's going bald.*

'I don't, but my guests do sometimes, and my brother likes beer. He's been staying here.' She nods towards the hall to intimate that her brother is at this very moment upstairs.

'Oh, is Matt here now?'

'Er, no.' Emily immediately berates herself for not lying and going through with the pretence. She sometimes has no qualms at all about being dishonest; at other times she feels compelled to tell the truth. *I have no idea why, but I really don't feel safe alone with Richard.* 'He's… out. He's due back soon,' she adds.

An awkward silence ensues between them. Then Richard speaks. 'When we talked on the phone, you said you were going to invite me round.'

'Yes. I wanted to ask you something.'

'I'm all ears.' Richard leans forward on the sofa towards Emily's armchair. She forces herself not to recoil.

'Richard, did you by any chance go to Christchurch Meadows sometime in March with a woman with dark hair?'

The question sounds very strange to Emily herself; she can only imagine how it must seem to Richard.

'No,' he says. 'I haven't been to Christchurch Meadows for a long time. I don't think I've been since I was a kid.' He chuckles again. Emily thinks his laughter sounds forced. 'And I haven't been out with a woman for a while, either,' he adds, focusing his intense stare on Emily again. 'Why do you ask?'

'A mobile phone was left in the park by someone who… looked a bit like you.' Emily can't bring herself to say that the thief saw the man scratching himself beneath his bald patch.

'I'm afraid I have no idea what you're talking about.'

Emily doesn't elaborate. She isn't sure if she should ask Richard what he wanted to confide in her. In the end, Richard brings up the matter without her prompting.

'Emily, I told you that I had a confession to make,' he begins.

'Yes, I remember.'

'Well, as I said on the phone, I have been umming and ahhing about whether to come and see you.' Emily hates that expression. Her father used to say it a lot.

'Go on.'

'I've been rather weak, you see.' Emily doesn't, but she nods. 'At first, I considered it to be a part like any other, a role I had to act out. Then I started to wonder why I'd been asked to perform that part. And so I reasoned with myself that it was just a practical joke. I was doing someone a favour, and being paid for it. It was harmless.' Richard drains his beer. He hadn't poured it into the glass, preferring instead to swig it from the bottle. 'But deep down I could see that it was cruel.'

'I'm sorry, Richard. I'm having trouble following you.'

'That's very ironic, Emily,' Richard says with another fake laugh, 'because I was paid to follow you.'

It takes a moment for the meaning of his words to sink in. '*You* were the one following me that night? But why?'

'I was asked to. I was told I had to check that you were all right.'

Emily feels her eyes widen in disbelief, and she tastes blood from where she has just bitten her lip too hard. She gets the distinct impression that Richard isn't telling her the whole truth.

'Didn't you realise that you were scaring me?' she asks.

'Well, yes,' he admits sheepishly. 'That was part of what I had to do.'

'Checking up on me and scaring the hell out of me are two very different things, Richard. Who paid you to do this?'

'I can't tell you that.'

'Why not?'

Richard ignores her question, but continues instead with what he has come to say. His voice is monotonous. It sounds to Emily as if he has learnt his lines off by heart.

'I realised something – that night – you know, when we kissed.' Emily shudders at that memory. 'I understood what a lovely person you are, Emily. You're kind and considerate. I like you, and I don't think you deserve to have all these tricks played on you.'

Fully alert now, Emily immediately picks up the plural.

'What else were you paid to do?' Narrowing her eyes, she leans forwards in her chair, and this time it's Richard who flinches.

It's a while before he answers. 'I was paid to dress up in a smelly old green coat and hang around in an art gallery for a couple of hours. I was told to let you see me, but only from behind. I didn't think you were going to show up, actually. I went for a coffee in the end. I felt rejected, to tell you the truth. It was just after we nearly… you know. I'd already agreed to do it, and well, I couldn't back out. I didn't know what it had to do with you.'

'It had everything to do with me,' Emily says. 'You must have realised the harm you'd caused when I chased after you! You ran away from me!'

Richard lowers his head, but not before Emily has glimpsed the hangdog expression on his face. She won't be mollified.

'Anything else you want to confess?' Emily sounds so scathing and abrupt that she hardly recognises her own voice.

'No.'

Emily isn't fooled. 'What else were you made to do, Richard?'

'Nothing.'

'I don't believe you.'

'I was asked to call you a couple of times. Breathe heavily. Use the name Alice.'

Emily raises her eyebrows. So, Richard also made the strange phone calls. 'Is that it?'

He shakes his head. 'I think it was the beginning of last autumn…' Emily already knows what he's going to say. 'I was asked to wear a red jumper and attract your attention while you were out running at Port Meadow.'

'You drove away in a black Range Rover.' Emily remembers clearly that the driver had raised his arm and hidden his face as he drove past her. He hadn't been deliberately concealing his identity. It was a nervous tic. He was scratching his neck. That was the clue that had been hiding in a corner of her mind.

'It was your husband's Range Rover. I was given the keys. I took it after you left the house, and parked it back in the driveway before you got home.'

Emily is seething.

'Richard, why did you do this? I don't understand how you could have done this!' Emily is almost shouting.

She moves her head down and around in an attempt to re-establish eye contact with him. But although his unwavering gaze had unnerved her before, now he won't even look at her.

She repeats her question, trying hard to speak more softly. 'Why did you do this, Richard?'

'I was broke. I needed the money,' Richard says. 'I didn't realise it would cause so much trouble.'

Emily doesn't really think this answered her question. She tries another one: 'Richard, who paid you? I need to know.'

'I can't do that, Emily. It's not who you think.'

'Who do I think it is?'

'I don't know. But if you tell anyone what I told you, I—'

'What will you do?' Surely he hadn't been about to threaten her?

'If you tell anyone about this and it gets back to the wrong person, I'll be in a lot of trouble myself.'

'Don't you think you deserve to be?'

'Yes, of course. But... what I mean is... I think maybe my life would be in danger. I don't think I'm exaggerating. Promise me you won't tell anyone. Not a soul.'

Emily considers this. Her father had used similar words the first time he'd raped her: *'You make me love you so much, Emily. Promise me you won't tell anyone how much I love you. Not a soul. Otherwise, we'll both be in trouble.'*

'I promise,' she tells Richard.

She'd never told anyone about the abuse before her father's death, although she felt sure that Will had guessed what was happening from the little she did confide in him. She hadn't intentionally kept her father's promise; she'd just felt too ashamed to tell anyone.

She wouldn't feel at all guilty or ashamed about breaking her promise to Richard.

'What made you tell me all this now?' she asks.

'I told you. You're a good person, Emily. I like you a lot. I didn't want you to think you were going mad. I feel terrible about the part I played in this.' He covers his face with his hands.

Emily tries once more to talk Richard into telling her who paid him, but he flatly refuses to say anything more.

After he has left, Emily replays the whole conversation in her head. She'd promised not to tell anyone, and she has no intention of keeping that promise. But she seems to have no one left to turn to. *Who can I tell?* she thinks. *Who can I trust?*

Chapter Twenty-Six

~

Oxford, North Devon and Bath,
1st – 4th May 2015

Emily no longer feels safe in her own home. Although Matt thought he would be away for just a few days, he has been gone for nearly two weeks. During his absence, Emily has tried to work on her paintings, but the slightest noise makes her jump out of her skin. She speaks on the phone to Matt every day, and she and Will send each other the odd text message. But apart from that, she has avoided seeing or speaking to anyone, and she leaves the house only to buy food or go for a run.

On one of these occasions, she comes back to find some of her things have been moved around. She'd tidied Mr Mistoffelees's bowl away in the cupboard, but it's now on the floor with cat food in it; her guitar has been taken out of its case and is on her bed instead of in the living room; the keys to the shed have disappeared from their hook in the kitchen and have been posted through the sound hole of her guitar. There's also a gift-wrapped package on the kitchen table.

At first, Emily just stares at the parcel. Then, with trembling hands, she picks it up and shakes it. In the end, she opens it carefully to discover the ugliest doll she has ever laid eyes on. Her blood turns cold when she sees the doll has a tiny, pink maternity bracelet around its wrist. She almost drops it on the floor. Holding her breath, she turns the plastic bracelet round to read the words written on it in Biro: 'Baby Cavendish'. Emily wants to scream. *I will not be beaten by this,* she says to herself, fighting back her tears.

'I'm coming back to Oxford,' Matt says when Emily tells him about all this over the phone. 'This has gone too far. In the meantime, Em, change the locks. We should have done that a long time ago. And get rid of Chucky!' If Matt wonders what the doll is supposed to mean, he doesn't ask. Emily's almost sure he doesn't know about Melody, though.

'I've already called the locksmith. And I've called Campbell. The police are on their way. I'll give them the doll and the wrapping paper.' Emily hopes that there might be fingerprints on the Sellotape of her parcel. 'But after that, I think I'd like to come down to Devon. I need to get out of here.'

'I understand. I've finished here, though. I'm free to come back now.'

'Well, I'll drive down today and stay for the bank holiday weekend. Perhaps we can travel back on Monday together. I'd like to visit somewhere on the way back.' Emily has a place in mind.

Matt seems happy enough with that idea. Emily knew he'd understand how desperately she needs to get away. Out of her house. Away from Oxford. Here, she's permanently jittery; she's justifiably paranoid. If she stays here much longer, she'll lose it completely. What was it that Richard said? He'd come clean about the role he'd played in her harassment because he didn't want her to go mad. *Is that what all this is about? Is someone trying to push me over the edge?*

Richard's confession has considerably narrowed down the

possible culprits. But Emily is trying not to think about that for the moment. She has been putting it off for several days, in fact. She has her suspicions, and she hopes she's wrong. Maybe she'll talk it over with Matt and Will. She certainly isn't going to tell Inspector Campbell about Richard just yet.

The Scottish redhead is unexpectedly sympathetic. She has arrived at the same time as one of the SOCO officers who had collected evidence from Emily's studio that day. He bags the wrapping paper and takes down notes while Inspector Campbell asks Emily questions. Campbell then advises Emily against staying alone in her house, even with the locks changed.

'OK. I'll get the parcel and doll off for forensic testing. I'll also chase up the results of the tests on the samples from the studio,' the SOCO officer promises, 'especially that long, black hair.'

'Long?' Emily asks.

'Well, it was longish, if I remember correctly, yes.'

'I didn't know that. Your colleague said forensics would confirm if it was a human hair. I thought it might turn out to be my cat's fur.'

'No. I'd say it definitely wasn't animal hair, but we'll know for sure what it was when the results come back.'

~

Emily has to make a phone call before going away for the weekend. To Will. She's very nervous about talking to him. She hasn't spoken to him since their conversation about the cat a fortnight ago. They've exchanged a few texts, but Emily isn't sure if his sentences are merely concise or if he's being brusque. Emily isn't a fan of electronic mails or text messages as she finds them lacking in tone. At least with the phone, she'll hear his voice.

She expects Will to be cold or detached with her when he answers her call. *If* he answers her call. Instead, he sounds delighted to hear from her and overjoyed when she asks if she and Matt can drop in on Monday on their way back from North Devon.

Other than Matt and Will, no one knows where Emily is going, or even that she is going away that weekend. She deliberately keeps it that way. Emily no longer knows who to trust, but she feels sure that she can have faith in her brother and her childhood friend.

Not only is the traffic on the M4 horrendous, but there has also been an accident on the North Devon Link Road near South Molton, and Emily arrives much later than planned at Josephine's house in Braunton. Matt has already prepared dinner, and they chat about his work while sitting in front of the muted TV with the trays of food on their laps. Emily feels both hungry and tired, and shortly after eating, she goes to bed and sleeps better than she has done for several weeks.

The following day, Emily and Matt buy flowers and drive out to Saunton Sands to throw them in the sea in memory of their mother. Then they walk along the beach. Emily paddles in the cold water of the Atlantic Ocean and is surprised to hear herself laughing at Matt's feeble jokes.

When they get back to their mum's house, Emily goes through the wardrobes. Matt has taken all of Josephine's decent clothes to a charity shop, but he hasn't touched the men's clothes as he doesn't know for sure whose they are. Even after all this time, Emily recognises several items of clothing as having belonged to her father. As she expected, the green Barbour jacket with the rip in the back isn't there.

She goes through the pockets of Graham Cavendish's trousers and a coat. She finds a paperweight, painted to look like a ladybird, which she vaguely remembers making in school for Father's Day when she was little. This upsets her, but she doesn't know why. Maybe it's because her father had kept her gift; perhaps it's because her classmates had given the same present to their dads, who in all likelihood deserved a gift for Father's

Day more than her own. She takes the paperweight and puts it in her handbag.

On the Sunday, Emily and Matt drive to Westward Ho! where they do some window-shopping in the boutiques along the seafront. Here, the juxtaposition of old and new buildings remind Emily of Greg, who had often joked that he was an old antique dealer while she was a young contemporary artist. Emily loves the creative feel to the place. She chats for a while to an artist who has set up his easel in front of his shop, and is painting children playing in the tidal swimming pool nestling among the rocks.

One of his paintings in the shop window catches Emily's eye. It depicts a long, cobbled street that leads the way between white-washed cottages down to the sea. She recognises the nearby town of Clovelly. She remembers playing here behind the waterfall on the pebble beach with Amanda when they were young.

Emily buys ice creams for herself and Matt and they eat them as they stroll along the beach, breathing in the salt air and listening to the screeching of the seagulls. When they turn around to head back, Emily takes the ladybird paperweight out of her handbag and hurls it as far as she can into the sea.

Matt drives back to Braunton along the coastal road. On the way through Instow, Emily's mobile starts to ring. The caller ID shows the incoming call is from Pippa. Emily lets her phone go to voicemail. She listens to the message Pippa has left her, but she doesn't call her back.

~

By the time they arrive in Bath on Monday, Emily thinks that she has avoided her problems for long enough. It has done her good to clear her head with the cool sea air, but now she is ready to voice her suspicions. She hopes that Will and Matt will be able to help organise her mishmash of thoughts and give her some clarity.

Will's sons are with their mother for the weekend, but Will introduces Emily and Matt to Chewie, his border collie, who gives them a very warm, wet welcome.

'Chewie?' Matt asks. 'Does he eat your furniture and shoes?'

'Yes, he does. It's an apt name for him. But it's actually because my elder son, Thomas, is a big *Star Wars* fan.'

'Ah, Chewbacca.' Matt nods his approval.

Will has made a quiche. He serves it with both oven chips and salad for lunch. Emily is amazed at how hungry she is. Her appetite has been insatiable over this long weekend.

When they've finished eating, Will makes coffee and suggests they drink it outside. The sitting room of his two-bedroom flat in Cavendish Crescent opens out onto a courtyard where there are three chairs around a small, round table. Chewie lies down under the table, resting his head on Emily's feet.

As she sips her coffee, Emily tells Will and Matt about Richard's visit. She has already mentioned bits of this to Matt, but she hasn't gone into any detail. This time she leaves out nothing of their conversation that evening, although she's careful not to mention that she kissed Richard in a car park in the centre of Oxford one evening or what had – almost – happened next.

Then Emily tells them about Pippa's phone call yesterday.

'I was wondering about that,' Matt says. 'What did she say?'

'She left a message, saying she'd just remembered going to Christchurch Meadows one day about two months ago with Imogen. She said it was at around four in the afternoon. Apparently, she'd arranged to meet up with her husband, Andy, and they bumped into Amanda and Charles. She wonders now if she could have been the dark-haired woman that Frank saw. But she says she knows nothing about a mobile phone being left behind that day.'

'Has Andy got a bald patch?' Matt asks. 'Frank described a man with a bald patch.'

'Yes, I think he has,' Emily says.

'Charles is definitely a bit thin on top,' Matt says.

'Richard was paid by someone, so logically that person knows both you and him,' Will says. 'And it's likely that this person is at least partly responsible for all the other horrible things that have been done to you. How many people know both you and Richard?'

'All the people Pippa claimed were in Christchurch Meadows that day: Pippa, Andy, Amanda and Charles. And Matt, obviously.'

'Let's concentrate on the people in Christchurch Meadows that day. That makes four people.'

'Yes.'

'Out of those four, do you have any idea who would threaten you?'

'Yes,' Emily answers. She's aware that both Will and Matt are staring at her now. She finds it hard to lay the blame on her best friend. But all the evidence seems to point to her. 'I think it was Pippa.'

'Why?' Matt asks. 'What motive has she got?'

'I can't imagine what motive any of them could have,' Emily says. 'But Frank described a woman with dark hair, and Pippa fits that description. He thought the phone belonged to the balding man, but maybe Pippa took it from my home and she was the one who forgot it. What's more, I heard a baby crying in one of my guest rooms, and I'm pretty sure that was Imogen. And, this might not mean anything, but Pippa never asks questions about my past. She's my best friend, but she has never probed into anything that happened during my childhood. I think she already knows.'

'Amanda might have told her,' Matt says.

'Maybe.' Emily is doubtful. Amanda doesn't tend to tell secrets or spread rumours. She has never been a gossip. She is used to keeping quiet about people's traumas; it's part of her profession.

'But surely Pippa wouldn't tell you she was at Christchurch Meadows if she was the one harassing you,' Will says.

'I think she thought I'd find out. She must have thought by admitting she was there she would look innocent.'

'Mmm.'

'The most damning thing, though, is the hair found in my studio. The SOCO officer said it was *long* and black. So, it can't be cat fur, but it could well be one of Pippa's hairs.'

She sees Will and Matt exchange a meaningful look. They're not convinced by her arguments, she realises. She can hardly blame them. It all seems a bit thin. It occurs to her that she now doubts her best friend when just a couple of weeks ago she didn't believe Will. She has no reason to trust him now, and yet here she is, confiding in him, relying on him. She sighs.

'Does Pippa have keys to your house?' Matt asks.

'Well, I've changed the locks now, but she did, yes.'

'Who else had keys?'

'Mum had a set of spare keys in Devon – they're the ones you're using; Mrs Wickens, my neighbour has a set of keys—'

'Why does she have keys?'

'I mislaid my keys once when Greg was away on business.' Emily pauses, wondering if he'd been with his mistress instead. 'And he thought it would be a good idea if Mrs Wickens had a key to the front door.'

'Who else?'

'Amanda.'

Emily sees Will shoot another conspiratorial glance in Matt's direction. The two of them seem to have invented some sort of sign language that Emily doesn't understand.

'You want to go first, Matt?' Will asks.

Matt shakes his head. 'After you, brah,' he says, as though he's holding a door open for him.

'Emily, the reason I didn't call you is, well, I've spoken to…

In the end I talked to my mother about... the cat incident...'
Emily realises that Will's mum would have been far more approachable than his father. 'I didn't want to be the one to tell you this, but—'

Emily is finding this preamble too long-winded. 'Just tell me,' she says.

'My mother saw your sister decapitate your cat. She used the axe my father owned for chopping up wood for our log fire. She'd stolen the axe.'

Emily doesn't say anything. She couldn't find her tongue even if she wanted to. She feels sick and knows her face has gone ashen.

'My mother was horrified and couldn't bring herself to intervene,' Will continues. 'When Amanda left the cat at the side of the road, my mum told me your cat had been run over. She asked me if we should bury it. I went to find Smokey, and, as I told you before, I tried to think of a way of putting his head back on or at least near his body. Then Graham found me and fetched my father from the farm. I got into a bit of trouble.'

Emily knows that Will is understating his punishment. He would have been beaten black and blue, she was sure of it. He'd already let on that his father's reaction had been a violent one when they'd spoken about this on the phone.

'For once my mum tried to stick up for me, although it was a bit late for that, and my father stormed off to your house.'

Emily can't speak for several seconds. Then she says, 'And Amanda said you'd killed Smokey. That's why you fell out with her.'

'Yes. I was so upset about the whole thing. The story of your cat being run over seemed unlikely to me even as a child. But I went along with it, partly for your sake, but mainly because I didn't want to get into any more trouble.'

Emily feels sorry for Will, and resists the urge to take his hand. Then a spark of anger flares up inside her.

'My sister decapitated a cat! She might not even have killed

Smokey. He might have been dead already. For all we know, he may actually have been run over! I'm sure you dissected animals during your training. Maybe Amanda was just curious.'

Curiosity killed the cat, says a voice in Emily's head. 'So, your mother started a rumour about an incident that took place about twenty years ago. And from that you deduce that Amanda is the one intimidating me? She was only a kid, for God's sake. Lots of children are cruel to animals.' Emily feels unsure of herself even as she raises her voice at Will. 'Aren't they?' she adds in a much softer tone.

Before Will can respond to her outburst, Emily's mobile rings. She takes it out of her handbag, which is hanging from her chair, looks at the caller ID and answers the call. She gets up to walk back into the sitting room, ostensibly for more privacy, but really she just wants to get away from Will for a moment.

'Hello, Inspector Campbell,' Emily says into the phone as she slides open the patio door.

'Hello, Mrs Klein... Emily. I'm calling to let you know that we've had some results back from the lab. Unfortunately, they don't appear to provide any clues we can follow up for the moment, but you may have something to tell us when you hear what I have to say.'

Campbell reveals that some latent fingerprints were recovered from the paintings. These fingerprints don't match Emily's; nor do they correspond to Josh, who had given his prints at Emily's request. However, they're not the fingerprints of a known criminal either, since they have yielded no match in the database. Campbell also tells Emily that a preliminary examination has revealed that there are fingerprints on the Sellotape, but Emily's own prints will again have to be eliminated.

'I'm hoping that the prints will confirm that the person who vandalised the paintings and the person who sent you the doll are one and the same,' Campbell says.

She then gives the details of the analysis of the hair found at the crime scene. Emily listens as Campbell gives her this information. When the police officer has finished, she waits eagerly for Emily's reaction. But Emily can hardly breathe, let alone speak. Her heart is beating so hard in her chest that it hurts.

When Campbell has ended the call, Emily sits on the sofa and takes several deep breaths. She waits until her heart rate has slowed down and the room has stopped spinning. Then she walks slowly back out into the courtyard and lowers herself into the chair. Chewie lifts his head, and puts it back down on Emily's feet. She's grateful for the contact. Emily now knows without a shadow of a doubt who has been harassing her.

'You had something to tell me, too, Matt,' she says to her brother. 'I'd like to hear it.'

'I'm afraid, like Will, it's a story that was told to me by someone else. And I haven't got a Scooby how she knew.'

'Who?'

'Aunt Mary.'

'Mum's sister? OK, go on.'

'Are you all right, Emily?' Will sounds worried. 'You look like you've seen a ghost.'

Emily nods, but she doesn't feel all right. Far from it. She feels as if her world is crumbling around her. Will places his hand on hers on the table. She turns her hand over and grips his tightly.

'Aunt Mary told me something recently. It was at Mum's funeral. I didn't want to bother you with it, Em, because it seemed so far-fetched. She has this… theory, and I, well… I didn't believe it. I couldn't take it in, I guess, at the time.'

'Go on. What did Mary tell you?'

'She said that while you were in the Children's Home, there was a fire in the stables at the Old Manor House where you and Amanda grew up.'

'I know that,' Emily says. 'We'd never had horses. Our father always said he would convert the barns, but he never did. Mum sold the house with the stables burnt down.' Will squeezes her hand. 'There were no horses,' Emily repeats. 'It was just material damage.' She sees Will shake his head out of the corner of her eye.

'Afterwards, the police said it was arson,' Matt continues. 'But Mary said it was attempted murder.'

'Attempted murder?' Emily echoes. 'I don't understand.'

'Mum had drunk a lot of whiskey, and for some reason she was locked out of the house. She passed out in the stables.'

'What happened next?'

'Mr Huxtable had seen the fire from his house, and when he arrived, he saw that the stable door was open. He pulled Mum from the building just before it collapsed. Mrs Huxtable had called the fire brigade, but the firefighters wouldn't have got there in time to save Mum.'

'Did you know about this, Will?' Emily asks.

'Not all of it, no. I only knew that the fire was arson and that your mum could have died. She was hospitalised for a few days. I had no idea you hadn't been told.'

Emily turns to Matt. 'And you think Amanda started the fire?'

'That's what Aunt Mary said. Mum was too drunk to realise, though, and Aunt Mary told me she'd had words with Amanda afterwards and left it at that. She didn't think Mum would ever get herself sorted out if…'

'If what?'

'What she said was that she didn't think Mum would ever sober up if she thought that one of her daughters had killed her husband and the other one had tried to kill her.'

'You do know Emily didn't murder her father, don't you?' Will asks Matt.

'No one told me what really happened that night, but I never thought Emily was capable of killing someone,' Matt says.

Emily barely hears them. She's still grappling to digest Aunt Mary's story. A realisation dawns on her. 'Oh my God!' she gasps. 'You think Amanda killed Mum, don't you?'

'I think we should call the police,' Will says. 'This is very serious.'

'I don't want to call the police yet,' Emily says. 'Amanda's my sister. We'll never be able to prove what she did in the past, and I don't understand what possible motive she could have for doing all these things to me now. She's always been so protective of me. I want to confront her about it first.'

Emily doesn't know if she's reluctant to involve the police because of some misplaced loyalty towards Amanda, or if she's refusing to face the facts even though everything indicates that her sister is undeniably capable of doing such evil deeds.

'I agree with Will,' Matt says. 'Let's call the police.'

'Please let me talk to her first,' Emily pleads. 'Face to face.'

Will and Matt look at each other again. In other circumstances, their coded communication would no doubt be comical, but right now Emily feels irritated and excluded. Then Will squeezes her hand again, and she realises she is supported and loved by these two men who only have her best interests at heart.

'The police just called me,' Emily says. 'That was Inspector Campbell. She wanted to tell me about the forensic results. There are fingerprints on the Sellotape, but obviously, it's too early to say if they match the fingerprints on my paintings. But Campbell was able to confirm that the long, black hair wasn't human.' Emily takes a deep breath. She notices that Matt and Will both have their eyes riveted on her as she adds, 'They think it came from a wig.'

'Amanda wore a wig for her play!' Matt exclaims.

'Yes, it must have fallen off her clothing when she was in my studio.'

'So we have proof that she was the one who destroyed your paintings,' Matt says.

Emily is willing to bet that the latent fingerprints retrieved from the canvasses will turn out to be Amanda's.

She wants to drive back to Oxford immediately, but in the end Will persuades her to spend the night at his place. The three of them will make the journey together the following day.

They stay up late, discussing what Emily will say to Amanda. They'll have to wait until the evening to go round to Amanda's house, as she'll be working during the day. Will makes emergency arrangements so that he'll be covered in the veterinary surgery for the next two days.

Emily takes a shower while Will makes up a bed for Matt on his sofa. He wants to change the sheets on his own bed for Emily and sleep in his sons' bedroom, but Emily won't hear of it.

'I'll sleep in your sons' room,' she says firmly. 'And Matt will pass out on the sofa.'

They look at Matt through the window. He's outside in the courtyard, smoking his second joint this evening.

Emily lies in bed for a long time staring blindly at the ceiling in the dark. She knows she won't sleep. She cries for a while. Then she creeps out into the sitting room to see if Matt is awake. As she predicted, her brother appears to be out for the count. The duvet is on the floor. She picks it up and pulls it over him. Then she thinks about making a cup of tea.

She hasn't made a sound, but from the crack under the door, she notices that a light has been switched on in Will's bedroom. She's about to knock gently to ask Will if he'd like some tea when his door opens. His chest is bare and she's suddenly filled with longing for him to hold her in his strong arms.

As she takes a step towards him, he takes her hand and silently pulls her into his bedroom, closing the door behind them.

Chapter Twenty-Seven

~

Oxford, 5th May 2015

Emily expects Matt and Will to insist on calling the police the next morning. To her surprise, they don't mention it. The three of them leave in Emily's car together with Chewie. The dog has been strapped in the back with a special harness, and is panting contentedly as he looks out of the window. Matt is sitting in the back seat next to Chewie; Will is driving and they arrive at Emily's home in the early afternoon.

It's as she's activating the electronic gate to her house that Emily spots the unmarked police car parked in the road. Inspector Campbell and Sergeant Constable are waiting, along with the two CID officers who came to Emily's home after her paintings had been vandalised. She watches, her mouth wide open, as the police officers get out of their car.

'Am I supposed to think this is a coincidence?' she asks Matt and Will, pointing at the four officers.

'Em, we did what we thought was best,' Matt says from the back seat. 'Amanda is dangerous. Jeez, she's probably a psychopath.'

When Emily doesn't respond, Matt adds, 'Oh, God, I hope she got her genes from her father.'

Emily turns round in the passenger seat so that she's facing Matt and raises her eyebrows at him.

'Whoops. Sorry, Em. I didn't think.'

Emily suspects Matt knew exactly what he was saying, and it makes her smile in spite of everything. She isn't really annoyed with Matt and Will for going against her wishes. In fact she almost feels relieved that they've called the police.

'Did you call Campbell from my phone?' she asks Will, as he pulls into Emily's driveway. Will winks at her, shrugs and gets out of the car.

~

At seven o'clock that evening, Emily rings the doorbell to Amanda's house. She's wearing a wire. Matt and Will have parked a little way up the street, and the unmarked police car is parked opposite the house with the four officers in it. Campbell has told Emily that there's also a police van a little further along the road, although she hasn't explained if this is to take Amanda away or if it's connected to the audio surveillance. Either way, Emily finds its presence reassuring.

Her sister looks happy to see her, and kisses her on the cheek.

'It was a nice surprise to get your phone call earlier,' Amanda says, stepping back to let Emily in and locking the door behind them. 'We haven't seen enough of each other lately. I've just this second got in from work, though. Would you mind making yourself at home while I take a quick shower?'

'No, of course not. Take your time. I'll make us some tea.' Emily can hear her voice falter, but Amanda doesn't seem to notice.

As soon as Emily hears the shower running, she unlocks the front door. Then she starts to look around Amanda's living room. She hasn't been to Amanda's house often; mostly Amanda has come round to Emily's. She notices how much black and red there is in this room. Abstract paintings with dark reds and browns as dominant colours hang on grey walls; there's a black leather sofa and matching armchair. A deep purple throw. A black fireplace. The curtains, which are drawn, are burgundy. *How have I never been struck by this before?* Emily thinks. *I'm an artist; I should have an eye for colours. Everything is sombre.*

She opens the drawers of Amanda's sideboard. She sees cutlery, glasses, coasters and placemats. *Nothing out of the ordinary.* She makes her way back into the hall and opens the door of the cupboard under the stairs. Amanda keeps the vacuum cleaner in here, and her shoes, coats and umbrella. *Oh, God! It's in here,* Emily says to herself as she gasps out loud. She has spotted her father's Barbour jacket. She turns it around on its hanger. Just as she anticipated, there is a rip running across the back.

All of a sudden, Emily is aware that the water is no longer running upstairs. Her heart starts thudding against her ribcage as she closes the cupboard door and heads for the kitchen to put the kettle on.

'Have you found everything you need?' Amanda is standing right behind Emily who didn't hear her come down the stairs or into the kitchen. 'Sorry. Didn't mean to startle you! The teabags are in the corner cupboard in a biscuit tin.'

When Emily doesn't react, Amanda reaches over her, opens the cupboard and hands the tin to Emily.

'Hey, isn't that Mum's?' Emily asks, catching sight of the golden bracelet Amanda is wearing. *Has Amanda taken that as some sort of trophy?* Emily wonders, grabbing her sister's wrist.

'You're hurting me,' Amanda says in a very even voice.

'Sorry.'

Emily releases her grasp. She can smell her sister's perfume. Amanda must have sprayed it on just a moment ago after taking a shower. The scent is intoxicating, and its potent blend is troubling Emily.

'Yes, it was her bracelet,' Amanda says. 'I kept it as a souvenir. Poor Mum. So sad.'

Emily scarcely takes in a word Amanda is saying. The heady fragrance of her sister's perfume is having an almost hypnotic effect on Emily. Suddenly she sees red. The red of her own anger. The red of Greg's woollen jumper. When she'd held it to her nose the day she'd come home from hospital, the pullover had smelt of washing powder, beeswax and polish. In short, all the odours that she associated with her husband. But there had been a more floral smell mixed with all of that, too.

This time, the memory forces its way to the surface before any defence mechanism in her mind can kick in and push it away. In a flash, Emily remembers word for word the argument she'd had with Greg seconds before the fatal car crash.

'It was you!' she hisses. 'I don't believe it, Amanda! It was you!'

Amanda gently pushes Emily out of the way and finishes making the tea. Then she picks up the two steaming mugs.

'Let's go into the living room.' Amanda is still calm. 'We can sit down and talk.'

Amanda's betrayal has nearly crippled Emily. This was Emily's guardian, her idol, her rock. Amanda has cared for her, advised her, looked after her and looked out for her all their lives. Emily obediently follows her sister, but it takes a lot of effort just to walk. Her heavy legs give way as she reaches the armchair. Amanda hands her a mug of tea. Emily puts it down on the coffee table.

'*You* were the one who had an affair with Greg,' Emily says.

Amanda sighs. For a moment, Emily thinks she's going to deny it. Instead, Amanda leans back on the sofa, looks her in the eye, and says, 'We fell in love, Em. We never meant to hurt you. We didn't want you to find out about us.'

Emily struggles to keep her temper. She is livid. She remembers Greg telling her that the relationship was over. It had crossed her mind in the car that he'd only admitted having an affair in the first place because his mistress – *her own sister* – was extorting money from him. Emily recalls her discovery in Greg's study the morning after her manic frenzy.

'Greg paid you a lot of money,' Emily says. 'I found the cheque-book stubs.'

Amanda doesn't miss a beat. 'I was having financial problems,' she says. 'I asked Greg to lend me some money to tide me over.'

Emily knows her sister is lying. 'He said you were blackmailing him and that you'd even threatened to kill him. You told him you'd killed someone before and could easily do it again. Greg said you were boasting. He asked me who you'd murdered.'

Who was it, Emily? Who was it?

My father. It was my father.

Amanda laughs. It's high-pitched and forced, like the cackle she used years ago for the characters of the witch or the wicked stepmother in the children's stories she would read to Emily.

'I was amazed that you hadn't told him the truth about Dad's death,' Amanda says. 'I needed the money.' She shrugs. 'I placed some stupid bets and lost. Greg had dumped me. I figured he should pay for that. Literally.'

Just as Emily is marvelling at how collected Amanda is being, her sister slams her fist down on the coffee table. Emily jumps.

Amanda's face has darkened. 'Then you killed him in the car crash,' she spits.

'It was an accident. I veered into the middle of the carriageway. Greg grabbed the wheel, but he pulled it down too hard and we crashed into a tree.'

'It doesn't matter how it happened! He was a good source of income!' Amanda springs to her feet and starts pacing up and down the living room. Amanda's ferocity scares Emily. Her eyes are wild; she makes Emily think of a large cat prowling backwards and forwards in a cage.

'Anyway, that's all in the past now, Em,' Amanda says, sitting back down on the sofa. 'Greg's dead.' Amanda's voice softens as she regains her composure. Her lips curl into a snarl. Emily is astounded at how quickly her sister's demeanour has changed. One instant she's annoyed; the next she's serene.

She is reminded of their father when they were children. He used to make them laugh by moving the palm of his hand up and down in front of his face. When he raised his hand up, he was smiling. But then he lowered his hand to reveal a scowl.

Emily decides to be direct. 'Yes, Greg's dead, and yet I received messages from him on Facebook. Did you write those, Amanda?'

Amanda feigns shock, but only for a split second. Then she grins. Emily thinks she looks proud of herself.

'Yes, that was me. I quickly came to see Greg's death as an opportunity. He wouldn't cough up any more. But I could make you pay. In more ways than one. So, yes, I sent you the Facebook messages. I wrote the text messages from Greg, too. I took his mobile from your house. That adulterous husband of yours was an idiot. He used his year of birth as a PIN code.'

'I already know you were responsible for sabotaging my paintings. Did you kill my cat, too?'

'Which one?' Amanda's chuckle is admission enough for Emily.

'But why?' Emily is aware that her question has come out as a wail. She clears her throat. 'I don't understand why you wanted to terrorise me.'

'Isn't it obvious? I wanted your money. You have more money than you know what to do with. You have far more money than sense. You've been living off Greg's wealth like a parasite. You don't even need to get a proper job. You don't deserve to live in the lap of luxury like a lazy princess. I was his mistress; he loved *me*. And yet I wasn't entitled to a penny.'

Even though Emily can hear how bitter and twisted her sister sounds, she still feels a pang of guilt. *Is Amanda right?* she thinks. *Don't allow her to make you think you are worthless*, a voice in her head says. It bolsters Emily's confidence.

'But why go to such lengths? You could have asked. I would have given you money,' Emily says.

Amanda snorts. 'Not as much as I needed. I've run up huge debts. You got life insurance from Greg's death. Your mortgage was paid off, and you got a substantial lump sum. If you died, Matt and I would inherit everything. Greg's life insurance, yours, your house, Mum's house, the works. Half of all you have would be more than enough for me.'

'You were trying to kill me?'

'Oh, no, Emily, no. I had no intention of killing you. I could have done. I thought about it when you asked me for that prescription. It would have been so easy to switch the pills. But I didn't want to get my hands dirty.' Amanda moves along the sofa, nearer to Emily's chair.

'I was hoping you'd do the honours and top yourself,' Amanda continues. 'You'd been showing signs of depression ever since Greg's death anyway, so I thought if I could just nudge you in the right direction, you might follow your husband to the grave. I wanted to drive you mad. When no one believes you, it can get very lonely. No one would ever have suspected me. No one would have suspected foul play. After all, you have a history of self-harm and psychiatric problems, and you tried to commit suicide once in the past, even if it was a pretty feeble attempt.'

Tears spring to Emily's eyes. She says nothing for several seconds, staring blindly at Amanda. *My sister wanted me dead. My own sister,* she thinks. *How can I have been so wrong about her?*

Amanda sips her tea. Somehow this gesture provokes a surge of fury, which overwhelms Emily. She wants to knock the scalding liquid into her sister's face. Emily wrestles with herself, taking deep breaths so as not to give way to her rage. She imagines getting up and placing her hands around her sister's neck, and squeezing.

For the first time ever, Emily feels the urge to kill someone. She hadn't wanted to kill her father. She'd only intended to hurt him. Badly. She'd gone to bed that night with a razor. She'd had it all planned. She would cut off his ear. Just like Mr Blonde had done to the policeman in the Tarantino film that Will had told her about. Just like Vincent Van Gogh had done to himself. Her father could live with one ear. He wouldn't hear quite so well. He wouldn't look nearly as normal. And he certainly wouldn't touch her again.

She wasn't sorry he'd been killed that night instead of injured. And yet, no matter how much her father had hurt her, abused her, damaged her, she has never considered herself capable of murdering someone. Until now.

But she won't do it. Emily is not a murderer. She has always admired Amanda. She has looked up to her and counted on her. She has often sought her advice and her approval. She has tried to be like her, emulate her. Now, however, she realises how different they are. Amanda has committed some unspeakably cruel deeds. But worst of all, she has killed ruthlessly. Not just the cats. Their parents. Both of them. Emily's convinced that Matt is right. But she'll have to ask her sister the question. She has to have Amanda say it aloud for the police who are listening in.

'What did you do to Mum?'

'Mum saw me leave your house after I'd put Greg's laptop back in his study. It was risky, but Matt had asked in front of everyone in The Grapes where Greg's computer was. So, I had to get it back into the house even though you were all there. I came up with some excuse for Pippa and Charles and drove back that day after the pub. Then I sped to Newbury to join them at the races. It took Mum a while, but she eventually put two and two together and confronted me about it. She didn't even do it face to face! She rang me. I had to drive all the way to Braunton to make sure she kept quiet. And somehow I managed to drive all the way back again afterwards.'

So that's why she had difficulty getting hold of Amanda to tell her that their mum had died, Emily realises. That's why Amanda was so tired on the way down to Devon again. They must have left very shortly after Amanda had got back to Oxford. No wonder Emily had to do all the driving!

'What did you do to her?' Emily repeats, making no effort to conceal her growing disgust for her sister.

'I forced her to drink whiskey. Jameson. Her favourite. Of course, I had to threaten her with a knife to begin with, until she got the taste back for her old habit. Then, when she was drunk, I pushed her down the stairs. And that did the trick.'

Amanda has spoken without compunction. Leaning forwards in the armchair and resting her elbows on her knees, Emily covers her ears with her hands, as if this will somehow block out the unforgivable atrociousness of Amanda's actions.

'She was never a mother to us,' Amanda says, her voice rising in both pitch and volume. 'She spent our entire childhood in a drunken coma.' Amanda has transformed again, from a self-important villain, bragging about her exploits, into a self-pitying victim, complaining about her mother's negligence. From guilty to innocent; from dark to light.

Emily glares at her sister in disbelief. She can't equate this dangerous monster with the caring sister she grew up with. How did she ever feel grateful to her? At this moment, she is filled with hatred and contempt. The feeling seems to be mutual. She can see her own emotions replicated in her sister's eyes.

'But, if you hated me so much, why did you ever protect me? Why did you shoot our father dead?'

'You really don't get it, do you? That was all your fault! You were always Daddy's favourite.' Amanda's face has become scarlet and distorted by rage. 'He called you his darling. His best girl. He never had a term of endearment for me! It was your fault. You took all his affection.'

Her father's words echo in Emily's head. He had blamed her, too, for making him love her so much. Too much.

'You were jealous?' Emily is incredulous.

'Of course I was. He never even looked at me. You were better behaved than me, slimmer than me, prettier than me. He was besotted with you!'

'But that's… sick, Amanda! I had no idea you were jealous of me! I confessed to killing our father because I felt indebted to you. You said that as a minor, I'd get into less trouble than you. I spent months in a Secure Centre because I thought you'd shot our father out of love for me.'

'You're so naïve, Emily. I would never have killed Daddy out of love for you. I was devastated that I'd killed him because of you. I was absolutely heartbroken. I missed completely.'

'I don't understand.'

'No, it never entered your little head, did it? Mum supposedly slept through the whole thing, and even she understood. I never considered the consequences. I just wanted Daddy to myself. I never intended to kill *him*. I wasn't aiming for Daddy; I was aiming for *you*, Emily!'

Emily doesn't register how it happened. She is reeling from shock. Amanda moves swiftly. Suddenly, Emily is being hoisted out of her armchair from behind, and Amanda is holding a knife to her throat. Emily catches sight of the open cutlery drawer in the sideboard behind her chair as she is hauled out of the living room.

Amanda half-drags, half-forces her at knifepoint along the corridor and into the downstairs bathroom. In the mirror on the door of the bathroom cabinet above the sink, Emily can clearly see their reflections. Amanda is crazed, her eyes bloodshot and dancing, her cheeks flaming. Emily is pale; her eyes wide open in fear. She also sees the knife in the mirror. It has a long, wide blade. A knife that could easily slice through vegetables. A knife that could easily slit her throat.

The reflections disappear as Amanda flings open the door to the cabinet with her left hand, all the while gripping Emily tightly against her with her right arm, and holding the knife against Emily's neck with her right hand.

'You'll swallow these, you little bitch!' Amanda says, grabbing a bottle of pills. 'Then when you're sedated, I'll take you back to your house in your car and cut your wrists open.'

Feeling the pressure of the blade on her chin, Emily forces herself to keep her mouth closed. She suppresses the scream rising in her throat. She has to breathe through her nose, and she's beginning to hyperventilate.

Amanda bangs the door of the cabinet closed. Emily can see the two of them in the mirror again. Amanda's lips continue to move, but Emily can no longer make out a word she's saying.

Suddenly Matt's reflection appears in the mirror as he pushes past two plainclothes policemen. She watches as her brother, her saviour, brings down the pedal bin as hard as he can on the back of Amanda's head.

It's not enough to knock Amanda to the floor, but as she releases her grip slightly, Emily pushes her sister's right arm away and ducks under it. She flees from the bathroom as the two CID officers rush in. Sergeant Constable envelops Emily in his arms in the corridor in front of the bathroom. He holds her against his broad chest until Emily sees Will and Chewie behind him and runs to Will's embrace.

Amanda spits at Emily as she is led away in handcuffs.

Will strokes Emily's hair as they stand with their arms around each other. The dog is desperately trying to push in between them and keeps licking the leg of Will's jeans. Emily senses Will move one of his hands down from her back to place it on the dog's head.

'It's over now, Em. She can't hurt you any more,' Will says again and again. Emily remembers Amanda saying nearly the same soothing words after shooting their father dead. *It's over now, Emily. He can't hurt you any more.* That had been Emily's mantra for a long time.

She tries to concentrate on what Will is saying, as if that can block out what her sister said earlier this evening. But she already knows Amanda's words will remain etched permanently in her mind. Her sister, her protector, who shattered her illusions when she said: 'I wasn't aiming for Daddy; I was aiming for you, Emily!'

Chapter Twenty-Eight

~

Oxford, July 2015

'So it *was* Imogen you heard crying! I don't bloody believe it. Shit!' Pippa is swaying precariously in her high heels and waving her flute of champagne around emphatically. 'How the fuck did she pull that off?'

'Apparently, one evening round at yours, Immie was particularly fractious. Amanda recorded her on the Voice Memos of her mobile, edited it and used that. She played the recording through a baby monitor, which she'd hidden in my guest room.'

'That was very calculating of her. She took a big risk with that nasty trick,' Pippa says.

'Yes, she did,' Emily agrees. 'And I nearly caught her, actually. I came hurtling down the stairs just as she made it out of the front door. I heard her roar off in her car, but I couldn't get a glimpse of the vehicle. She'd left the baby monitor under the bed upstairs, and had to come back and get it later when I was out. If only I'd thought to hunt all around the bedroom for clues!'

Emily sees Will wave at her from the other side of the garden where he's talking to Andy. She smiles back.

'That's not the only time she nearly slipped up,' Emily says.

Emily and Pippa walk towards the outdoor table and sit down on the chairs. Emily thinks Pippa looks lovely in her long, flowery summer dress, her dark hair loose and shiny. Immie was dressed up in beautiful clothes for the occasion, too. After the informal, non-religious naming ceremony, conducted by Andy in the back garden, the eight-month-old baby was put in her cot for a nap. Champagne and canapés are now being served.

The godfather, Joe, a friend of Andy's, has told anyone who'll listen all about his year-long backpacking experience 'Down Under' from which he has just arrived back with a healthy bronze glow to his skin and an annoying Australian twang to his accent. Joe met Imogen for the first time minutes before making his speech.

Emily also made a speech, which had taken her hours to prepare with Will's help. Pippa and Emily now have other, more pressing things to talk about. They've chatted a few times on the phone, and Emily has brought her friend up to speed with Amanda's arrest and confession. However, they haven't seen each other until now, mainly because Emily has hardly been back to Oxford since it all happened in May, preferring to stay at Will's flat in Bath. She has only been to Oxford two or three times to sort out the sale of her house and the preparations for her exhibition in December.

After all this time, Pippa is keen to hear all the details.

Pippa lifts her flute, sees that it's empty and shakes it, as if more champagne will magically appear, and then puts the glass down again looking disappointed.

'Oh?' Emily has never known Pippa to be so inquisitive. 'Were there other times when Amanda nearly screwed up?'

'Yes, on several other occasions she was nearly caught out. For example, she put in the wrong code in the security system when she came to steal Greg's phone. She told the police that she was almost spotted by Mrs Wickens, my neighbour, who kept a lookout after she'd heard the alarm screeching. Then there was the incident at Port Meadow. She made Richard put on Greg's jumper and drive his Range Rover.'

'Richard did that?' Pippa's eyebrows have shot up into the middle of her forehead.

'Yes. He was so in love with Amanda. He knew she was manipulating him, but he would have done anything for her. Anyway, he got the car back to my house before I arrived home, and Amanda put the car keys back in their place, but they left with Richard still wearing the red sweater. Amanda had to hide it under my bed the day we were boxing up Greg's stuff. She admitted to the police that it was a blunder, but it contributed to making me, and everyone else, think I was going mad, because I knew I'd checked under the bed for Greg's sweater. So, Amanda wasn't too bothered about that in the end.'

'It seems odd. She had everything planned and then she was careless.'

'I don't think she was careless, really. I think that after each narrow escape, she felt more and more invincible. I reckon Amanda got a kick out of taking risks.'

'It certainly sounds like it. Did she make any other mistakes?'

'Well, Amanda had synced Greg's iPhone to mine, and then she left it on the bench that day when you were all at Christchurch Meadows. That was careless of her, right enough.'

'The woman with the dark hair that man saw – what was his name? Frank? – it *was* me!' Pippa exclaims.

It strikes Emily that Pippa seems quite pleased with her and her baby daughter's involvement in all this. But who could blame her? Emily's story has been all over the news. Pippa was even asked by *The Sun* to give an interview. Without any hesitation, she refused. (Andy said his wife replied: 'If you pay me enough, you can take a photo of me with my tits out, but I'm not giving you any dirt on my best friend or her sister.')

Emily felt an immense wave of gratitude and affection for

271

Pippa when Andy had told her that earlier. After Amanda's unpardonable betrayal, Emily is all the more thankful for Pippa's steadfast loyalty.

'I never knew Amanda was so good with smartphones and computers,' Pippa says. 'She managed to sync that phone to your mobile so she could spy on you, and she hacked into yours and Greg's Facebook accounts. I wouldn't have thought her capable of all that.'

'Me, neither. Apparently she'd taken evening courses in IT a while ago. I vaguely remember her telling Greg about it – he was interested in computers,' Emily says. 'She'd become quite tech-savvy and was able to put all of that to good use. She even managed to Photoshop a picture of Greg by a black Range Rover in front of the Old Manor House, where we grew up. And she somehow made it appear on my computer as a pop-up ad. I had no idea that was even possible!'

'And I have no idea what a pop-up ad is,' Pippa says. Both of them burst out laughing.

Emily can laugh now, a little bit, but until just a few days ago, she'd been a mess. Amanda failed her in the worst imaginable way, just as her father had done. The hardest part for Emily is the feeling that a large chunk of her is missing. A huge piece of herself has gone away with Amanda. For so many years, her elder sister had been the biggest influence in her life. Her sister's absence, along with her deceit and hatred, has left Emily feeling exhausted and empty. In just one year, she has lost her husband, her mother and her sister, and with it part of her own identity.

A few days ago, however, she discovered something. Something that's going to change her life for ever. It came as a complete shock at the time, but Will has been so enthusiastic, and Emily is becoming more and more excited about it.

'Ah, the lady needs a refill!' Joe observes, picking up Pippa's empty champagne flute. He disappears briefly, then comes back with a bottle, and fills up Pippa's glass.

'A true gentleman,' Pippa says, jerking her champagne in Joe's general direction to toast him.

'And you, Emily, the fairy godmother. Still not drinking? You're next for this Name Day business are you?' Joe asks. He points the bottle at Emily's flat stomach. Emily doesn't answer.

'Oh, no,' Pippa says, 'Emily doesn't drink.'

Joe, unruffled by his socially inept comment, staggers off in search of more empty glasses to fill.

Emily still says nothing.

'Joe's harmless, Em,' Pippa says. 'He's just a little clumsy. And drunk.'

Emily notices Will and Andy heading over to join them.

'E-em?' Pippa somehow draws out the diminutive of Emily's name to make two syllables. 'You're not, are you?'

Before Emily can answer, the men sit down at the table.

'Will was just telling me you're about to start house-hunting in Bath,' Andy says to Emily. He moves his chair closer to Pippa's and puts his arm around her shoulders.

'Yes, at the moment we're living in Will's flat, but ideally one day soon we'd like to buy a house,' Emily says.

'Ooh, you didn't tell me about this,' Pippa says. 'What sort of house are you looking for?'

'It will need to have five bedrooms so that Thomas and Oliver can each have their own bedroom and so you guys can come and visit. We want a large garden for Chewie, of course, and it has to be situated not far from the boys' school and close to Will's veterinary surgery. I'd like a studio, or room to extend the house to add one.'

'The boys are very motivated about helping us visit places,' Will adds. 'At the moment, they're spending a lot of time on the Internet looking at online estate agencies.'

'And your house has been sold, Emily,' Pippa says, a note of melancholy in her voice. She sips her champagne.

'Yes, we're putting most of my stuff into storage in Bath.

273

Tonight is the last night I'll ever sleep in the house on the Woodstock Road. There's a removal van showing up at some unearthly hour tomorrow morning for my furniture and boxes, and then I have to hand over the keys to the estate agent.'

'Are you at all sad?' Pippa asks.

'No.' It's the truth. Emily can't wait to get out of here.

'You can stay with us whenever you want to come back to Oxford, you know.'

'Thank you. I'll be back to get ready for my exhibition in October or November, and then for the big day itself in December. I'll let you know the exact dates and see if that's convenient.'

'It will be,' Pippa says. She turns to Will. 'What about your flat?'

'I'm about to put it on the market. It's in a great location, so I'm fairly confident it will sell quickly.'

'So, what were you two nattering about?' Andy enquires.

'Amanda,' both Emily and Pippa answer at the same time.

'Ah.'

There's an awkward silence until Pippa asks Emily, 'Do the police really think Amanda did everything on her own? I mean, clearly she used Richard, but isn't it possible that she had an accomplice?'

'According to Campbell, the police were initially convinced that she must have had an accomplice. In fact, they interrogated Charles.'

'Ah, yes, Charles, of course,' Andy says. 'I read in the paper that a man in his late forties was helping police with their inquiries. I should have realised it was him.'

'He and Amanda were very close, romantically involved, in fact, and so he seemed the obvious partner in crime, I suppose,' Emily continues. 'But I knew Charles wouldn't have abetted Amanda.'

'Too honest?' Will asks.

Andy chuckles. 'No, he's not that honest. He helped Greg with that antique scam, didn't he?'

'Yes, he did,' Emily says. 'And that worked against him in this instance. Somehow all of that got dragged out into the open.'

'What was that poor antique dealer's name? He had a funny name, didn't he?' Andy furrows his brow.

'Mr Kipling,' Emily says.

'That's right. Mr Kipling.'

'It's funny you brought him up. Quite a coincidence. I saw him only yesterday,' Emily says. 'He came to pick up all of Greg's antique furniture from the house. I'd rung him to tell him he could have the lot. He was over the moon.'

'I'm sure he was!' Andy says. 'That will more than compensate him for his broken vase!'

'What's this about a broken vase?' Will asks.

'What makes you so sure Charles didn't help Amanda?' Pippa asks before the conversation goes off further along this tangent. Will would have to hear the story about the Chinese replica another time.

'Well, do you remember, Pippa, you suggested asking Charles for advice when I received all those messages on Facebook? And when we did tell him some time later about it, he urged me to contact the Help Centre. There was also an evening in The Grapes when he offered to take a look at my computer. And I noticed that on all three occasions, Amanda was trying hard to keep Charles out of it. She didn't want him to get involved. The first time, she tried to change the subject. The second time, in the pub, she suddenly needed a cigarette even though she doesn't smoke. And finally, when he offered to help me, she practically sulked until he took her home.'

'Do you think she was worried that he might find a trace of her hacking on your computer?'

'Possibly, although I remember Charles saying that it would be extremely difficult to do that. But in any case, he obviously didn't suspect for a moment that Amanda was the cause of the problems I was having. I was quite sure he wasn't tangled up in her scheming.'

After a while, Emily senses with relief that they've exhausted the topic of Amanda, so she gets out her phone to show Pippa the photos she took of her god-daughter earlier in the day. The two women coo over how cute Imogen is. Will and Andy, visibly less interested in this subject, saunter off to join Joe who is having a slurred, incoherent conversation with Andy's parents.

As soon as the men are out of earshot, Pippa puts Emily's phone down on the table and looks at her, her eyes bright with excitement.

'You are, aren't you?' she asks, picking up from where they'd left off before the men joined them.

'I am what?' Emily knows full well what Pippa is getting at.

'You're pregnant!'

'Shh. Not so loud.'

'Doesn't Will know?'

'Of course he does!'

'How far gone are you?'

'Only about eight weeks. I only found out three or four days ago! We weren't intending to tell anyone until I got past three months. How can you read me so well?'

Emily isn't complaining. She's delighted to be able to share this secret with Pippa. She has kept too many secrets from her in the past.

'Your silence spoke volumes. And *five* bedrooms? You're transparent, my dear,' Pippa jokes, tucking a strand of her hair behind her ear. 'Was this planned?'

Emily is surprised at the directness of Pippa's questions today, but she tries not to show it. 'No. But we're both thrilled about it.' Emily's voice belies her words, and her face falls.

'Bu-t?'

'I'm anxious about becoming a parent.' Emily realises she was about to bite her nails, so she sits on her hands. 'I loved my mum, really I did, but she was a terrible mother. And the less said about my father, the better. I don't feel I've had a role model.'

Pippa reaches across the table and takes both of Emily's hands in hers. 'Emily, you'll be a wonderful mum,' she says.

'Do you think so?'

'I know so. You've only had examples from your parents of how not to do it, but you'll find your own way.'

'You're an excellent mother, Pippa. I do have a good example after all.'

'Oh, don't copy me!' Pippa feigns horror.

'No, seriously. Your kids are turning out great.' Emily looks over at Harry, who has been playing on the swings and slide in the garden with his older cousins all afternoon. 'Have you got any tips for me?'

'Well, when you really love your kids, you carry them for nine months, and then spend the rest of your life trying to work out how to get them back inside your womb so that you can protect them! You're wasting your time. Take it from me. It can't be done. But that's the most important part of your role: love and protection. And you'll love them unconditionally. You'll see. You'll be fine. I know you will.'

Emily squeezes Pippa's hands hard. *How did I ever suspect that my best friend could harm me?* Emily thinks. *Pippa has never been untrustworthy. She has never been anything but reliable.* Emily doesn't want Pippa to know she has ever doubted her, but she vows to herself to make it up to Pippa for letting those suspicions enter her mind.

Shortly afterwards, Will and Emily get ready to go. They have things to organise before Emily leaves her home in Oxford for good tomorrow morning.

Pippa hugs Emily tight, and whispers, 'I'm happy for you, but so sad for myself. I don't want you to leave, you know.'

'Pippa, you're my best friend. You won't keep me away. And you can come and visit us, too,' Emily whispers back.

'You know,' Pippa says, holding Emily at arm's length and examining her, 'for someone with such a fucked up family, you turned out all right.'

They both grin.

EPILOGUE

~

Oxford, December 2015

With hindsight, Emily realises that they should never have driven by the house in the Woodstock Road. It had been Will's idea. And it turned out to be rather a bad one.

The exhibition was a huge success. It ran for a week and attracted many visitors. An art collector offered her an astronomical amount of money for the *Colour Triptych*. Emily was very pleased with her acrylic paintings on wood panels. Entitled *Dark Side*, *Breaking through the Blue* and *Into the Light*, the bright colours gave life and movement to her works.

For Emily, these paintings symbolised her life story. She was almost reluctant to sell them. To humour Matt, she'd also displayed her twin canvasses *Death to Art*, complete with the knives, just as he'd suggested. Contrary to Matt's prediction, these vandalised paintings did not sell for a fortune, but they sold nonetheless.

Emily stayed at Pippa and Andy's during the days leading up to the big event. Will had driven her to Oxford with the remaining paintings, and then he'd returned to work in Bath. He drove back to Oxford for the last day of the exhibition, leaving Chewie and the new feline additions to their family – Mungojerrie and Rumpleteazer – in safe hands.

Matt took the train to Oxford to support Emily; and Rosie, Emily's friend from the Ruskin School of Art, also came to see her exhibition. Emily hadn't seen Rosie for years and was delighted to catch up with her. Even Lucinda Sharpe showed up on the Friday evening, and Emily received a congratulatory email from Mr Latimer, her art teacher at Exmoor Secure Children's Centre. He hadn't been able to come, but was following her career with interest.

A lot of people turned up out of curiosity. Rather than fame thanks to her artwork, Emily had gained notoriety because of her sister's crimes. As her trial had just begun, Amanda was in the local and national news more than ever. She'd pleaded guilty to all the charges laid against her, and journalists and lawyers predicted that she would be sentenced to life imprisonment, possibly with a recommendation that she never be released.

Amanda hadn't attempted to contact Emily in the seven months since her arrest. This surprised Emily, but she didn't really know why. At the same time, she felt relieved that her sister hadn't written to her.

Emily had secretly contemplated changing her name. But what would she change it to? She certainly couldn't go back to being a Cavendish. Her maiden name was Amanda's family name. And if she adopted a new surname, what name would she choose?

Emily felt that changing her name by deed poll would be a drastic change of identity, and she wasn't sure she could cope with that at the moment. She was still trying to reconstruct herself without her sister and her husband, after all. But Emily finally felt as if she belonged to a family, and she was looking forward to Christmas for the first time in years, finding Tom's and Oliver's enthusiasm contagious.

Although she hadn't discussed changing her name with Will,

he provided the solution to her dilemma when he asked her to marry him the previous week. Emily was so thrilled at the proposal that she only realised the following day her name would change when she married her childhood friend. Feeling like a besotted teenager, she'd spent hours practising her signature as Emily Huxtable. That name had a nice ring to it, but at the same time, she found it hard to believe that it would be hers.

~

Will uses that name now, even though their wedding isn't set until February: 'So, Mrs Huxtable, would you like to swing by your old house? Or shall we head on back to Bath?'

They're standing next to Will's car and his hands are on the growing bump of her stomach.

Emily hears herself answer although she isn't conscious of having made up her mind. It's as if someone else is speaking the words for her: 'Let's make a detour. Just to say goodbye.'

Will parks in the Woodstock Road in front of the Victorian house Emily had shared with Greg. Emily gets out of the car, stands in front of the gates, and looks at the building for the last time. She feels no nostalgia, no twinge of regret. A family live there now. The Hardings. Emily met them on their second visit to her house with the estate agent. She hopes the three young children will give the place a soul. She imagines that for this family, this house could be a home.

She's about to get back into the car when Mrs Harding comes running down the drive towards her. She has an envelope in her hand.

'I thought it was you,' the new owner says. Will steps out of the car, and greets Mrs Harding.

'Hello,' Emily says. 'We were just passing.'

'You're not thinking of moving back in, are you?' Mrs Harding jokes.

'No, no. We've just put in an offer for a house in Bath.'

'Oh, that's so exciting. We're very happy here, you know. The children love the garden. My husband has put up a trampoline for them.'

'What a good idea.'

Mrs Harding is holding out the envelope through the bars of the gate. 'This came for you. I was going to ask the estate agent to forward it.'

'Oh, thank you,' says Emily, taking the letter.

After some small talk, mainly about Emily's pregnancy, they say goodbye.

Will seems to be more curious than she is, but Emily waits until they're on the motorway to open it. The name and address appear to have been penned in Emily's neat, rounded handwriting. An SAE? But it is unstamped. And Emily is almost sure she has never laid eyes on this envelope before.

She tears it open, and takes out a small piece of paper. On it is written a single sentence in the same script. Emily reads:

You no longer have your sister by your side, but I will always be with you,

Em.

A chill runs down Emily's spine. She rereads the sentence, frowning. But it still isn't clear. Is it addressed to 'Em' or did 'Em' sign it?

What could this mean?

Emily doesn't want to think about it for now.

Will places his hand on her thigh. 'What is it, Emily?' he asks.

'It's nothing, just an ad,' she replies, scrunching up the piece of paper and the envelope. She turns to him, and feigns a smile. 'I can't wait to get home!'

Dear Reader,

We hope you enjoyed reading this book. If you did, we'd be so appreciative if you left a review. It really helps us and the author to bring more books like this to you.

Here at HQ Digital we are dedicated to publishing fiction that will keep you turning the pages into the early hours. Don't want to miss a thing? To find out more about our books, promotions, discover exclusive content and enter competitions you can keep in touch in the following ways:

JOIN OUR COMMUNITY:

Sign up to our new email newsletter: po.st/HQSignUp

Read our new blog www.hqstories.co.uk

🐦 *: https://twitter.com/HQDigitalUK*

📘 *: www.facebook.com/HQStories*

BUDDING WRITER?

We're also looking for authors to join the HQ Digital family!
Please submit your manuscript to:

HQDigital@harpercollins.co.uk

Thanks for reading, from the HQ Digital team